The Long Walk Home

Manreet Sodhi Someshwar trained as an engineer, graduated from the Indian Institute of Management, Calcutta, and worked in marketing, advertising and consulting. An award-winning writer (Commonwealth Broadcasting Association), she is a book critic for the *South China Morning Post*, Hong Kong. Her debut novel, *Earning the Laundry Stripes*, was released in 2006 to critical acclaim, with *India Today* calling it 'an enjoyable tale of a sassy girl's headlong race up the corporate ladder…' She also featured at the Man Hong Kong International Literary Festival 2008.

Visit her online at www.manreetsodhisomeshwar.com.

The Long Walk Home

Manreet Sodhi Someshwar

HarperCollins *Publishers* India

a joint venture with

New Delhi

First published in India in 2009 by
HarperCollins *Publishers* India
a joint venture with
The India Today Group

ISBN: 978-81-7223-828-5

2 4 6 8 10 9 7 5 3 1

HarperCollins *Publishers*
A-53, Sector 57, NOIDA, Uttar Pradesh 201301, India
77-85 Fulham Palace Road, London W6 8JB, United Kingdom
Hazelton Lanes, 55 Avenue Road, Suite 2900, Toronto, Ontario M5R 3L2
and 1995 Markham Road, Scarborough, Ontario M1B 5M8, Canada
25 Ryde Road, Pymble, Sydney, NSW 2073, Australia
31 View Road, Glenfield, Auckland 10, New Zealand
10 East 53rd Street, New York NY 10022, USA

Typeset in 11/14.5 Adobe Garamond
InoSoft Systems

Printed and bound at
Thomson Press (India) Ltd.

For Papa, always
And Mama, maawan thandian chaawan

Contents

THE BHALLA FAMILY TREE

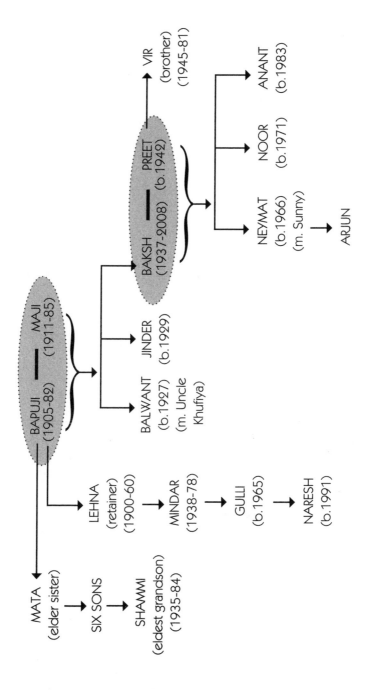

If they answer not to thy call walk alone,
If they are afraid and cower mutely facing the wall,
O thou of evil luck,
Open thy mind and speak out alone.

If they turn away, and desert you when crossing
    the wilderness,
O thou of evil luck,
Trample the thorns under thy tread,
And along the blood-lined track travel alone.

If they do not hold up the light when the night is
    troubled with storm,
O thou of evil luck,
With the thunder flame of pain ignite thy own heart
And let it burn alone.

Walk Alone
Rabindranath Tagore

PROLOGUE

Harbaksh Singh Bhalla, Advocate, Punjab and Haryana High Court—Baksh to his parents and siblings, Bhallasaab to colleagues and others. At five feet-ten, ninety kilos, with a forty-five-inch waist, Mr Bhalla was heavy-set. His younger daughter Noor measured his ample girth every time they met by ringing her arms around his belly. Of course, they never closed in a loop. Even when her father sucked in his stomach and insisted questioningly: '*Some* weight I must have lost?'

Mr Bhalla's fondness for sweets and his evening tipple contributed to the flab. To rectify matters, he ate raw garlic flakes in the morning, only egg whites at breakfast—to the delight of the dog who got the ball of yolk—and rukha roti, thin and puffed like a poori but minus the oil, at mealtimes. He religiously underlined health-related articles in his morning newspaper, *The Tribune*, and scrupulously followed the prescription—'a glass of warm lime water first thing in the morning helps break down fatty deposits'—until such time that he decided to favour a new one.

On those 'health drive' days he wore his slimming belt—the one that promised weight loss without exercise; it just needed to be worn, for three hours in the morning—consulted *Webster's Dictionary* for the meanings of words he had jotted down on the paper's margin as he read, and had the general cheer of one embarking on a new and wholesome venture.

The 'health drive' days, however, were erratic. What was regular was the morning walk—exercise, though, was only an ancillary benefit.

He woke up early because he slept early because his tippling started early. In the initial days, walking was a way to while away time. But as alcohol strengthened its hold on him, the morning air became essential to clear his mind. At some point of time, the walk became a friend. In a world of broken dreams, lost chances and corroded love, walking became a reassuring fixture that didn't cost anything, didn't change loyalties, and always listened.

A diabetic and a heart patient, he got his blood pressure checked frequently. He took the prescribed tablets of Disprin and Sorbitrate daily. He also took his drink daily: Bagpiper Whisky of Mohan Breweries, on the rocks, at times with water, accompanied by salty fried chana, or chicken tikka on the days he stopped by at the Green Hotel on the way home.

Husband of one, brother to two, father of three, he succumbed to a much-prognosticated heart attack—having suffered two prior angina attacks—witnessed by one brother, one servant and a rickshaw puller. He died in the same town he was born, just short of his seventy-first birthday.

One could say that Harbaksh Singh Bhalla hadn't travelled far in life, literally and figuratively. A lifetime in one place can imply many things: a lack of wanderlust, an inordinate attachment to one's roots, risk-aversion. Or inferences more practical can be made: lack of opportunity, ancestral property, family matters. Then there exist tenuous notions like the air of a place and how the spirit resonates to it, the smell of the earth and its connection with something deep and primitive within us, the songs of home and their dance in our veins.

It could well be a concoction of all the above—a heady mix of conflicting elements that gives rise to an equation at once complex and elementary. But equations, however tortuous, can never sum up a person. The best way to know a man may still be the only way: to walk in his shoes and live his life.

DAY 1: ANANT

As the bus trundled into the city, leaving behind the stretch of green fields fringed by lonely electric poles, the break in scenery was almost surgical. The greenery vanished completely, replaced by dour brick houses—single-storeyed, double-storeyed, some low-roofed triple-storeyed—running into one another. Varnished hoardings sat astride legs of steel or were plastered on the road-facing wall of a convenient attic.

Anant chewed his inner lip and looked out of the bus window. TV antennae sprouted unevenly on rooftops, like a haircut gone awry. A mangled kite, its flailing thread stuck in the jaws of an aerial, lifted its limp body in the dust draughts raised by roaring four-wheelers. Enclosure walls, customarily blotched with piss stains, were spanking in places with bright painted murals of soap and fertilizer brands and radiant visages of hero-heroines in the latest Hindi film posters.

'Kent di savvari, Kent di savvari,' shouted the bus conductor, announcing the arrival of the cantonment bus stop.

The driver had shaved thirty minutes off the usual travel time of three hours. Spurred by the light morning traffic, he had driven with relish, tipping the bus in zealous overtakings, firing the horn incessantly at those refusing to make way for the Punjab Roadways Goliath-on-wheels. 'Speed Thrills But Kills' signboards routinely popped up on the highway, courtesy Rotary Club, Moga, or The Lions Club, Ludhiana Chapter. Written in English, ignored by the drivers, they served as ironic warnings only to the few literate passengers who clung to their seats during the daredevil ride. For even if he could read the signs, the driver, a burly Punjabi—by temperament if not size—would surely have guffawed at such delicacy of sentiment.

Fast, the bus had reached very fast—the Titan wristwatch looked back at Anant as he turned his wrist over.

Not fast *enough*.

Something told him he was late. Too late.

It was a short halt that did not occasion shutting off the engine which growled noisily as people scrambled out and in. The morning sun glinted off the driver's rear-view mirror. It shimmered on the red-and-green plastic flower garland draped around a framed picture of Guru Nanak standing upright on the dashboard. A passenger avoided a seat where the sun shone on the Rexine in an amber patch. The steel latches of the front windows caught the rays and Anant inclined his head to avoid the incandescent glare. Not yet May, but the sun was seemingly ignorant of the calendar—a couple of hours and the heat would be rising in thin wisps from the tarred road. A couple of hours, and...

'Cha! Garama garam chaaa!'

The exhortation floated in from a tea stall, the whiff of fresh brew on its wings. Ordinarily, Anant would have grabbed a glass of tea. But today he felt sluggish, like he had popped a few Calmpose tablets. He pursed his lips, moved a lump down his throat and rubbed his right hand on his thigh; the palm was swollen, the fingers blanched yellow. He had probably gripped the steel rod of the backrest of the seat in front of him through the journey. His palm now smelt of metal—a tart smell that only an antiseptic soap would slough off. He knew. The same smell came from holding a hospital bed's railing.

The conductor blew his shrill whistle. Outside, the air was thick with the mad caper of people stirring to life. The bus rattled away from the stop, honking and ploughing its way through the buzzing melee of morning commuters. Rickshaws were piled high with schoolchildren drooping under the weight of obese schoolbags. Thelawalas scurried with their push-carts to grab their coveted spots on the footpath. The resident pavement dweller, 'Desi Hakeem', rearranged herbal potions and bottled lizards beneath his faded khaki tent. He enjoyed *protected* status—every new constable who came tap-tapping his staff was taken through the delights of tiger penis and rhino horn guaranteed to turn him into a Kama Raja! King of Passion, and free of charge! Which foolish constable would reject such offerings?

How many infernal summers and crisp winters had they withstood—that contraption, its owner and the pickled bugs? They were there when Anant had first started bicycling to school. The sight of the creepy-crawlies, swimming in a yellow liquid, had made him pedal ever so slowly as he tried to figure out if they were alive or dead.

Scooters and mopeds weaved intricately around their four-wheeled brethren, braving the exhaust fumes as they slithered forward. A farm tractor thundered along, the driver casting imperious glances at the cars, especially the matchbox-sized Maruti 800s. The bus driver craned his neck out of the window to toss an invective at a wayward cyclist. Familiar sights and sounds. Things Anant had grown up with. Things that would be there tomorrow. And yet, they would not be the same.

Like *Great Expectations*. He had read it in Class X. And read it again, years later. The book was the same; his understanding of it had changed. 'Pre' and 'post' and, in-between, a defining experience that changes how we see things.

❧

The bus stopped before the railway bridge.

Anant clutched his red backpack, descended and glanced across the road. A board sat in a half-loop atop a gate. It announced in Gurmukhi, then English: Amar Hospital.

Amar: Eternal.

Immortal hospital. Mortal patients.

Inside the hospital compound, he looked around the cement courtyard, whitewashed rooms forming its perimeter. Some years back, it had been a bus depot. In the depot-to-hospital makeover, the bus bays had been roofed over, resulting in those hovels. To the left of the quadrangle, a queue of patients sat on wooden benches in the corridor outside the OPD. An important-looking nurse in a blue salwar-kameez was issuing queue numbers. Aside from this hive of activity, and the ubiquitous background babel of traffic, the place was quiet.

Why had they brought him here? Mission Hospital was right next door... Funded by American missionaries, it offered a semblance of reliability in a city where a surgeon, in the process of slitting open an anaesthetized patient, could find the OT plunged into sudden darkness, the emergency power supply having petered off in a day of twenty-hour power cuts.

Then, with a searchlight and some candles, the surgeon would proceed with the cutting, a sweat drop shakily finding its way into the patient's bloodstream. *flesh* ...

Anant walked towards the cubbyhole that said 'Amerjansy' in Gurmukhi, 'Emergency' in smaller letters below.

As a final-year medical student, he walked hospital corridors daily. He knew death and disease intimately, he met them every day. They whispered into his ears as he moved the stethoscope over a prostrate chest, sprang at him from an erratic pulse, stared at him as he watched the ECG ticker flatten, socked him in the eye as he pumped a recalcitrant heart. They were a regular fixture of his life, like shitting and swotting. Death and disease were twin tutors who helped a trainee doctor rehearse for the day he would be a practising doctor. On rare occasions, though, the proscenium arch fell away, the stage vanished, and life became all too real. The Case became a Patient who became a Person.

Like the little girl who had to sit in a particular posture to survive: arms clasped tight around her chest, hands clutched together beneath the chin, a position of constant supplication. The moment she eased up, the hole in her heart would commence draining out the life source. That was the way she had lived all of her five years, the embrace steadily tightening its hold on the growing body and the enlargening aperture, until she came to Har Anand Medical College and Hospital.

She was an anomaly: an *unusual case*. The student fraternity, galvanized by the departure from TB, malaria, hepatitis, descended. For two days she satiated the curiosity of the trainee doctors, then died. And the bemused look traversed from her eyes into Anant's heart.

Was that why most doctors were fatalists? Because they were bewildered by their own profession: the endless mysteries to which there were no answers, the erratic nature of medication which worked perfectly for one body and misbehaved with another, the omnipresent element of chance that mocked any certainty in diagnosis or treatment? When *Gray's Anatomy* and other tomes did not yield answers, the profession collectively turned to the one-with-all-the-answers, presumably.

The Ultimate One: the one who issued ultimatums.

❦

Opening a netting door, Anant stepped into an anteroom. A ceiling fan circled breezily over a figure slumped on a table. The air was cool and redolent with medicinal odours, phenyl—that accursed aroma of Indian hospitals—predominating. A green—hospital green—curtain was pulled across a grilled window next to the table. It flapped with the fan's breeze and light peeped in to play grill-patterns on the table's surface. The door swung back on its loose hinges and fell shut in a low moan.

The man half-raised his head. 'Hanji?'

'There was… is a patient who was admitted in the morning… with chest pain.' Anant searched the attendant's sleep-heavy face for clues.

'Heart patient? Buzurg?'

'Yes.' Buzurg. Elderly gentleman. Papa had been that for many years. Premature greying and a patient demeanour had combined early on to lend him an old man's air.

'And you would be…?' Sweat-stained circles were visible beneath his underarms as he pulled the sleeves up.

'Anant. Anant Singh Bhalla,' he said, hoping the weight of his full name would dispel the attendant's dismissive look. 'I am his son.'

'Oh!'

The attendant surveyed him: the curly hair that fell almost to the shoulders, the unshaven face, the faded jeans cuffed at the ankles, the dirty backpack.

'I thought his son was a doctor.'

Anant was used to this. To the pointed scrutiny and the false assumptions. College professors, senior doctors, most classmates' parents, colleagues—all found him disconcerting. As Bihari, the dhaba owner at Har Anand, said, 'Doctorsaab, you are a little hat ke.' *Hat ke*, distinct. Conceptually different, like namkeen laddoo, a salty sweetmeat. In a match-the-following, a solemn face with a stethoscope slung around the neck of a white coat would fit the descriptor 'doctor'. While *his* mug, depending on the proclivities of the illustrator, would fall anywhere between 'rocker' and 'ruffian'.

Bohemian looks and the pursuit of medicine were invariably at odds. Just as the slim volumes that lay scattered amongst his medical tomes: Tagore's *Gitanjali*, Seth's *All You Who Sleep Tonight*. His hostel mates found it baffling that he could recite 'Jodi tor daak shune keu na aashe tabey ekla chalo re' in a distinctly non-Bengali accent, the first two lines that is, and the complete verse in English, and not know the lyrics to the raging Bollywood ditty of the week.

'I am studying medicine. Where is my father?'

Disbelief and pity washed over the attendant's face. He shook his head, saying, 'He passed away.' Then, glancing at the clock on the wall behind him, he continued, 'It's been an hour now. Heart attack.'

He passed away. Heart attack.

Anant processed the words—coming to him in a slow, punctuated motion, one at a time—even as the dreadful import of the disclosure impinged on his brain right away. His instinct had been right. What had Jinder Tayaji said on the phone? 'Baksh is in hospital. His urine has stopped...' Cardiac shock can produce low blood pressure, reduced urine levels and cellular abnormalities—the notes on 'Severity of Heart Attack' had streamed ticker-tape fashion through his head.

Papa was no more.

He was dead.

He would be lying down and not breathing.

He would not smile again, or speak again.

He would not look at him with those gentle brown eyes, equal measure of hurt and love, and sadly say, 'When I go away, you will realize...'

Now, he had truly gone away.

The words piled into him now, seeping in a sluggish descent to his heart, and someplace deeper. The epiphany dawned: there was no such thing as the *bottom* of a heart. Nothing contained the feeling that tunnelled into him. It was heavy and deep and sinking continually. A sharp ache, with a dense permanence. It filled his eyes and crushed his face. His left hand, balled, plugged his mouth. His shoulders shook with acceptance of the foreboding he had carried with him since the telephone call at daybreak.

'Sit down, please... sit, sit.' The attendant pulled up a chair, laid a hand on Anant's shoulder and propelled him downwards. He stood watching Anant for a while, went to a water cooler beside the door, and fetching a glass of water, placed it in front of Anant. He sat down in his chair and, leaning forward, said, 'His brother was with him. And a servant.' He spoke slowly, offering information like a salve. 'We called Dr Sharma right away. He told us to give the patient a Disprin while he hurried over. Checked his ECG and BP.'

'MI?' Anant looked at the attendant.

'Yes. MI.' He nodded. 'He was given injections. But Doctorsaab said the patient had delayed coming to the hospital. It had got too late to save him. His brother took the body.'

MI. Myocardial infarction. The arteries must have blocked. The doctor would have given thrombolytic injections: prescribed treatment for opening of blocked arteries. But it had not worked.

'Can I see the doctor?'

'Right now he's in the OT. Some operation. Maybe if you come back in a couple of hours…'

Anant nodded, then wiped his glasses on his shirtsleeve. The lachrymal glands had had their run for the moment. He bit the skin inside his mouth and, sighing, proceeded to get up.

'Your father was strong.' The attendant obviously felt he had to say something. Something of the father's last moments the son could carry with him. 'Even in that pain, he was calm.' He patted the young man's hand and said softly, 'Kalle aaye Nanaka, sadde uthe jaaye.'

When He calls, it is time to go.

ॐ

His father lay on the chowkidar's folding bed in the front veranda. His face was calm, except for a slight crease on the right corner of the lips, as if the mouth had frozen in a last grimace of pain. The turban had moved back, exposing the high forehead with its clear division of tanned skin… and a bruise mark! A welt on the upper right half of the forehead. A couple of inches long. Reddish-brown stain where the blood had clotted, crested by thin white torn skin. It looked fresh, recent. Had Papa hit his head somewhere?

Gently, he touched the skin. The mark was rough, the skin around it warm, fleshy, lifelike. Instantly, he put a finger below the nose. And with his left hand, touched his father's wrist.

There was no pulse.

'I tried to help reach on time but he had made it too late, very late, even Preet was not at home...' Jinder Tayaji was saying something. His usual fast speech had derailed entirely—he was chugging incoherently. The sudden death of a younger brother had rattled him. The printed mauve turban peppered with pink squares was incongruous with his bewildered visage. Pacing the tiled floor, he appeared like a mad Lear to Anant—the unfurled end of his turban jerking with each step, the crumpled shirt clinging to his concave chest, the wrinkled bejewelled hands quizzing the air. Anant set his jaw and returned his attention to his father.

Papa's white beard looked unkempt: the knot below the chin had loosened. He wouldn't like that. Anant smoothed the hair that had pried loose. Patted it back. It felt like twine: stiff, stringy. Old white hair. When was the last time that he had touched his father? Been so near him? Near enough to know what his white hair felt like? Frail ridges around the eyes spread outwards like the veins of a peepul leaf. Flaccid eyebags. The eyes drawn shut.

'Were they that way when he breathed his last?' Anant's question broke his uncle's whispery monologue.

The old man looked at him uncomprehendingly. Like he had been interrupted in the middle of a trance.

'Were his eyes already closed?'

With his right thumb, Jinder Tayaji flicked at the corner of his eye, shook his head vaguely, and resumed his brisk pacing and his whirling soliloquy. 'What could be done, the rickshaw driver came to inform me, when I reached he was already beyond recovery, the doctor tried, he gave Reteplase, but heart had given up so what could be done…'

With an index finger Anant lifted an eyelid gently. The familiar brown iris. It was looking straight up. It did not look back at him. He softly settled the lid back and sat down near his father's feet, head bent. The chowkidar stood some distance away, conversing with a few of the office staff who had turned up. Manua, the servant, squatted on the floor, looking from Tayaji to Anant, waiting for directions. The watch showed nine-thirty.

Anant had to think fast. No one else was at home. He had to force his mind out of the morass of depression, at least for now. He would grieve later. There were things to be done until Mama came back. Pasha was howling from the balcony upstairs. There was an edge to his bark. Each raucous yowl was followed by low growls and moans, as if he was in pain.

'So sorry to hear about Bhallasaab. We came right away.'

Anant inclined his head sideways and watched Mehta Uncle take both of Tayaji's hands in his, offering condolences. He was an old family friend of sorts. His children had studied in the same school as Anant and his sisters. And he was a lawyer, like Papa. Three other colleagues were with him. Anant had met them at some time or the other. They walked over to the bed and patted Anant on the back as he continued to look downwards.

'Must have been a bad attack.'

'Bhallasaab was never very careful about his health.' There was no attempt to mask the reproach, the voice was peremptory.

In downcast arcs they swayed their heads to the tune of piteous tch tchs, glanced at the body, then regrouped around Tayaji.

'What can be done, God's will...' Tayaji wrung his hands, massaging them over and over, Lady Macbeth-like.

All the perfumes of Arabia... Anant's disoriented brain sang.

The ground floor had been rented out to an insurance company. People from the office now approached him to offer their sympathies. 'This is really unfortunate... It is only appropriate to keep the office closed today. We will inform the others who arrive. We are also putting up a notice at the gate.'

Anant nodded his response. It was best that the ground floor stayed shut for the day. When the family arrived, they could do without an audience. The office employees would certainly welcome a holiday—even if it was because the landlord had expired.

The gathering of lawyers around Tayaji had swelled. There were ten–twelve people in the veranda now, engaged in a drill of sorts: shaking hands, gawking at the prostrate body, spinning their hands skywards in resignation, commenting on the ways of God, huddling in the garden to air their individual take on the matter at hand.

'Where is the rest of the family?'

'Mrs Bhalla has gone to Chandigarh on official work,' supplied a knowledgeable source who had earlier requisitioned the answer.

'When is she coming back?'

'How long do you plan to wait—the children live far off, don't they?'

The queries flew in from each cluster. No one wanted to be left behind in this display of concern for the departed. Anant watched the assembly closing in on his uncle, firing questions, hurling conjectures, suggesting solutions to what was clearly none of their problem. Precisely why there was such evident relish for the task. They looked like people eager for a performance. They wanted *something* to happen. And were keen to orchestrate its happening.

'We say, Jinderji, that you don't delay the cremation too long. Not good. Not good.' The proponent wore a world-weary look, as if he dished out this sort of advice daily, and twitched his nose. 'How long will you wait? And the smell…'

'Bhallasaab's daughters stay far away. Getting here will take twelve hours minimum—that is, if tickets are available.'

'With no family around, we all have to decide.' The tone was smug in its conclusive rendering of the finale to the discussion.

Anger curdled inside Anant. He wanted the pesky, solicitous guests to leave, and take with them their baggage of good intentions and noble plans. This was not some Open House. Why was Jinder Tayaji not saying something? He stood there, head lolling on his gaunt frame, the slouch in his back more pronounced than ever: an apologetic question mark. Making an effort to rein in his anger, Anant focused on the mosaic floor, trying to think ahead.

'What time is the cremation, beta?' Mehta Uncle's feet had approached him to enquire. Lawyer legs stood in a dense semicircle behind him. From the corner of his eye, Anant saw a couple of the office staff lingering at the fringes, furtively entertaining themselves. The air was suffused with the breaths and smells of too many people: dried talcum sweat, cigarette smoke, ghee, paan masala, unbathed body odour—the last, probably his own. Pasha's plaintive moans hovered above—slow, ascending, plateauing, only to begin again.

An assortment of footwear swarmed Anant's line of vision: open-toed Bata sandals, mud-caked Punjabi juttis—one embellished with golden paisleys, Hawai chappals, white slip-ons, a couple of black shoes. Funny, the mind! Even in that haze, it was registering the state of feet on display: unkempt toenails, chapped heel, an unusually fair pair of feet…

'Beta?' Mehta Uncle again.

'I don't know,' Anant said, looking up at him. 'I have to wait for Mama.' *Move back. Allow some air for Papa.*

'But that will be too late, beta…' Mehta Uncle said, his voice matter-of-fact as he picked his nose, then examined the dried piece of snot on the tip of his index finger.

Late? For what? For whom? Anant sat still, his hands on his lap.

'Listen to your elders. In matters like these it is best not to delay.' The semicircle stepped up now.

'After all, we are well-wishers, puttar.' They ringed around the bed. Fidgety for action, thirty or more pairs of well-wishing eyes bore into him. Jinder Tayaji stood disconsolate at the fringe, still unsure of what to do with his hands, or with the gathering's galloping cremation plans.

Bizarre. These people would not let even a dead man be.

'NO.'

Mehta Uncle's hand, journeying towards his nose, darted backwards, as if singed by an electric current. Discordant rumbles rippled through the gathering. 'What are you saying? Do you even know how these things are done? After all, Bhallasaab meant something to us also. We worked with him for so long—we will not let his body rot while you sit around doing nothing. Your uncle here is okay with our suggestion—'

'Out! OUT of here!'

He would not stand here and let others decide how the family spent its last moments with Papa. With folded hands, he looked them straight in the eye, 'Bahut meharbani. Thank you for the concern you all have shown. But now, it's time you leave us to our matters.'

The abrupt dismissal made the gathering skittish. The lawyers had rallied to bereave a dead colleague, they were offering support. Instead, the young son, flouting all social norms, was packing them off! 'Hain! Look how he talks! Nashaee hai. Takes drugs. Just look at his hair—unkempt like Majnu's. Do doctors sport hairstyles like this? What else can you expect from today's children? Chalo, let it be. He's a child… Such children… Good that Bhallasaab can't see all this. God rest his soul in peace.'

'Please LEAVE.' Anant stood up. At six feet-four, he towered over them all. The crowd became a receding wave. 'MANUA!' Anant turned to the servant who had not risen from the floor and was watching everything, stricken. 'Bolt the gate after they leave.'

The party trooped out, remarking on the etiquette of today's children, their regrettable ways, and clucked even louder to underscore their own astute observations.

Jinder Tayaji flapped about, distraught. 'Anant, what have you done? You have sent the biradari away—'

'To hell with the community! What are you saying? Don't I know why their tails are on such fire—so the saskaar is done while the sun is still bearable! What would I tell my mother and my sisters? And why were you not supporting me?' Anant's voice rose from the gut, laced with unshed tears. His chest heaved with the effort to contain his anger and frustration and hurt and loss.

The raised voice and the sight of the crowd hastily filing out of the gate attracted curious onlookers from the Mall Road in front of the house. They peered over the bougainvillea hedge, trying to fathom what was happening.

Shakespeare got it wrong, Anant thought. The world is a circus, not a stage, Schadenfreude its defining exhibit. He watched the gawkers feeding on his misery, gaping idly, speculating on what had transpired; watched his uncle, frail and afraid and vulnerable; watched his father, in repose amidst all the tumult; and suddenly, he felt very alone and very adult.

With his head he motioned to Manua. The servant lunged for the gate, noisily bolting it and shooing the vagrants. 'Take a hike! Don't have anything to do or what?'

Meanwhile, Anant pondered how to shift his father's bulky frame through the long corridor and up the flight of steps to the first floor. His training as a doctor left him ill-equipped here: after pronouncing a patient dead, he was accustomed to a swift exit.

❧

Anant stepped out of the STD/ISD phone booth beside the BP petrol pump, pocketing the billing scroll and change. He had gone there to call his two older sisters, Neymat in Delhi and Noor in Bombay. His mobile phone was out of charge: he had not thought of picking up his charger when he had scrammed pre-dawn, and there was no cell phone in the house—his parents were technophobes—and the landline allowed only local calls.

Papa had had the facility for national and international dialling cancelled after a bill for ten thousand rupees landed in the mail one day and everyone at the telecommunications company—the clerk, manager, the department head—insisted he pay the bill first, then apply for a refund. Perhaps somebody had pinched his line, they wagged their heads in commiseration, and made all those calls, but a bill was a bill and a middle-class respectable man had no option but to pay. So Papa had paid, cancelled the facility, and left thieving to the thieves who would find another line to filch.

The aunty with whom Mama had stayed while in Chandigarh had informed him that Mama had caught the morning bus. Her official work had wound up earlier than scheduled, so Mama was already on her way. Anant glanced at his watch—eleven: she would be near Talwandi now. Half an hour and her bus would reach Ferozepur.

Should he try Noor's number again? It had been unreachable. Who knew which part of the world she was in: her job, traipsing over the globe as a management consultant, would shame Phileas Fogg. Later, he would call Delhi again—Neymatdi had not answered on the first few attempts. His eldest sister was a doctor at a Delhi hospital, her job and the associated commute made her work hours unpredictable.

A farm trolley pulled into the petrol pump, its exhaust beating a raucous phut-phut as it popped out nimbus clouds in the air. The road was brimming with traffic. He had better hurry to the bus stand. As he walked to his scooter, a voice interrupted him.

'Daktarsaab?' He saw a rickshaw puller stop by the roadside and look at him enquiringly. 'You recognize me? I—'

'Yes. I know.' One of the rickshaw drivers who had routinely ferried Papa to the district courts or the bazaar.

'It is very sad about Bhallasaab. Very nice man he was. Wish we had reached the hospital earlier.'

'You drove him there?'

'Hanji. Not well at all he was. In great pain. But you know Bhallasaab—still spoke calmly…'

'What time was that? When you picked him up?'

'Must be around six—hunh, six—the Mail passengers were going by.'

Punjab Mail—the train came in at six, the days it was on time. Anant sighed involuntarily. He proceeded to kick-start the scooter.

'But why was Bhallasaab walking about so early?'

'What early! He usually walks at that time, at times earlier.' Anant shrugged and sat astride his whirring machine.

'No, Daktarsaab. He was walking at three in the morning.'

'What?'

The rickshaw puller rode his vehicle closer to Anant. 'Aye-ho—why was Bhallasaab walking about at three?'

'Three o'clock!' Anant snorted. What was the man saying?

'I am telling you, Daktarsaab. I saw with my eyes. He was walking near the City Chowk around three in the morning. That's where we sleep in the night. In the open, near the main bus stop.' He stepped down and angled the front wheel to park the rickshaw. Then he took the striped cotton scarf hanging around his neck and wiped his face unhurriedly, his eyes intently watching Anant.

'Something woke me up… I turned on my side, some dogs barking. I was about to sleep when, there, I saw Bhallasaab. He

passed under a streetlight, his face was clearly visible. Slow steps
he was taking, and his face had a faraway look—jiven neend vich
tur rahe hone. I thought to call out to him, but then I let it be…
That's when I looked at my watch.'

'And then you picked him up at six again?' What was the
man getting at? Baksheesh? Some money, perhaps, for having
done a favour to his father in his last moments?

'Sure! That is the time I take my first passenger. Bhallasaab
was walking back from the bazaar side. Badi peed vich son—'

'Yes, I know. You mentioned that. Why was he walking
around at three in the morning?' Anant's voice had risen; a few
passers-by turned to stare.

Beneath Anant's irate gaze, the rickshaw puller fidgeted a
bit. Thrusting his hands outwards, he said, 'Daktarsaab, that is
what *I* am asking. What was Bhallasaab doing walking about so
early? If I had known what was to happen, I would have taken
him to the hospital then itself.'

Walking at three. Sleepwalking.

Anant shook his head. The rickshaw puller was probably
fibbing, concocting stories. Casting himself in a bigger role in the
entire episode. But what if he *was* telling the truth? That Papa
had spent the last three hours of his life roaming the city…

Where did he go? What was he looking for? And when
did the pain start? Surely he could have attempted to reach the
hospital earlier—he was familiar with angina pain… And he
must have passed the Haveli. Then why not knock on Jinder
Tayaji's door for help? Admittedly, the brothers had their
differences, but still… The pain must have started three to four
hours before he breathed his last at seven-thirty… How did he
manage to move with the pain shooting through him?

Questions, questions... Anant's mind was a maze of questions confounding him as rode to the bus stand, mulling over each improbability, attempting to decipher the information, sifting through it for bits that made sense.

At the bus stand, lost in his thoughts, he was oblivious of the racket around him as conductors announced their destinations, each wrung out like a medley; vendors hollered to be heard above the din of idling engines; buses barged in; horns blared; passengers boarded, alighted, hurried, bargained, purchased; and all departed in a clang of metal, clink of glass and plume of smoke.

BAKSH

THE LAST WALK

Baksh woke up with a heavy feeling in his chest. What was it? He had not even had a drink last evening. And it had taken so long to get to sleep. Now this… it was as if somebody was giving him a massage inside the chest… but the pressure was almost unbearable, the grip vice-like. He turned on his side and sat up in bed.

Niveous moonlight filtered in through the netting door and lit the room dully. It picked up the green sunmica trestle table, his reading glasses lying unfolded on some page of the Bhagavad Gita he had been reading the evening before. Bhagavad Gita, the Song of the Divine One, one of many searchlights to help him pick his way through an inscrutable world… On the battlefield of Kurukshetra, Krishna advised Arjun to do his karma. Doing one's duty, regardless of consequences, was a central tenet of the Gita. Yet, it confounded Baksh: was doing his duty the equivalent of doing what he believed was right? When the great warrior too seemed confused, Krishna revealed his celestial form, saying, 'Now I have become Death, the destroyer of worlds.' Thus he illustrated to Arjun that the world as Arjun saw it—the battlefield, his enemies, his relations—was illusory, since absolute reality was beyond human perception. Yet, Arjun could not escape his physical condition except by fulfilling his duty.

Baksh sighed. In his seven-decade-existence, there was one thing he had gleaned with certainty: living was bewildering.

His gaze lingered on the Bhagavad Gita before turning to the adjoining untidy pile where brown and khaki folders sat, tendril-edged with age. They belonged to court cases he had been pursuing for a while. Shiny folders—harbingers of new court cases and healthy income—were a thing of the past. His focus on a 'lost cause'—how the other lawyers sneered, albeit politely—had led to lost cases and dwindling clients.

Then, he felt it again. The pain. Blunt, thick, like a fog rising inside. He put a palm on his chest and moved it gently. Maybe a trip to the toilet…

He got up and slipped his feet into the Bata sandals, the back strap permanently tied and flattened against the heel. The stillness of the house filled with a rhythmic thap-thap. In the veranda, Pasha stirred and cocked an ear towards him.

Walking across his room, the girls' bedroom, then his wife's, he got to the bathroom. He was reaching for the light switch when he stumbled.

When he came to, Pasha was by his side, studying him. The pain in his chest had receded. How long had he lain there—five minutes, ten? He was aware only of his bent knee and the buzz around his head. He tried to clear his head, get his bearings. His right arm was distended, the upper half cushioned part of his face. The left had fallen in a limp fold alongside his chest. His legs were sprawled, the right one as if half-attempting to climb a step. Awkwardly, he swivelled on an elbow until his back collapsed against the floor. Weakened by the effort, he gulped in air.

Another angina attack? Possibly a heart attack? He needed to see a doctor. At this hour? Who would be awake? He had to try—sitting there would not help. The pain could return; nobody else was at home.

He managed to make his way to his room, where he picked a turban from the top of the wooden almirah where it lay: fresh ones in neat stacks, worn ones in merry hillocks. Setting it on his head, he secured it until his ears crept beneath the folds. Gingerly, he walked out of the room, Pasha close behind him, sliding his body past the door.

He picked the house keys up from the wooden lock-shaped key hook. From the fridge he extracted a plastic container and overturned the sticky red remains of chicken tikka into the dog's bowl.

A remote sniff test, then Pasha spun around and tailed him.

Baksh crossed the veranda, patted his back pocket for the curve of folded notes and paused by the main door, meeting Pasha's expectant gaze. Jabbing an index finger in the direction of the terrace, he urged, 'Cat, Pasha. Go for the cat!'

Lured by the vision of the cat that routinely escaped him, Pasha spun and arched his body in a distant reconnaissance of the stated part of the house. Deftly, Baksh stepped out, shutting the door behind him. As he turned the bolt, frantic short barks rapped at him in the silence of the night.

As was his custom, he turned left at the gate and started on the path of his regular morning walk. He walked slowly, not wanting to jog the pain awake. His doctor's clinic was in the main bazaar, beside the flour mill from which Preet got fresh-ground wheat every month. After thirty-nine years of service as a government teacher, Preet had retired, though she continued to work with the teachers' training institute as a consultant. That was why she had gone to Chandigarh—to sort out some provident fund issues at the secretariat.

Preet... he shook his head. They had been married for forty-six years. However, unlike other families where the husband and wife maritally osmosed over the years, Preet and he continued to be out-of-step: his movements languid, embracive; hers purposeful, independent.

How focused Preet was, how determined—with a talent for persevering. Neymat was barely a year old when Preet was interviewed for and got a teaching job in a London school. In the 1960s, the English were following an open immigration policy and qualified professionals were in great demand.

'It is our chance to start life in a land of opportunity,' Preet had said. 'Rab rakha, with hard work and our talent, we will make good in England. Why just us? So many Punjabis are packing holdalls for London.'

He had pondered. The plan was for Preet to go ahead, start with her job, find a place to stay, and within six months Baksh and Neymat would join her.

'Kismet does not knock on the door twice,' she had cautioned as he sat thinking.

In their case, it certainly did not: Preet and he never travelled to a foreign land. That passport, though, Preet had held on to. On some occasions, rifling through the safe of her Godrej steel almirah, her fingers would make contact with that faded repository of a dream. Normally, she would shove it further back, but if one of the children chanced upon it, they would demand to see it. Particulars in brown ink, the photo of a young Preet—beautiful, wavy hair, resolute chin, eager eyes—would look back at them.

*They would cluck, comment on their mother's erstwhile beauty
and the frittered chance of becoming English citizens.*

*'O Papa, if only you had not dithered. Then for us also, it would
have been Balle! Balle! Birmingham.'*

'221-B Baker Street!'

'London fog, Scones with butter…'

*It was expected—from children who had grown up on a diet
of Blyton and Dickens, but in a land where the equivalent of OBE
was NRI.*

*However, he never thought of that missed chance at becoming
English. For him, Chandigarh had been a closer aspiration. But
what if he had allowed Preet to go ahead? Had not dampened her
enthusiasm through his ambivalence? Life would have turned out
differently, that was certain, but would they have been happier?*

*His shoulders lifted in a shrug as he smoothed down his
moustache with his right hand. Who could say? When so much of
happiness depended on the air of the place one lived in… Beyond
the petrol pump, before the alley that led into the Housing Board
Colony, stood a milestone. He seldom failed to notice it, the quaint
reminder of days gone by. What sense of nostalgia kept that stone
alive while most of the modern infrastructure crumbled around?*

*Lahore 20 miles—that was what it said. And his mind started
to journey down a path from long ago.*

1946

Jinder Paji's Lahore, the city without seeing which, Baksh was
informed, he may as well consider himself not born. 'Jis Lahore
nahin wekhya, o janmayan nahin!' Now that Baksh was nine,
Jinder Paji had decided it was time his kid brother grew up and

got some real education. Seeing the 'Paris of the Orient'—where Jinder Paji and Cousin Bitta studied at F.C. College—was part of the agenda.

When Baksh awoke the first morning in Lahore, he discovered Jinder Paji and Cousin Bitta in the midst of a lusty debate. Over a leisurely breakfast of stuffed parathas, the two were devouring headlines from *The Tribune.*

'In Lahore, two educated gentlemen refuse to continue to eat their food, or even pay for it, when they discover the bearer, as well as the caterer, are Muslims,' Paji read out a news item. 'Have they gone mad?'

Cousin Bitta snorted. 'Hypocrites all! In the evening these same men will be sleeping with Muslim girls in Heera Mandi.'

'Look at this one.' Jinder Paji tapped the newsprint with his right palm. 'Another article on Pakistan. Here, listen. "Sir Khizar Hyat Khan accuses the British of being the mother and father of Pakistan." Then it goes on—"The Sikhs are agitated. They will resist it to the death."' He flung the paper on the table, tilting a teacup.

'This is British jiggery-pokery—they are doing what they indeed have always been good at. Divide and rule.' Cousin Bitta stroked his moustache with both hands, twirling it into elegant upright tips at the ends. 'But what do they take us for? We have our lands here—do they think we will just walk away? We are wearing bangles, hunh?'

'Stuff and nonsense!' Jinder Paji's knee shook erratically. 'Lahore is a cosmopolitan city. A true representative of the Sufi culture…'

'Cosmo-polly-ten… what's that, Paji?' Baksh was intrigued by the significance his elder brother attached to the word.

Jinder Paji looked at him, folded his arms across his chest and knitted his brows. It was not like him to instruct. His way was to let a person loose in the environment, a helpful nudge now and then, and the answers would ultimately reveal themselves. But evidently the question was important for, after some thought, he spoke up. 'Lahore is an ancient city—some say it was founded by Loh, the son of Ram. Ram, the God, hain? For the last one thousand years it has been the capital of Punjab. Ghazni, Mongols, Mughals, Sikhs, British—all have descended on the city. Some made it their home, others looted it and went away.'

He started to walk up and down the garden, hands clasped behind him, eyes on the grass. 'But you know what? The city just grew more vibrant and alive: it absorbed the multiple cultures, made them its own. You have seen how beautiful it is: lustrous Mughal edifices, Sufi shrines, stately English buildings, charming lanes filled with the most incredible flavours, a concert at every corner, mauseeki in the air... And its people truly know how to live: zestful, never-say-die—whatever their community. Because what unites them is their spirit!'

There Jinder Paji paused to look at Baksh. 'Lahore is the visible soul of the Punjabi. How then can anyone apportion it by religion?'

The look on his brother's face reminded Baksh of Cousin Bitta when he spoke of a certain lady friend.

It would only be many years later that Baksh would truly understand the meaning of that look. That it is possible to love a place like it is a person. That during Partition, when people crossed the newly created boundary line with their families intact, they *still* left behind a member of the family. That a place is never just its physical coordinates, for its location is often in the heart. Thus, it can be carried around forever, and passed on to one's children, with all its lingering memories and wistful fragrances.

Only later would Baksh learn how the violation of an early love forever numbed his elder brother to another love.

At that moment, Bitta decided to make things simpler. 'Listen Baksh. Lahore is like the makhni daal cooked by Maasi.'

Baksh knew his cousin was referring to the black lentils his mother, Bitta's aunt, cooked.

'It simmers in the pot through the night with its various spices. And when you taste it in the morning, can you tell whether the flavour comes from clove, or cardamom, or cumin?' Bitta jiggled his eyebrows.

That was true. Yet, as Baksh spent time in Lahore, the idea of Pakistan—an independent Muslim nation to be carved out of Hindustan—acquired some kind of reality day by day. In his hometown of Ferozepur, nobody had seemed to care.

❧

The fifth day of his stay was Basant. And all of Lahore turned out to celebrate the traditional festival announcing the end of winter and the onset of harvest. The scent of mango wafted through the air and teased the bushes laden with roses. The dazzle and shimmer of the mustard fields was matched only by the dance of yellow kites in the skies above.

Qasur, midway between Lahore and Ferozepur, was a spot for the professionals: the most viciously competitive breed of kite flyers. Since they did not claim to be those, Jinder Paji and Cousin Bitta were to meet at their friend Kareem's place in Mozang for patangbaazi. Kareem's house was an old haveli; the rooftop terrace was ideal for kite-flying. The area was more crowded—that would ensure sufficient competition. Baksh was to assist with holding the string and would get to fly a kite only after they managed to snare some.

It was a lovely day in the middle of February—deliciously, pleasantly cold. A breeze buffeted the kites as people clambered atop their roofs to commence flying—a lead flyer, an assistant holding the string and numerous observers munching sesame-seed-coated jaggery riyoris and gachak, hollering encouragement and proffering counsel.

By mid-morning, all three friends had flown kites, lost some and won many. Wires overhead and streets below were beginning to be spattered with mangled kites.

Baksh had managed, with a fallen tree branch, to snare a couple of kites as they trailed past the rooftop. In addition, Kareem had divulged an ingenious lassoing technique: a nylon thread to one end of which a pebble was tied. He moved the lasso in quick arcs, flung it high over a floating string, and the weight of the pebble sagged the thread until the kite came within catching distance.

Kareem's ammi sent fennel tea and samosas with a servant who deposited the tray on a stool, hitched up his lungi and hunkered down to watch the action. They had the tea in turns—the post could not be abandoned!

Soon Bitta was engaged in a neck-and-neck duel with a kite flyer from the opposite rooftop. As the others cheered raucously, Bitta moved back and forth, his shoulders rippling beneath the kameez, the skin on his index finger raw from the abrasive thread.

'Dhil de! Dhil de! Loosen the string!'

Baksh let the spindle roll recklessly inside the thumb-index finger hoops of both hands. The servant sprang to move the stool out of the way of Bitta's vigorous backward shuffles.

'Bo-kata!' yelled a lusty voice from the other rooftop as Bitta's kite lost its anchor. 'Oye! We have shown you! Better go play in your own lane.'

Cousin Bitta was hardly the type to take such an insult. 'Is this your father's lane? I didn't see his name plastered anywhere.'

'Watch your tongue, or we will cut it off! Just like we cut your kite!'

Bitta was now almost leaning over the railing, the carved wooden structure in danger of breaking apart. He flung his right arm at the opposite party, the index finger returning to jab at his jutted-out chest. 'Oye! Who dares touch even a hair on my body?'

'Hrr hrr…' went the other team, having succeeded in riling Bitta. Some men slapped their thighs in imitation of kabaddi, as if they were readying to tag him down.

'The lunds!' Bitta marched to the corner where the kites lay. 'I'll show those machods.' Then he proceeded to bandage his index finger and thumb with a thin strip of muslin. All the while, he kept tossing determined glances at the opponents across.

Bitta was now going to use the manjha, the string coated with performance-enhancing ground glass. Baksh chuckled to himself. The duel was set to be fun!

At the first available opportunity, Bitta tacked his kite onto the opponent's, and in a few concentrated tugs, sent it plummeting. He allowed himself a lusty 'Balle! Balle!' before setting off on the other one. It was as if the slanging match had roused the invincible kite flyer within him. There was no stopping him until one of the rowdies from across, grievously mortified by the loss of his kites, hovered over the ramparts of his roof terrace and spat in the direction of Kareem's haveli. 'All Sikhs and Hindus will go Jamuna-paar, across the Jamuna we will pack them! Haramkhor!'

That was hardly guaranteed to chasten Bitta! 'Oye, bastards!' He marched towards the corner that was closest to the aggressor's, stringing his kite along. The others also joined him. 'Rein in your tongue, you fools! Was Lahore part of your mother's dowry?'

Something was flung across the gap and landed on their side: an old rubber piece from a cycle tyre. They were getting desperate! 'Listen, if you don't know how to dance, why get on the floor?' Kareem hollered, laughing loudly. 'Go downstairs and sit in the women's quarters!'

'Hindu–Sikh murdabad! Jeevey, jeevey Pakistan!'

'Ullu da pathha! Come down and we'll show you...'

Kite-flying had suddenly taken an ugly twist. Kareem's father, hearing the commotion, came up. Gauging the black mood and sullen invectives hurtling to and fro, he ushered them all downstairs.

❧

On his last day in Lahore, Baksh and Jinder Paji mounted the buggy to the station, where they would catch the Punjab Mail to Ferozepur. It was a cold day and the sun showed no signs of emerging from beneath its sheet of clouds. It was almost as if Basant had incorrectly heralded the end of winter.

They rode in the chilly air, the horse's hooves clicking sharply in the quiet of the Sunday morning. The buggy had rounded the corner of Mall Road onto Bedan Road when a crowd surged into view. It was standing at the edge of the road, engaged in intimate debate. The people were congregated around something, pointing, signalling, alternately peering down and drawing away. On Paji's instruction, the driver pulled the buggy close to the kerb and hurried off to enquire.

He returned in a few minutes, his walk becoming a sprint, and he leapt up to his seat. 'It's a young Sikh's body. He's been stabbed in the chest and left to die.'

That was the last Baksh saw of Lahore. How was he to know then that Zinda-Dillan-e-Lahore, the city of life and lively people, would soon be littered with corpses? And true to its cosmopolitan nature, the carcasses would be of all denominations.

DAY 2: NOOR

For the rest of her life Noor Bhalla would associate Da Vinci with loss.

It was at the Leonardo da Vinci airport, as she stepped into the Arrivals lounge, that her mobile jingled: 'Dhoom macha le dhoom macha le dhoom.' The popular Bollywood number was Noor's ringtone of the moment—she changed it frequently and was no longer surprised when a firangi lip-synched the song in places like Brussels or Budapest.

'Can Bollywood go Global?' *Harvard Business Review* had recently debated in an article. According to Noor, it already had. In Montreux, tourists visiting the Chateau de Chillon came stumbling out of the dungeons to bask their chilled hearts under the radiant mug of Aishwarya Rai on a giant billboard for Longines. In the Bollywood beauty, the Swiss watchmaker had finally found the elegant successor to Audrey Hepburn. In the ten years that Noor had been travelling overseas, the assaults from saffron-clad blonde devotees of Hare Krishna Mission at airports had given way to folks who ambled up, chanted 'Namaste! Namaste!' then thrust their T-shirted chests at her, usually sporting the screen-printed visage of King Khan, his eyes goggling at her from atop two perky breasts.

Now Noor unzipped the side pocket of her IBM laptop and half-smiled at the happily nodding co-passenger. 'Anant' beamed the phone's green monitor. Strange! Her younger brother seldom called, proffering his perpetual shortage of cash and his sister's extreme affluence as excuse.

'Ant?' she queried, using the moniker that a bemused Mama routinely disapproved of. 'You can't reduce a name like Anant, which means "one with no end" or "infinite", to *Ant*!' To which Papa would grin and add, with a toss in Mama's direction, 'Ants in her pants!'

'Hel-low?' The poor connectivity added to her unease, which she summarily quashed—what could be wrong?—as she scanned for the exit, right hand pulling her Tumi suiter along. 'Ant, what's up?'

'Have you returned home?'

'Home? I am in Rome.'

'Rome? Weren't you in London last week?'

'My moronic client,' Noor said, huddling against a pillar, 'needs on-site assistance for one week. So, last minute, boss kicks me and, Roma, here I come.'

Static blips. Noor adjusted her head as garbled words came in spurts over the distance: '… need your…'

'Can't hear you!' she shouted into the phone.

What was it? Last time around, Anant's bike had skidded as he had roared out of the college gate—he had blamed the loose gravel, she had assumed he was trying to impress some chick—and he had called on her for money for the bike's repair and to make her an accomplice in his charade to avoid visiting home for a month. 'Don't want to bother them needlessly with all these bruises…'

Concerned, she had asked, 'How bad *is* it?'

'The surgeon is hopeful,' he had said, before pausing, the sudden sobriety tremulous on the phone line, 'that the medulla oblongata, currently in vibration mode, will suture with the spinal cord again.' Then he had guffawed. Noor half-smiled at the memory. What was it this time around?

'I won't be in Bombay anytime soon, Ant. I have an assignment for the week that I may barely accomplish by Sunday night. Then I have to be back in London—'

'Papa's...'

Had Anant gone silent, or was it static?

'... no more.'

No more. The noise in Noor's ears was thunderous. Why was the airport in such commotion? She glanced around: people ambled past, lugging luggage, chatting into cell phones, craning their necks for flight information, business as usual... The roar was in her head. She willed herself to stillness. *No more.* The words crashed down on her: her eardrums were runways; hammer, anvil, stirrup pounded with the touchdown; her brain braked to sudden comprehension.

⁂

Mama sat on a white bedsheet on the floor. Her hands, forlorn in her lap, a pair of autumn leaves. Her head, covered with a white chunni, reclining against the wall, a snapped twig. As Papa's elder sister, Balwant Pua had staked her position beside Mama, from where she massaged her arm and issued soothing words, her bark-textured skin quivering. A couple of colony-aunties scurried around. Noor picked her way through, hugged her mother and kissed the papery skin before resting her head against her bosom. Mama's eyes looked vacant. Noor remembered a time once before when they had hollowed out similarly—as if they had walked out in pursuit of the lost one.

In the large courtyard, Neymat, who had arrived earlier from Delhi, had taken charge, not surprisingly. She had met Noor with a tight hug, her dry eyes red-rimmed, motioned with a chin towards Mama and gone back to supervising the cotton mats being rolled out in anticipation of those who would come to condole. A solemn Arjun was helping his mother straighten the ends and pat them down. Not for the first time Noor wondered how Neymat did it.

Neymat was the eldest child and, at four feet and eleven inches, the shortest. But height seldom had much to do with stature, as Napoleon had demonstrated, and Neymat's epithet in the Bhalla clan was '*Madre Gallina* Two'. The second mother hen. But for Neymat, Mrs Bhalla's nine-to-five job at a teachers' training institute would have created a supervisory vacuum when the children returned home from their school at 1:45 p.m. While the maid warmed the food and set the table, Neymat ensured that Noor and Anant changed out of school uniforms, discarded the sweaty shirts into the washing machine which doubled as laundry basket, hung the pleated skirt/pants to air, placed their black Bata school shoes on the shoe rack, deposited their silver-buckled plastic red belts and blue ties in their almirahs, washed their hands, sat down to eat, and amidst the exchange of school gossip, bickering, pulling faces, actually managed to consume their meal. After that, it was siesta time in summers, or straight to homework, by the end of which Mrs Bhalla would be climbing the steps to their first-floor home.

Neymat was no master puppeteer and the children—feisty Noor, unruly Anant—were less marionettes and more warriors who engaged in daily skirmishes and lusty yelling, despite the age difference of twelve years. Since Noor's nose was perennially buried in books, the mischievous Anant had figured out that the best way to rile her was to hide her book the moment Noor took a break. When Noor stopped leaving books around, he startled her with a whole-wheat lizard—toasted on an iron griddle, black lentils for eyes—flung from behind so that it mimicked a house lizard plunging from the ceiling. Yet, the fractious members, much in the manner of the jousting members of the Indian Parliament, managed to pull together and conduct business under Speaker Neymat.

Noor saw a group of men walk in and Sunny Vir, as the elder son-in-law, approached them. By turns they clasped his extended hand in both of theirs, nodding, speaking softly. Then they sought out Jinder Tayaji, who sat in one corner, hands in his lap, opening-closing-examining them, as if for lost contents. He was her favourite uncle, whose bobbing pennant, as he ascended the steps to the house, his face hidden behind brown-paper bags of toffees, paperbacks, pens and scented erasers, invariably got the children grinning. And yet, Papa and he had always shared an uneasy relationship. Often, in summer, the kids would spend their entire vacation in Chandigarh, the family of five taking over the two-roomed bachelor pad. Months later, they would hear from somebody that Jinder Tayaji had visited Ferozepur, but the children had not received a visit, which only meant that the brothers were in the non-communicating phase.

Balwant Pua poked Noor and asked her to fetch a glass of water. Then she returned to scanning the gathering, her eyes ferrety behind the outsized glasses. Nestled in her neck, like a lizard, was a thin henna-dyed braid. Once inside the dark kitchen, Noor studied Balwant Pua.

She was the unfathomable one: never properly married, she had two girls and 'Uncle Khufiya', the mystery man, for consort-spouse, as well as the lion's share of her father's vast inheritance. She was, for all practical purposes, the villain of Noor's childhood. Courtesy whom the 'Will' surfaced at Bapuji's deathbed, allocating the family property disproportionately, and causing those deep silences at the occasional mandatory family gatherings.

The next instant a group of white-clothed heavy-assed aunties jigged around the corner, abruptly blaring their trumpets of sorrow. Noor grimaced and glanced towards Mama. She had not stirred. This condolence was a dreadful piece of Punjabi theatre. She watched them approach Mama, palms outstretched, pretending to beat their chests, torsos swaying in rhythm with their keening, before burying their faces in their white chunnis as they squatted amongst the other mourners. Having delivered a perfect piece of Punjabi siapa—all vocal, no lachrymal—they started to whisper with their neighbours. Balwant Pua leaned forward to supply answers, nodding her head lugubriously.

Noor lingered in the kitchen, attempting to stay her irritation. Balwant Pua was a childhood scab. The children, Anant and Noor—perhaps because of age or temperament, Neymat was above such puerile conjectures—routinely weaved wild surmises around the colourful aunt in relationship with a mystery man. They had never seen Uncle Khufiya, Neymat's claim of once having sighted a tall man with an elegant silver goatee was put down to her genteel nature which habitually skirted scandal. In any case, Uncle Khufiya was rumoured to surface in Balwant Pua's life at night-time, though people—those with idle minds and loose tongues—said how could they know there was one Uncle Khufiya and not more? Anant and Noor would look at each other goggle-eyed, before clasping a hand over their mouths, laughter sputtering through.

Noor wished Anant was here now. It was he who had picked her up from the railway station, his shirt sticking to his back though it was early morning. He had been running errands, he had said.

'What errands?'

'Arranging ice,' Anant had replied quietly. 'I have been requisitioning ice for twenty-four hours now.'

In the fierce heat of April, Papa's body would start to decompose. First Anant had gone to the cold drink stall that stood right outside the house. But the owner had sorrowfully informed him, 'You will require a couple of *blocks* of ice for this, puttar.' Anant had then thought of Azad Tent House, the regular supplier of sundries—chairs, jute carpets, tents, drinking water fountains—for weddings and parties. Upon reaching there he had found Azad, the proprietor, standing in the midst of ice mounds, sweating profusely as he oversaw the hacking and loading. When Anant had placed his order, Azad had barked, 'So much ice? Should you not have placed the order in advance?'

But Anant wasn't around: he was riding his scooter through the alleys of Ferozepur's bazaar, running more errands in preparation for the cremation.

The Complete Idiot's Guide to Human Combustion: Put a person atop piled logs, pin him down with more, the face last, until a pyramid of wood emerges. In elliptical perambulations, splay ghee on the wooden tombstone, covering maximum surface area. Next, strike a match and feed the fuel. Watch it devour the clarified butter and grow. Watch the slimy pustules scramble out. Watch the hungry flames yearn for the skies, reaching out with black fingertips. Watch him combust. Hear him crackle and disintegrate. Smell him roast. Behold the blazing wooden stump sag from the hand of the incendiary, Anant. Around the coliseum the crowd stands.

❧

In the evening, with the cremation done and the mourners gone, Noor made her way to the terrace of the second floor. She watched birds fly in batches across the darkening firmament, soundlessly hurrying home. From the Mall Road came the sound of their human counterparts scurrying around on their bleating-hooting motors. In the regular manner of people who died, Noor's father had upped and left abruptly. Yet, Noor could not shake off the feeling of being short-changed. Parents were meant to hang around, be there, watch from the sidelines, whatever, even when the children grew up and went about their lives, calling infrequently, visiting seldom…

In the fifteen years that she had been away from home, Papa had changed, Noor knew, in the same way that one is aware of global warming—it seldom impinges on one. Papa had become reticent, he had fewer questions about college or friends or work—even the exotic foreign cities she travelled to didn't evoke much interest. But the mere presence of a parent meant one could be a child, one could come home to lick one's wounds when the world got to be too much. In that lay comfort, one that Noor had never disrupted by attempting to enquire about her father's increasingly worn-down self.

Pursing her lips, she now gazed into the distance, past the railing, in the direction of the lawn. Many years ago, a gulmohar tree had stood there. In the manner of an amputee who continues to feel pain in a leg long gone, every time she returned home, Noor saw the gulmohar first, then the empty space. Its blazing flowers had been her companions as she had spent countless days of summer vacations reading in its generous shade, an auburn leaf gracing a page every now and then with its careless, gentle fall. One day she came home from Chandigarh for a mid-semester break in her engineering course and found the gulmohar gone. When she quizzed the gardener, a gaunt man who seemed to have poured a lifetime's energy into making the brilliant azaleas, roses, sunflowers and lilies bloom, he said it had got hollow from within. And one morning, it had just toppled over.

That night, Uncle Bitta arrived, his usual mischievousness muffled in the suddenly grieving home of his younger cousin, old friend, Baksh. The house was quiet, the guests had departed and Mama was resting in her darkened bedroom. Five days ago he had stopped overnight and spent time with Baksh before catching the morning train to Lahore, Uncle Bitta informed the children as Neymat handed him tea.

Uncle Bitta was part of the contingent of businessmen that had travelled with the prime minister on his first foray to Pakistan—six months back—to improve trade relations. Since then, he had followed up with individual exploratory trips. 'Scouting for business,' he had grinned at Noor while discussing his business plans during her previous visit. 'The potential is immense. For Pakistani exports *other* than terror,' he had said with his trademark wink.

Now, he opened his suitcase, withdrew a packet wrapped in brown paper and handed it to Noor. 'You might find use for this.'

'What is it, Uncle?'

'Green tea and niyoza—your father asked for it.'

Niyoza. Pine nuts. Papa loved those. On an average winter day, Noor could plunge her hand into the deep pockets of his chocolate-brown overcoat and expect to come up with a handful. The dainty black nuts, however, were tough to crack and Noor always waited for Papa to relax on the terrace and start to skilfully snap them with his thumb and index finger. As the tiny glistening cream-coloured spindles emerged, Noor would thrust her hand forward for a few, and Papa would deposit them in her palm.

Tears stung Noor's eyes. Uncle Bitta patted her head. Gruffly, he said, 'Baksh is probably looking down at us right now'—he thrust his chin skywards—'seated atop some cumulus cloud cushion, enjoying his whisky.'

When Noor started to sob, he wrapped a burly arm around her. 'All right, let me divulge the joke then. I was saving it for Baksh, but seeing that I have made you cry, let me see if I can make you smile. Un-hunh?

'I was in Jamrud, which is right at the doorway to Khyber Pass, to see the fort. If you remember your history, Jamrud was conquered by Hari Singh Nalwa, Maharaja Ranjit Singh's commander—something even the English never managed!' Uncle Bitta snorted. 'And there I got talking with a burly Pathan who asked for a list of places I had visited in Pakistan. Hearing my reply, the Pathan chuckled. "So, where did you find Pakistan?

Lahore is like Dilli. Islamabad, of course, is a very nice city, green, clean. But so far from Pakistan, no? And Peshawar, well, Peshawar is the city of Pathans–Afghans. Good luck, Mr India, in your hunt for Pakistan, and when you find it,"' Uncle Bitta jogged his brows as he aped the Pathan, '"do enlighten us."'

Noor smiled. Papa would have enjoyed the joke.

The bell rang. A policeman stood close to the meshed screen door, his protuberant belly sporting black and white checks where the light reflected through the net. Noor held her breath as a decade and a half collapsed in front of her eyes. Many years ago, a bell had rung in the same way, a fat policeman had arrived unexpectedly, and carried into the house news that would forever upset the equilibrium of their home. He looked like the same policeman… What was it this time around?

Uncle Bitta and Anant trooped out and led him to the corner of the terrace, where they stood for a long time, their heads lowered in soft conversation. The conference over, the policeman left. Anant informed them gruffly that he had come to offer condolences. Uncle Bitta patted Noor's head and beamed a reassuring smile at all. There was nothing to worry about.

But the policeman had awakened a past memory and, though no one spoke about it, each felt a dread settle within.

BAKSH

THE LAST WALK

*B*aksh *was dimly aware that he had reached the chowk. A pack of strays ambled about, their yowling stirring the night air even as bodies sprawled beneath sheets continued their undisturbed roadside slumber. The lottery stand stood in its usual spot, shuttered. An erstwhile hand-driven cart, it had grown into a tin shack with permanent residency on the footpath and now sold Archies Cards, dailies and magazines. Gul, the proprietor—whose Afghani ancestor had fallen for the Punjab plains years ago while selling Kabuli almonds and dates—had been selling him lottery tickets ever since he missed the Sikkim lottery by one digit.*

One digit, the children sighed whenever they heard, reheard, overheard the story of the Ambassador car they had almost had. Until one day Neymat announced, 'A miss is as good as a mile, Papa,' and retreated into her botany book. Preet, chopping vegetables, gave Baksh a glance-over and shook her head. The story he had stopped rehashing since, but Gul, he persisted with. The retelling of his narrow miss over the years had made the four-wheeler, and everything related to it, a part of his life. In any case, Gul's trove of couplets—they swapped one each day—was unparalleled.

Gul: Urdu for flower. He should switch to Guldan, flowerpot, the children guffawed. But they still had to learn: wisdom and beauty—how unlikely the places where they could sometimes reside. Like in Miansaab, his henna-bearded Urdu tutor…

Forgotten memories started to stir within him again, like cold vapours in a winter courtyard warming to the sun's honeyed rays.

1947

A truck of Muslim soldiers had fired at the gurudwara in the city, killing the priest and the devotees inside. The women, they had carried off. Later, a gunny bag filled with chopped breasts had been found in the chowk…

Despite the rising murmurs on the eve of Partition, Miansaab, like most others, had decided to stay put, driven both by inertia and an inability to imagine the worst. A day after the disclosure of the Radcliffe Line, 18 August 1947, the Urdu tutor found himself afloat in a sea of incredible transmutation. After hundreds of years, a nation awakened to emancipation.

And two hundred years after Ahmad Shah Abdali first crossed the Indus river, the marauding hordes returned once more. Then, Abdali had returned from Punjab with fifty cart-loads of heads of Sikhs, leading the Sikhs—in the subsequent eight invasions—to resist a stronger army through guerrilla warfare. Now, two centuries later, the progeny of the erstwhile warriors readied to shed blood again and Punjab, the historical battleground, prepared for the next Ghallughara. Men locked their mothers, daughters, wives and young children inside the house—the weak fortified with pellets of afeem—armed them with petrol cans and matchboxes, with instructions to ignite if they failed in the guard outside. While fireworks lit the sky above Delhi, Jauhar fires, greedily licking the bodies of women seeking refuge in death, roared in Punjab.

Bapuji hid Miansaab in the hay barn beside the cowshed—it was the only safe place, in case somebody came checking. The cowshed stood against the wall of the haveli's eastern courtyard. Two water buffaloes were tethered inside. Since the attack on the gurudwara, the city had been lit up at night by fires in Muslim localities and rent during day by ominous shrieks, banging doors, crackling timber, gunshots, slash of knives.

Raj karega Khalsa, aaki rahe na koi… The truth will prevail, no enemy shall remain…

The cries grew louder, the air ponderous with dread, thickened by smoke, warm with flesh smells. A loud banging on the nail-studded wooden gate of the haveli announced the arrival of the pack at their door.

Bapuji, in white kurta-pajama, the white beard tied in a loose knot beneath the chin, a muslin turban on his head, motioned to Lehna, the odd-job man at the haveli, to open the door. Then he sat down on the charpai beneath the mango tree, hands clenched in his lap, trying to project the semblance of a calm householder interrupted in his evening rest.

'Waheguru ji ka Khalsa, Waheguru ji ki fateh,' rang forth as a crowd of fifteen–twenty Sikhs leapt into the courtyard. Some held flaming torches, some glistening kirpans, a few brandished their scythes and swords.

'Where is he? Where is the Urdu master?' shouted one agitated voice.

A man in the front motioned to those behind with an outstretched left arm. 'We have no fight with you,' he said to Bapuji. 'Hand us the Muslim master and we will leave.'

Baksh, standing behind the cot, recognized the leader. He had come to the haveli a few days earlier, collecting money for buying arms and raising a Khalsa Army. To protect our innocent Sikhs, he had said. That agenda had obviously grown to include the killing of others, innocent or otherwise.

Bapuji stood up, a white dwarf against the heaving manticore spewing fire and steel. 'Bhai, you have been misled. The master is not here. We have not seen him since a week when he came for the last class that Baksh attended,' he said, pointing to his younger son.

'We have proof that he is hidden here. It does not behove you to hide a Mussalman in your house.'

'This is a community of curs!' one mobster declared. 'Why do you want to side with them against us? Do you forget what all our people have faced at their hands?'

'But a dog is a loyal animal,' Jinder Paji spoke from the rattan chair where he had been lounging, his books piled around the table lamp. 'Everyone acknowledges that.'

All eyes turned to him and Baksh wondered how wise it was of him to interfere.

'They are no one's friends. Right from the time of our gurus, the Muslims have been an enemy of the Sikhs. Such atrocities they have committed. Such zulm! Now is our turn to avenge it all.'

But Jinder Paji was not giving up. He spoke calmly, only his leg shook convulsively at the knee. 'In the battle at Anandpur Sahib, Guru Gobind Singh instructed Bhai Kanhaiya, the water-carrier, to give water and first-aid to *all* wounded persons, Sikhs and Muslims alike. Then how can you forget the Guru's actions and behave differently?'

One particularly fierce mobster sprang forth and waved his spear at Jinder Paji. He wore the blue shift characteristic of the Nihang Sikhs, a towering blue turban decorated with miniature steel implements, a kirpan slung across his waist. 'Three of our gurus were killed by the Muslims. How do you forget *that*?' Then throwing a look at his comrades behind, he said, 'Who will take their revenge?'

'Aaho. Revenge!' rose a chorus.

'Enough lecturing, I say. Let's find the bastard!'

'Oye, come with me. I told you he's hiding in the barn.' Their next-door neighbour came from behind the crowd, a sword in his right hand. He looked from Bapuji to the leader. 'What are we waiting for?'

What a strange fit of amnesia it was, Baksh thought. This man routinely shared chai or hookah with Bapuji beneath the peepul tree. He had called for assistance when his buffalo had birthed early. Why, the two families chatted over the rooftop terrace on starlit nights, when sleep proved elusive.

The throng surged towards the eastern wall of the courtyard. Fervent cries suffused the air. The barn door was thrust aside and the men leading the charge rushed inside. Hacking indiscriminately through the pile of dried straw, they sent the twigs zigzagging, poked behind the clutter with their spears and flung the clanking pans, pails and pots about. Others looked on for evidence of a limb sailing through.

No sound came, nobody jumped out and fell at their feet begging for mercy, or life, or both. The hay lay scattered all around, the wheel and buckets were kicked viciously, but there was no one.

They turned on the neighbour. 'Didn't you say he was here?'

'Definite-definite. Why else would plates of roti and dal go inside the barn three times a day? Have buffaloes started eating our food, hain?'

'Maybe he has run away.'

'Or maybe,' the neighbour's eyes were alight with cunning, 'he's hiding elsewhere in the house.'

Baksh shivered. Jinder Paji tensed in his chair, the knee-dance freezing momentarily.

Bapuji folded his hands together, held them in front of his chest and addressed the leader who was looking around. 'Look, you have searched what you came for. Now you must leave. We are simple people. We have no fight with anybody. Whoever you are searching for, please continue it elsewhere.'

The leader looked ready to assent. Bapuji had given him money for buying weapons—maybe the memory of that made him less aggressive than the rest. Jinder Paji's eyes darted from Bapuji to the hesitant leader.

'*No-o!*' yelled the neighbour, jumping in front. 'Why give up without searching the house? I tell you,' he thrust his sword vehemently in the direction of the living quarters, 'I am right.'

The leader motioned to two men to begin a search through the living quarters. One carried a flaming torch, the other a scythe, as they started from the western perimeter. First was Jinder Paji's room. Besides a bed, a study table and books strewn all over, they found nothing. Next, Balwant's Pehnji's room—unoccupied since her marriage.

The northern wing consisted of the kitchen, pantry, a bare room for guests and Bapuji and Maji's large two-bedroom set.

The search through the kitchen and pantry was over soon and then they were at the threshold of the master bedroom. They proceeded to step over the threshold. Every eye was riveted on the door when a female voice rang out, 'Stop!'

The men halted, unsure. The voice continued, 'There are women inside. Have you no shame?'

The leader stepped forward and spoke gruffly, 'We just want to take a quick look. Why don't you step aside while—'

'Have you no ma-pehn in your family that you want to come inside searching women's rooms?'

A woman emerged from within, a chunni covering her head, the lace framing her stern features and the queen-like forehead.

Maji! What would happen now? His mother seldom spoke against anything, preferring to show her anger by stroking the ladles harder in the pan, or steeling her mouth in a stiff disapproving line.

She held the chunni in her right hand, partially framing her face. 'What excuse is this—in the guise of religion, you want to enter the women's quarters? If you are a Sikh, then remember, I am a Sikhni.' Maji stood tall and straight, left arm clasped across her chest, eyes unflinching, seeing ahead but refusing to look at the strange men. 'I dare you to enter!'

Thank God that Cousin Bitta's mother had moved in with them a week back. Maji's sister, she had come visiting, but trouble broke out soon after and she was forced to stay on. A cot had been added to the divan in the living area, next to the master bedroom. The chairs and table had been removed to make space and were placed in the courtyard. Normally, Maji was the only woman who lived in the house and there were no women's quarters as such. But her sister's extended visit had changed that. The neighbour-turned-aggressor being aware of this, his mouth puckered in confusion.

The leader nodded his head. He sheathed his kirpan and turned to the throng watching the unfolding spectacle. 'Let's go, after all, we have seen most of the house.'

Rumbles burst forth from the gathering as he folded his hands to Bapuji and motioned to the crowd to move.

'But...' the neighbour protested.

'Who but a eunuch would hide behind a woman's kameez? Let's go. He's not worth the trouble.' The leader looked at his throng hesitantly shuffling about in the yard. 'We have *other* business to finish, or have you forgotten?' A swift flick of his raised right hand and ominously he started to walk towards the main door.

Their collective manhood declared, future intent established, the mob sallied forth. A rustle of lungis, scraping of leather juttis, sputter of leaping flames, and the visitors were gone.

Lehna jammed the heavy bolt into its slot, then slumped against the wooden door.

❧

Early next morning, Lehna fed the horse and got the buggy ready. Bapuji had two tall brass tumblers of warm milk, egg bhurji and ten parathas for breakfast in the master bedroom itself. Then he left for the cantonment, a couple of kos away.

Baksh and Jinder Paji conversed softly with the servants in the courtyard, discussing the fresh reports of violence they had brought. Later that day, Bodh Singh, the caretaker of the extensive Bhalla farms, arrived from Rakhri farm on the outskirts of the city. His strapping frame stooped with the weight his heart was carrying. The Muslim tenants who had stayed on after Partition were dead. A Sikh mob, some fifty-people strong, attacked their tenements at dusk, setting fire to the houses. The fields were spared because they belonged to Bapuji, a Sikh. When people ran screaming from the flames into the open, they were speared or slashed with a kirpan. Heads lay scattered amongst the crops, the blood drying in brown trails on the soil.

The elderly farmer sat on a stool, his shoulders slumped, and touched his ears repeatedly with his fingers. 'Tauba, tauba. Such evil! A toddler who escaped from one house was speared and his body held aloft as the mob departed for other villages. Where does this bestiality come from?'

Bapuji returned before sunset. He had managed to make contact with Colonel Gurbaksh Singh, a relative in the interwoven network of a Punjabi clan. He was escorting some trucks to Lahore with refugee Muslims.

Maji prepared a dozen rotis and cumin potatoes, folded them in a cotton napkin with mango pickle and packed them in a date palm leaf basket. An outsized aluminium trunk that had come as part of Maji's dowry was brought out of the store and emptied of woollen sweaters and blankets. It would now carry Miansaab.

Around ten, an army one-ton arrived at the haveli. Crouched in the trunk, foetus-like, Miansaab looked defenceless and vulnerable as he thanked Bapuji with mute tears. Three jawaans carried the trunk through the darkened courtyard and hoisted it onto the army vehicle. Baksh watched from behind the latticed window of Jinder Paji's room as the vehicle executed a swift U-turn and sped off towards the cantonment. Two Sikh soldiers with rifles bobbed grimly in the back.

DAY 3: NOOR

A raucous trilling had begun on the first-floor terrace. A gaggle of sparrows fluttered in the air, landed on the railing, hopped onto the concrete floor before clambering onto the large earthen bowl, pecking inside with their beaks, even disappearing into its cavernous shell. Noor watched them disinterestedly. 'Feed them some dough balls, they have come in search of those.' Her mother came up behind her. 'Usually, I put it out first thing in the morning.'

Noor took the kneaded flour from the fridge, rolled small balls with her right thumb and index finger, then walked out to the terrace. The birds were unafraid and hopped gingerly around Noor. She emptied the dough balls into the earthen pot and changed the water in the drinking bowl.

Soon two pigeons flew down, edging the sparrows off the rim of the pot. Next came a parakeet, its green neck ringed by a brilliant red, its beak twitching as it sat and ate the atta. The next instant a caw-caw filled the air as a big black crow swooped down, landed on the terrace floor, its wings held aloft as it angrily marched towards the pot. The other birds flew away. The crow's coat shone a lustrous blue-black, its beak was pincer-like and, funnily, it had only one leg. It hopped onto the pot on that leg and started to greedily consume the rest of the food. Mama joined Noor and wistfully said, 'Your Papa used to call him Long John Silver. "Saala kaan!" he would say. "Early morning who wants to listen to his caw-caw? Perhaps we should get a scarecrow." "That will scare away the other birds too," I said. "Hunh," he grunted. "Why do the English say one thing and mean another? Shouldn't a scarecrow do just that: scare crows?"'

ha

Later in the morning, Noor ushered Jinder Tayaji inside. He walked briskly, his pennant bobbing, as he rubbed hands in front of his chest. 'How is everything?'

Neymat nodded. 'And you?'

'Changa. Fine-fine.' He glanced around, settled into the armchair that Anant proffered and resumed his hand massage. Abruptly, he announced, 'I want a photo of Baksh. Nice photo, haan, colour, black and white—any will do. Better, give both. Black and white... good for the newspaper, colour for the symposium.'

'Symposium?'

Noor sat on the divan beside Neymat, facing her uncle. He seemed to have recovered from the daze that had seized him since Papa's passing. Had the idea of a symposium energized him? To Noor, he epitomized idiosyncrasy. Perhaps it was to do with the fact that he was so different from everyone around. In a culture where marriage was a rite of passage into adulthood, he was a bachelor. In a religion where smoking was taboo, he merrily lit his Gold Flake anywhere and everywhere. His turban was a brilliant printed muslin, a jaunty contrast to the pastels sported by most Sikh men. He even wore it the old-fashioned way—instead of neatly tucking the folds in, he let one end unfurl and stand upright on his head. Eccentric, idiosyncratic Jinder Tayaji—that was how she always saw him.

Noor's eyes swept warmly over her uncle who now sat crunching the pleats of his pennant with both hands, firming its uprightness. His bejewelled fingers—topaz and sapphire set in silver or gold, a total of six rings—had the texture of old potatoes. He had certainly got more eccentric with age.

'Some privileges I have,' Jinder Tayaji spoke, addressing the three children, 'as president of the Retired Officers Association. I have proposed a symposium on Baksh. To recount his life, his contributions to the city, to the Bar Association, etcetera. The local reporter for *The Tribune* has confirmed he will print an article on Baksh.'

'Why do we need that?' Noor piped up.

Jinder Tayaji's hands, dangling from the arms of his chair, clenched and unclenched. His clear eyes gazed at Noor as he said, 'You children of today don't understand the importance of such things—'

'But... but it sounds so highfalutin. Like some... some Rotary conference on... on ending Indo–Pak hostilities.' The next instant Noor bit her tongue at her gaffe: Jinder Tayaji led candlelight peace vigils at the Hussainiwala border every Independence Day.

'Interesting word: highfalutin. High-fa-lu-tin. The usage of which confers on the user the very same quality.' He fixed his gaze on Noor. 'Personally, I prefer *pretentious*.'

For a while, everything went quiet.

After several minutes, Jinder Tayaji offered, 'It's a way to honour him.'

Neymat looked at Noor. 'No harm.'

Anant shrugged.

But Noor continued to remain doubtful. 'I don't think he would have liked it.'

'Really?' Poking an index finger into his jumbled beard, Jinder Tayaji riffled through the white, russet and black hairs. 'How well did you know your father?'

※

Dusk lashed the indigo sky with vivid streaks: swathes of flaming orange, slivers of fuchsia, blips of white. Noor walked the length of the rooftop terrace: the railing overlooking the Mall Road at one end, the solitary room left unfinished at the other. It was fully constructed, windows and doors in place, but no paint, no furnishing, since neither Papa nor Mama could decide what to do with it. In any case, Papa never consulted anyone on his building sprees. Once, he had commenced re-flooring the bedrooms a fortnight before her pre-engineering exams.

'Don't you know,' she had ranted, 'hammers chipping away in the background are not conducive to comprehending the structure of Benzene, or solving quadratic equations?'

In answer, Papa had shrugged.

It was time to go down and assist Neymat with dinner. Not that she knew much cooking, but she was a useful handyman of the chopping onions, cubing tomatoes, laying the table variety. She cast a last glance at the sky—a sunset was perhaps the only thing that redeemed an Indian summer.

An elderly woman sat in the veranda, conversing softly with Mama. Noor wished her—a quick bow, hands folded—and proceeded to the kitchen where Neymat was straining milky tea into a cup. Placing it on a tray, she motioned to Noor to take it outside.

'Who is she?'

'A neighbour from the Old House.'

'Hmm...' Noor patted her eyelids—the overworked tear duct did not help her contact lenses, rendering them foggy or dry.

'Her son, Prince, was implicated in some terrorist incident—Papa had taken the case.'

'Yes... I recall the name!' Noor nodded in remembrance. 'Prince! The old woman, I had named her Queen—'

Neymat raised her eyebrows.

'Well, what else do you call the mother of a Prince, hunh? Queen was my morning wake-up call for most of tenth class. She would be here before Mama had finished making the first cup of tea and stay until Papa departed for the courts. She would refuse food, sit quietly in a chair, wait for Papa to offer some news, something with which she could depart and spend the rest of the day before returning the next morning. Funny...' Noor shook her head. 'Papa couldn't have had concrete information to give on most days—after all, her son was held under TADA.'

Noor walked out to the veranda with the tea, offered it to the woman and sat down beside Mama, the tray tucked between both hands. Queen was probably older than Jinder Tayaji. She blew on the tea, sucked it in slowly, licking her lips after every swallow.

'I would have come early. Baksh had given us support in our days of need... But my knees—they just jam up. Doctor says... these old bones.' Extending a wrinkled hand, she sought Mama's forearm. 'Baksh... I had seen him since I got married and came to my husband's house—then he was some nine–ten years of age...'

This woman had seen her father that young! What else could she tell about Papa? How did he look? What was he like? Playful, naughty, or was he the serious type? And studies? Absorbed in her thoughts, Noor had missed part of what the woman was saying.

'—I thought to go out and call him. But my poor knees. And when I finally looked out of the window again, he was walking down the lane.'

Who? What? When?

'Who? Who was walking down the lane?' Noor shot the question at the bent figure.

'Baksh. Your father.'

'When?'

'The day he died.'

The *day* he died? Did the woman know he had passed away by 7.30 a.m.? She could not see the old woman's eyes, sunk deep in her flaccid face. Her head drooped over a sagging frame, like the Pope whenever he appeared on TV: in urgent need of puppet strings to prop him up.

'W-what time did you see him?'

The woman sipped the tea, her throat bobbed, the folds ringing the neck pulsed like a pond into which a stone had been thrown. 'Must be some… I heard the carpenter's cock crow… four, four-thirty. Sleep doesn't really come to me, puttar, so I lie awake most of the time. Night, day—they become the same in old age.'

'Four in the morning? You saw Papa at four in the morning the day he passed away? Where?'

'The steps of the haveli,' she said, rising to leave.

A taste, like she had bitten into an old almond, seeped into Noor's mouth. She looked at Mama, who sat recumbent, head tilted, against the wall behind. Her eyes were shut. Had she even heard what the old woman had said? What would Papa be doing at the haveli steps at four in the morning? And why? Why was he there? Why not upstairs with Jinder Tayaji? Tayaji had not mentioned any such thing—so was he unaware? But, four was too early for his walk—he usually left around five-thirty, six...

Mama was shaking her elbow. 'Help her with the steps.'

As she escorted the woman, Noor learnt afresh that Papa was sitting on the haveli steps. In deep thought. Then he walked in the direction of the gurudwara. Through the miasma of age and ailment, the information emerged in bits, and Noor processed it. Most likely, the woman was mistaken. She must have seen somebody else, some homeless person... Or she had mixed things up. After all, she was so *old*. Even Jinder Tayaji did that at times—mixing up events and dates. Yet, he would be convinced that he knew what he was saying.

At the gate, Noor hailed a rickshaw and helped the old woman climb into it. Her gaunt frame was limp and weighty, a sack of coal.

As the driver started to pedal away she turned her head in Noor's direction and said, her words fading away in the roar of the traffic, 'One more thing, puttar. As he sat there, he was massaging his leg and shoulder—the left side.'

꥟

The cement floor was cool. Noor placed her palms on it. Then transferred the coolness to her eyelids. The air-conditioner hummed, and reassurance sallied on its cool sweeps and rhythmic whirr. In the backdrop, the generator's muffled thundering buffeted the house like a rough hand rocking the cradle to the accompaniment of the AC's soft lullaby.

'How well did you know your father?' Jinder Tayaji had asked, the look in his eyes saying he knew the answer. Was she right in her assumption that Papa would not like to be fussed over for the sole reason that he had died? His picture, though, had appeared in the paper once.

She had been attempting to figure out the differential rate of change, limit approaching infinity, when Papa had placed the day's *Tribune* next to her calculus book and pointed to a picture at the top. The upper half of the folded paper, page three, showed a group of black-coated lawyers flanking the Punjab chief minister who had wound up a discussion with members of the Ferozepur Bar Association. Papa stood to the extreme right, a little removed from his fawning colleagues.

With raised brows, he had pointed to the picture, a mischievous grin playing hide-and-seek in his unkempt morning beard. 'So?'

Preoccupied with wading through d/dy of functions, Noor had returned a vague smile, the back of her mind processing the gap in the conclave. Like a disgruntled child coaxed into a birthday party snapshot? Or was Papa an *independent* in a group photograph? The cause behind the visible void she had learnt later.

If not for Mehta Uncle, Noor would never have got to know. He had come to pick up his wife, who was their social sciences teacher, and on sighting Noor, as she cycled out of the school gate, he had commented to his wife, 'Is she as headstrong as her father?' Noor had pretended not to hear but had slowed down to catch the ensuing conversation between husband and wife.

Apparently, the chief minister, on his first visit to the Ferozepur Bar Association, had been lambasted by Bhallasaab on the issue of young boys being detained under TADA. The other lawyers had remained suitably silent, as per decorum, and in any case, who wanted to bell the cat? But Bhallasaab, no—he had berated the chief minister on his government's human rights record, citing specific cases! The Bar didn't know what to do with him! He was a senior lawyer with too much indiscretion for either a *senior*, or a *lawyer*.

Reaching forward, Noor picked up a notebook from the trestle table. It was a school exercise book, the kind children use for mathematics, the pages marked with neat squares. On the first page, Papa had written some names. Against each name extended a series of numbers. At the bottom of the leaf was a date. Roughly two months back.

Quickly she turned the pages. The pattern was repeated throughout. The book was more than half full, the last date was two days before he died.

It was his lottery notebook. Where he penned the names of various lotteries. What were those numbers though? Probabilities? Calculations on which one would win the jackpot? Heera, Moti, Lakshmi, Kanshi—innocuous, nondescript names: what promise had they held?

She did not know. Nor did she understand. For, amazed that a sane man could be taken in by such a venture, she had always observed his 'legalized gambling' with faint disdain.

Abruptly, Noor got up and opened the teak almirah beside the bed. She moved a hand against the suits and shirts hung from the wooden rod, feeling the soft twill, the well-worn jacquards, the winter pinstripes, the undulating seersucker on which her hand, and mind, now paused.

'Seersucker or sheer-shakar?' Papa had asked her, one turbulent evening in the 1980s, when trouble brewed outside, and at home. After another battle with Mama, he had retreated to his cane chair on the front balcony. Mounted on a wall behind him were the twin portraits of the two gurus that could be found in every Sikh home: Sobha Singh's rendition of the first, Guru Nanak, and the tenth, Guru Gobind. Between them, they spanned a faith from its pacifist start to its militant transformation. A syncretist and a crusader. A shah-fakir and a soldier-saint. Somewhere on that scale lay most followers of the religion, Noor had thought. Those like Papa tipped the left, the ones like Mama weighted the right. Seersucker? Whisky glass in hand, Papa had elucidated. 'Sheer: milk, shakar: sugar, together they give the name to the cloth that looks like milk with bumpy grains of sugar in it! Yes, the English took it from us and made the joyous sheershakar into the washed-out seersucker!' Papa grinned. 'When Timur invaded India, he borrowed sugar from us; in turn, we borrowed the Persian term sheershakar for our striped summer wear until the English, their tongue toiling over Hindustani, made it seersucker!' He sighed then, his face suddenly vulnerable, his voice slurring, and said, 'Despite all the chauvinist nonsense around us nowadays, Noor, we are all palimpsests, remember that. Our histories are written in layers—peel them sufficiently and, underneath, we are all alike.'

There then was Papa—surging up in memories of young militants and lottery tickets and striped linen, a constantly shifting collage. Tears welled up in Noor's eyes. How well could any child answer the question: how well did you know your father?

BAKSH

Even after all these years, Baksh couldn't shake off the feeling that Miansaab's departure had marked the end of a certain way of life. He remembered he had been painting a portrait of Guru Nanak at the time. After Miansaab left, he resumed work on the picture, but the result surprised him. The Guru in the painting looked frail. His shoulders, draped in a phulkari shawl of blue and saffron squares, were not as broad as those depicted in the famous painter Sobha Singh's widely copied portrait of the Guru; the forehead was not smooth, but marked by a clutch of wrinkles. The painting lacked the munificence that radiated from Sobha Singh's portrait. The Guru's eyes looked tired and, yes, afraid. The painting was still with Baksh. It hung from a wall in the dim-lit storeroom, hidden behind piled-up steel trunks and the bedding rolls.

The Sutlej glistened in the distance. Baksh started to trudge through the bramble, making for the riverbank. Reaching it he took a deep breath and, as was his habit, opened himself up to the tryst—after all these years, when most certainties had seeped out of him, his affection for the river still held strong. Moonlight bound the man and the river together as Baksh studied the ripples from beneath which a river dolphin could be sighted on a lucky day; felt the river's languor as it wove down the plain, segmenting the alluvium into India and Pakistan; twitched his nose to the odour of effluents that besieged the river; inclined his head to catch the faint sibilant sound the river made, imperceptible except in solitude.

The river and he had known each other all his life, the relationship—like any long-standing one—was rocky. But that was not unusual. Punj-ab was the land of five rivers, and Punjabis had gained vigour from the waters, changing the course of the rivers to harness even desert land. But water has memory and every once in a while the mighty rivers conspired to halt human breaches.

With the Sutlej, of course, Baksh felt a special kinship. The longest of the five rivers, it journeyed along the northwest boundary of his town Ferozepur. During Partition, when time came to apportion the vast plains of Punjab, its rivers became natural boundaries. Ferozepur was Muslim dominant, and the laws of India's division allocated it to Pakistan. But Ferozepur was also a large military arsenal for the British, as it had been through history. They had used it as a strategic outpost to rein in the wily one-eyed Sikh Maharaja Ranjit Singh who, after driving the Afghans out of Punjab—a historic reversal—took Lahore as the capital of the first Sikh kingdom, smack under their twitching English noses. Therein lay the quandary of Ferozepur—a place that lived perennially in the shadow of Sutlej and Lahore. No wonder Partition saw a befuddled Ferozepur, one that didn't know whether to go left, or stay put. What Cyril Radcliffe demarcated, Mountbatten obliterated, thus forever marking Ferozepur as the border district of India. A region with fifty-five per cent Muslim population, which owed its foundation to a Muslim, was granted to India.

Baksh sighed: can a shadow be severed from its source?

Over the years, Lahore made repeated attempts to reclaim the sutured umbra, through two wars, intermittent cross-border firing and, finally, a sponsorship of Sikh militancy in the hope that it would carve Punjab out once again and graft it to its separated western twin.

Baksh watched the river's gentle careless sweep as it continued on its journey—how different it was from the fearsome foam that had once invaded his house, his neighbourhood, his horizon. Baksh had to sit down. As the weeds scrunched underneath, a recollection swamped him.

1947

It was afternoon when they heard: the Beas waters had submerged the railway bridge outside Amritsar. Harike, the confluence of Beas with Sutlej, was in such proximity to Ferozepur that they knew it was their turn to flee from the growing rage of the combined waters. For the past few months, the air had been thick with stories of how the Punjabi farmer—that hardy harvester of golden wheat, sunny mustard and downy cotton—had morphed into a mass-murderer. In turn, the caravans of partitioned people, heading east and west, begged for mercy—from the attacking hordes, from the stalking sun, from their God. But in the pantheon of deities that stayed unmoved, Indra, the god of rain, proved the most recalcitrant: the monsoons failed. Instead, rivulets of blood streaked the parched earth. The dry riverbed became a night halt for the refugees. Ravi, Sutlej, Beas—the mighty rivers tumbling from the Himalayas—foamed at this transgression. Swollen with molten snow, they now burst upon the plains like village louts lusting after a young widow. The aqueous phalanx, the rumours reaching them claimed, was higher than an average house.

Bapuji, a heavy cotton satchel bundled under his arm, accompanied by Lehna, hurried to the market to requisition a motorized vehicle—truck, jeep, van, whatever—at whatever cost. Maji packed a couple of suitcases, her chant of 'satnam, satnam' interrupted only when she drew a long breath to invoke God's mercy: 'Mehar kar, Waheguru, mehar.'

Baksh stood with Jinder Paji at the haveli door and watched the floor of the lane turn clayey. Soon the water seemed to ooze out of the earth, rising by inches. Within an hour the muddy water began to clutch at fleeing feet.

Mata, Bapuji's elder sister, sat on a cot in the courtyard while Maji locked the rooms. Widowed early in life and with six young boys to raise on her own, Mata had turned to her brother for help in managing her sprawling estate. She was visiting him that summer, as she did frequently. Now that the sons were married, they had each taken their share of the estate, the farms had been divided, and Mata was set free and homeless.

Maji had secured the doors to various rooms, even deposited the brass cooking vessels on the wooden shelves lining the veranda kitchen—the one used for cooking during the summer when the draft blew the smoke away and cooled a moistened brow—and Baksh wondered how high the water would rise. It was already level with the haveli's first doorstep. In all, there were three, each roughly a foot high.

'The water is rising fast…' Maji was beside them at the door, her voice steady, but her breath coming rapidly.

'Hanji,' replied Baksh needlessly, looking from the lane to his mother. Had she seen a flood before?

'They have been gone a while...' Maji tugged and patted her chunni, already in place around her shoulders and covering her head, arranging, rearranging the drape.

Residents of the lane were quickly decamping. Thick brown water, like jaggery syrup, tugged at a man shouldering a pregnant wife on one side and balancing a bamboo stave sagging at the ends from two makeshift cloth sacks on the other. A stray dog plodded ahead, alternating between yelps and high-pitched barks.

'Tch, tch. Chal! Tch, tch! Shabash!' A bullock cart trundled past, the driver urging the animal to lug the trap—heaped with a cot, clothes, suitcases, canisters, family members and a goat—through the sludge.

'He will be here soon,' Jinder Paji spoke in his soft hurried voice, not looking in Maji's direction. 'The water will take a while...' He scanned both ends of the lane.

Baksh looked from the lane to his brother and back. Everywhere people were stirred up. Amidst excited shouts, commands and fearful screams, doors were being slammed shut, bolts snapped; buffaloes, cows, horses galvanized; carts hitched and mounted. Suddenly, one man on a bicycle trilled past, energetically weaving his vehicle through the panicky crowd, a steel trunk lashed with jute rope to the carrier. 'Paran maro! Paran maro!' he shouted with a frantic bobbing of his head, even as his chest leaned way over the handlebar.

Go die elsewhere!

Baksh gulped down the constriction in his throat and shivered. Suddenly, death, that had hovered in the air like breath on a winter morning, that had been the inevitable fill-in-the-blank when mournful conversations petered out, was clamouring in their lane, surging at their doorstep. Fear constricting his throat, he tried to decipher his elder brother's expression. Jinder Paji's brow was furrowed in concentration, the inner lip bit at the corner, his lean body taut like a kite's spine. Suddenly, his hand shot out and clenched Baksh's arm as he commanded, 'Baksh! Quick, move!' and half-dragged him across the courtyard.

With frantic fingers Paji opened the door of the master bedroom and hurried inside. Baksh followed. With much laboured breathing and short stop-go breaks, they heaved, pulled and shoved the divan into the courtyard. It was a handsome structure made from tahli wood, large enough to seat five people comfortably, and sat on sturdy high legs, gaily lacquered.

'What is this, puttar? What are you doing, Jinder?' Worry and perplexity fought for dominance in Maji's face as Paji stooped over to catch his breath. Then he raised an index finger and said through ragged breath, his head cocked to the lane, 'Li-sten!'

The surrounding babble had risen, but added to the cacophony of human wails and animal snorts was a new sound. A roar could be heard approaching from a distance.

'The lane is flooding!' Mata yelled. 'Rabba!'

'Quick!' motioned Paji. 'Let's hoist the cot on top of the divan. That will give us some five–six feet of height… Baksh, you keep a lookout near the door. Yell if you sight either Bapuji or a wall of water.'

Wall of water! Baksh staggered to the door. Could the water really be that high? And that strong? He looked down and saw his feet were wet. In the lane, the water level would be three feet at least!

'Oye kaka! What are you doing standing there?' A voice came from the escaping throng. 'Get going at once!'

In the courtyard, the women were now perched atop the cot perched on the divan. Mata was counting her prayer beads, eyes fastened on the door, lips moving softly. Jinder was locking the bedroom door. Inside the cowshed, the buffaloes were tethered loosely. They were mooing sonorously now and stamping their feet, flinging straw across the floor.

The roar was growing frighteningly close. As if the haveli stood on the Sutlej's bank and not three miles away. A deafening swoosh, and Baksh saw the river plunge into the lane from the bazaar end. Every pore in his body screamed flight, but his feet had sprung roots. Fear pulsed through his static body and erupted in a bellow: 'Pa-a-a-ji!'

Jinder was beside him the next instant. The wave rode high, tree branches, knotted bundles and debris floating on it. It swamped the lane, knocking those fleeing on foot, reached the carts scurrying away, and then tugged at their knees. It was cold and strong and both brothers gasped at the suddenness of the assault and clung to the heavy door.

'Jinder! Baksh! Come here quickly,' Maji shouted and motioned frantically. The water was halfway up the divan's legs.

'I will watch for Bapuji from here. Baksh will join you.'

'No!' Tears rolled down Baksh's cheeks. 'I'll also wait here.' Jinder frowned, then squeezed his brother's shoulder and held up a reassuring hand to his mother.

The water had found its level and now occupied all open spaces. The buffaloes were bellowing and straining at their ropes. How long before they broke free? And then what? Where could they flee? The street was a confused medley of humans, animals, household items, farm implements—buoying, sinking, striving not to drown.

'I see them now. They are at the corner.'

Mata's voice floated over the chaos, barely audible. The milky beads still turned in her hand, slowly, though; her eyelids shivered tremulously, like she was awakening from a feverish sleep. Mata was known in the family as an occasional clairvoyant. There was no set pattern to her talent—it could not be tapped on demand. She saw things, at times, and spoke them out loud. If someone happened to be around, her statement was noted; she herself seldom remembered what she had uttered on such occasions. Her visions were generally known to come true.

Jinder and Baksh scanned the end of the lane from where the wave had rolled in. Sure enough, a buggy came into view, the horse struggling in water that almost covered its legs.

'They are here!' the sons shouted in unison.

'Rabba, tera shukrana!' Maji clasped her hands in relief, shaking them fervently, then hugged Mata, who wore a blank look.

Lehna Singh brought the buggy to a halt at the door. Behind him followed a truck, Bapuji and a driver seated in the front. 'Load whatever you can in five minutes,' said the driver. 'There's no time to lose.' Then he reversed the truck until its rear almost touched the haveli's door.

Lehna was the first to descend into the flooded lane. Jinder held the horse's reins while Lehna dropped the truck's tailgate from its hinges. It fell into the water that hovered just below the truck's floor. It was a weather-beaten goods truck with wooden side panels and wooden floorboards—the kind that plied the highway carrying grain from farms to the mandi. Bapuji was lucky to have found one in the bazaar at a time like this.

Jinder first carried Maji to the truck, followed quickly by Mata. The water was above his stomach now and he strained to hold his arms up high as they ferried the women from the divan to the truck. Baksh was the next to wade through the chest-high water and hop in.

Lehna fetched a wooden plank and placed it between the threshold of the haveli and the truck's floor. Then he tried coaxing the two buffaloes in. The animals shied and jerked their heads at the sight of the swirling water. But Lehna's soothing sounds and comforting pats encouraged one, then the other, to climb the plank onto the truck. There, Baksh wound their ropes tightly to the side panel.

Next, Lehna released the horse from the buggy and tried to get it to follow the buffaloes. He coaxed the animal, smoothed its coat, whispered near its ear, even rapped its rump. But the horse refused to budge and stood quaking in the water, its white coat rippling spasmodically.

'Shall we, Sardarji?' the driver queried Bapuji. He had not shut the engine, it alternated between low shudders and long rumbles. He probably did not trust it to restart.

'Tie his rein to the back of the truck,' suggested Jinder. 'That way, he may follow.'

The water now stood four feet high. And was continuing to rise, swamping the floor of the truck. The buffaloes jigged their hoofs, lifting one, then another, attempting to dispel the water. Maji patted them.

'Is everything in?' Bapuji asked Jinder from the front seat as the driver cranked the gear shaft.

'The suitcases! They are still inside.' Jinder tapped his forehead with the base of his left palm. 'I will get them.'

Bapuji waved a hand in dismissal. 'Jinder! The water has risen very high. It's not worth the risk.'

'I'll get it,' spoke Lehna, now sitting astride the horse. 'Hold the rein.' He motioned to Jinder, then climbed down from the horse and plunged into the water. It came up to his chest. Baksh quelled a shriek. Lehna retrieved a rope from the buggy, threw one end to Jinder and proceeded to tie the other end around his waist submerged in water. 'If I lose balance or fall, pull me in.'

'Watch, oye Lehniya!' Bapuji was standing hunched, head thrust out of the window, his arm held aloft. 'Tainun gava ke mainun kuj nahin milna.'

'I'll be back, Sardarji. You don't worry.' Then he was cutting through the water with strong strokes.

Baksh knew what Bapuji was thinking—Lehna had been with him since his marriage; his father had served Bapuji's father. He belonged to that breed of employees who were more aides than servants—rapidly disappearing, like everything else that had once been familiar.

Soon, Lehna waded back, holding his chin high. The suitcases were balanced on his head, the water rode up to his shoulders. He had returned quickly enough, but the excruciating wait had seen Bapuji collapse in the seat, head sunk low, holding his turban with both hands.

Lehna handed the cases to Jinder. Baksh clasped his hand and gripped the side panel as a soaking Lehna hoisted himself up. As Lehna stumbled into the truck, one of the suitcases sprang open. Jewellery—gold necklaces, gem-encrusted kundan sets, Maji's diamond and ruby wedding tikka, elephant-headed gold *fagin m o lwer-*

bangles, beaten-gold jingles—flew out and thumped heavily into the muddy swirl below. Jinder's left hand clawed the air in front, even as his right hand struggled to tilt the bag inwards. He toppled back into the truck as Maji and Lehna supported him, and Baksh made to grab the lid shut. But the contents had mostly slipped out by then.

The driver jerked the truck into gear and started to reverse the vehicle. 'Sardarji,' he said in a gruff voice to Bapuji, 'my bargain with you is to take you to safety. Therefore, please don't ask me to stop on the way—come what may.' As Bapuji nodded limply and the others listened, he continued, 'This is only for your safety—and mine. If we stop even once to give help, the truck will be run over...'

As it felt the pull of the truck, the horse raised its head in confusion. The rein held tight and tugged at the animal. The truck roared slowly into the oncoming rush of water and the animal began to plough its way at the rear.

The family clung to the side panels of the truck. The water had been too strong to raise back the wooden tailgate that would have latched the truck shut. One loose grip and a person could sink down the truck bed and roll into the muddy depths outside.

All around them was evidence of the havoc caused by the Sutlej's flooding. A cow struggled to stay above the water; a chair was adrift, its legs sticking up in the air; lungis, shirts, turbans twirled like coloured ribbons at a Baisakhi fair. They passed a family perched atop a peepul tree. A man and a woman were festooned in the branches, arms gripping overhead tree limbs, feet planted on a sturdy bough, their child, saddled on the father's waist, gripped a wooden hand-painted bird in one hand, the other latched to his father's shoulder as a muddy sea lumbered at the trunk—a montage frozen in fear.

'Rabba! Waheguru! Waheguru!' Maji muttered and closed her eyes.

Suddenly, the horse neighed and tossed its head wildly. It flicked its hind leg and thrashed at the water. An arm was lunging for it from beneath the muck. But the current was strong, the hand trailed, and the horse's leaden trot continued unhindered behind the truck. Floating on the muddy waters, an embroidered tapestry came into view. Sprawled out were geometric patterns, woven in silken gold thread on a red handloom cloth. The intricate motif could only be a Bagh—that women of the house embroider over many months, is first worn on the wedding day, is passed down from mother to daughter, and can never be bought in a market.

As the party looked solemnly at the river-lane and the flotsam strewn across the water's surface, Mata broke the silence: 'Money will not last in this house…'

Baksh did not know it then but Mata was to prove prescient. Partition lines would be drawn between siblings. And the enemy, once again, would be within.

DAY 4: ANANT

Back home from his second visit of the day to the municipal office, where he had gone to make out an application for the death certificate, Anant placed the Studds helmet on the sideboard, wiped a sweaty forehead on the sleeve of his T-shirt and grimaced as he sat down.

In the morning, the clerk responsible for registration of births and deaths had been missing—a rash of unexpectedly itchy proportions had assailed his chest, leaving him incapacitated for anything but fanning himself in front of a stool-mounted fan, the shirt unbuttoned, hands feeding the itch with periodic scratching. Consequently, all *other* work had been relegated to the afternoon.

'Clerk says… these things take time.'

Neymat crimpled her mouth and said, 'He's looking for money.'

'A *death* certificate—for heaven's sake!' Noor waved her right hand. 'Are they this heartless?'

'Death. Birth. What is it to them?' Anant tugged at his T-shirt repeatedly to cool the rivulets of sweat streaking down his torso. 'For humanity's sake, I told him, show compassion. Know what he said? "I am a government officer first, human being later. And a servant of the Government of India cannot possess a kindly heart. If he does, he has to keep it under lock and key. Otherwise the one billion population of our bilious nation will leach it with their individual petitions.'"

His hand motioned towards the refrigerator. Neymat brought out a one-litre bottle of Pepsi. From the lower rack of the sideboard, she retrieved a glass and poured the drink.

Anant downed the cola in one gulp and settled back in his chair. 'Maybe somebody else should go. The clerk will not want to see my face in a hurry.'

Neymat looked up from examining the vegetable tray in the refrigerator. 'Why?'

Anant stayed silent.

'Perhaps we should just pay him,' Noor interjected, 'and get it done with. How much does he want, Ant?'

'For a *privileged* family like ours, I guess his rate would be four to five thousand.'

Noor made to get up. 'Let me fetch the money—I withdrew some cash at Delhi airport—and let's get this over with.'

'Five thousand rupees is a lot of money,' Neymat offered quietly.

'It will also solve a major headache,' Noor pointed out.

'And where will it stop? God knows who else will ask for money tomorrow—these things get around.'

'I agree with Noor,' Anant said. As his sisters looked at him, he hunched forward, resting his elbows on the tabletop. 'I told the clerk he was a shameless bloodsucker. A privileged leech in a government job. Other worms have to try harder.'

An 'Oh!' escaped Noor as Neymat sat back in her chair, her arms crossed.

'Sorry, Neymatdi,' Anant shrugged.

Neymat shrugged too. 'Let's see if we can get it right. I will go meet the clerk. Meanwhile,' she paused, 'there's something I wanted to suggest. Now is as good a time as any. So many people will be coming for Papa's bhog ceremony—relatives, friends, colleagues. You could get a haircut.'

'So I am on display that day?' Anant clenched his fists, twisting his mouth into a sneer.

'Nobody is on display. But certainly, you can look appropriate—like a responsible son. You are the man of the house now.'

'Tch!' Anant straightened up in agitation. 'Why should anyone be bothered if I wear my hair long? Do I go into their homes and advise them on hairstyles? Hain? And what has responsibility got to do with a haircut?'

'Ask Noor.' Neymat pointed a confident chin in the direction of her high-flying consultant sister, who made dollars from dishing out marketing counsel. 'It is about creating the right impression. You are going to be a doctor in less than a year—why not look like a pro?'

'Oh-ho, Neymatdi! Does *Gray* also illustrate how a doctor should appear?'

'Be practical! If you were ill and had to choose between two doctors—one who looked like you and another who looked like... like...'

'Like you,' Noor offered.

'Okay, me... Whose sight would you find more reassuring?'

'Of course, you. Like McAloo Tikki Cheese, McDonald's top-selling burger in vegetarian India, you are the ultimate

Doctor and Florence Nightingale Combo!' He did an elaborate namaskar before dragging a chair to sit beside her.

'Packaging is important—that is a fact of today's world. Why, no one will buy a Lux bar if the wrapper is dirty… they will pick another soap.'

Anant wiggled his brows at Noor. 'What is the marketing wisdom?'

'Long hair is chic. And it goes with your image—enfant terrible! But Neymat is right. Packaging is the name of the game. It's the age of style over substance. In Bombay, currently no wedding dinner is complete without crab cakes, Perignon and Perrier.'

'You know what is hot in Delhi nowadays?' Neymat asked. 'The Buddha Bar theme wedding! This one has a statue of Buddha decked in zardozi, with diyas lit all around. They play some strange music called *Buddha Bar* in place of wedding songs. And you can sample any world cuisine: Thai, French, Malaysian… So people hop from one stall to the other, picking and pecking at goose liver, prawns in coconut sauce, Thai green curry. But the longest queue continues to be for, guess what?' Neymat clicked her fingers. 'Tandoori!'

'In Ludhiana,' Anant laughed, 'all marriage pandals are designed on the lines of Bollywood sets. People get swimming pools emptied so they can convert them into dance floors—like they saw in *Monsoon Wedding*! So much fuss so two people can sleep together!'

The three siblings burst into laughter and looked at each other. It felt good, this momentary respite from the grief that had gripped them.

When the laughter died down, Neymat sighed and sat upright. 'For the bhog, Anant, you have to look beyond *your* interests. Remember, *you* are the man of the house now. And there are responsibilities that go with it—'

'What is this *responsibility* business?'

With no answer forthcoming from Neymat, Anant leaned towards his sister and asked, 'Neymatdi?'

Neymat shrugged. 'You *are* responsible now for Mama.'

'Which means what? First, you ask me to cut my hair. Next, you will prevent me from going to the US for higher studies. Third—'

Neymat's right hand waved in the space between them, indicating he lower his voice lest Mama hear them.

'And who's responsible for my dreams?' Anant asked, his voice crushed. 'Help me understand this... When we were growing up, we were all equal. As Papa said, "You are all my sons." And now, he's gone, and we are unequal.'

Neymat watched the agitation on her brother's face and said softly, 'Some things don't change, Anant. You *are* the son.'

Anant moved his foot over Pasha's warm belly and the dog stretched out, pleased with the attention. Lately, he had taken to trailing Anant, and got agitated when someone from the family, particularly Anant, left the house. He ran in circles around them until someone leashed him. Now, one foot soothing Pasha, Anant chewed his inner lip. Early in the morning, one of Papa's colleagues, a certain Kapoor, had arrived. Anant was previously acquainted with that semi-colon of a man—a large head and thin legs—who worked as a sub on Papa's court cases. Kapoor, however, had irritated him. Rather, the lawyer's inquisitive brand of condolence had.

He had rummaged through Papa's papers, claiming he was looking for a case file they were working on together. Why, then, was he peering into Papa's diary? Then he had launched forth on a bizarre discussion of the Iran–Pakistan–India gas pipeline and how it was changing the face of Ferozepur's real estate. Which, of course, Anant would know, considering how interested Bhallasaab had been in that particular development, IPI. He called it Ippy, like it were another Punjabi kid affectionately named Happy, Puppy, Guppy by his fawning parents. Then he had launched into a monologue on the various benefits of IPI, such as the vastly improved Indo–Pak relations...

Anant had sat and listened, then stopped listening, before bringing the rambling Kapoor to an abrupt halt by declaring it was Pasha's 'walk' time. The Dalmatian, he informed Kapoor, was so frisky with pent-up energy that if his walk was delayed by a few minutes, he usually went for the first pair of strange legs in the house. Upon which, Kapoor eyed Pasha who was spread-eagled beneath Anant's chair on the cool concrete. Pasha, his jaw hanging loose in the April heat, returned Kapoor's enquiring look with an impressive display of angular teeth arrayed like knives on a chef's board. It had sent Kapoor packing and left Anant with an unpleasant taste in his mouth.

There was something furtive about Kapoor's manner, the way he studied Anant's face as if searching for something, all the while inanely talking about some gas pipeline. It made Anant wonder what Kapoor's motive for coming to the house was—he, clearly, was not grieving.

❧

Balwant Pua minced down the concrete pathway, her photosensitive glasses tinted brown, one shade darker than her skin, one lighter than her hennaed hair. Finding Anant seated on the stretched-out folding bed in the veranda, she sat down, her baggy purse spilling out of her meagre lap. She had come to see Preet before heading off to Chandigarh, she informed him.

'Chandigarh?' Anant asked.

Balwant Pua pursed her lips, as if swallowing a terrible thought.

Anant wondered what she was thinking. Lately, she had been distressed over the future of her two daughters. Lovely had done a most unlovely thing by marrying a man of her choice and setting up house a block away from her mother's. Initially, Pua cribbed to all: 'He is a moneylender's son, he's only after my money.' Until Lovely, griddle-dark, bamboo-tall, uniquely cynical, declared, 'Half your money is legally mine and only enhances my market value.'

After Lovely's marriage, Pua had placed a steel plate filled with mud balls beside the entrance gate every night for thirty days. The pandit's prediction of a divorce within a month of marriage did not materialize. Lovely, on discovering her mother's deviant plan, paid some urchins to splay her house with sodden earth. So savage had been the daughter's night-time retribution that the mother had had to repaint her house.

Dimple, prematurely named for the dimples which disappeared from one cheek and then another as she grew, answered better to Dumpling. Matric-fail, thirty-plus, she had fallen way behind in the matrimonial race. But Balwant Pua had found the solution to her problem: a house-husband. A fair complexion and mother's wealth would throw up a suitable groom—it was only a matter of time.

Even the pandit had thus forecast. And this was Pandit Gopinath, the brightest and most revered astrologer in the whole of Punjab! Why, hadn't he predicted a decade back, when Sonia was not even in politics, that she would one day lead the Congress party? Of course, an assortment of forecasters, soothsayers and astrologers were on Pua's regular rolls. So profitable an employment it was that when she relocated to Ludhiana, one pandit uprooted his Ferozepur practice and followed her.

Now, extracting a worn-out picture from her purse, Balwant Pua handed it to Anant. 'Looking through some old photos I found this. It is of your papa.'

Anant scanned the black-and-white photograph, speckled white where the print had peeled off. It was a wedding picture from a bygone era. A man, decked in a groom's finery, mounted on a horse; a young boy, his sarbala, peeped from behind. People ringed around the horse: women in crinkled chunnis covering their heads, men in loosely tied turla turbans.

'That is your papa—the sarbala.' Pua nodded with her chin.

'Papa! How old was he then?'

'Six–seven… near about.'

'Wow! The earliest photos I have seen of him are the hockey ones. He is eighteen–twenty in those.' Studying the picture, he said, 'He looks like Arjun—rather Arjun looks like him, no?'

'Notice the curly hair.' Pua tapped at the picture with her index finger. 'He refused to get a turban tied on his head. Was never fond of it as a child—would run away while Maji called after him. On that wedding day, too—the marriage procession was getting late, so your grandfather said to let it be.' She paused.

Anant looked up and saw his mother behind the kitchen's mesh door. She stood very still. He knew why she was eavesdropping—she did not trust her sister-in-law.

Balwant Pua resumed her story, her voice low. 'How small he was then... Always trailing me, Pehnji this, Pehnji that...'

Anant gazed at the photograph, trying to connect the man he knew as Papa with the little boy who peeped shyly from the photo, an aureole of curls ringing his clear face. The boy was dressed in a silken achkan in a dark colour, a lighter motif visible on it.

'He went too soon.'

Anant raised his head and saw his aunt's face mired in some emotion: remorse, sorrow, love?

'This is not the right order of things... not the natural order...'

He watched and listened.

'The firstborn is usually the first to go. Baksh was the youngest. There was still time...' Her chin quivered, her fingers lying in her lap jerked. 'So much he has left behind... unfinished.'

Suddenly Balwant Pua was agitated. 'But I have to be off to Chandigarh now. The tenants—susare! Not paying the rent on time. Raising needless demands. Repairs, paint, this, that...' She dabbed her face and neck with a chunni end. 'They know I am an old woman—so they create mischief.'

Wearily she looked at Anant. 'Perhaps you want to accompany me? Just a day?'

So that was what she was here for! Anant was relieved. Some things never changed, and it was comforting to have Balwant Pua revert to form. He couldn't help a short snorting laugh.

She eyed him curiously.

Behind the mesh door, he saw Mama stiffen. And he remembered a story she had told him once.

Mama and Papa had started to build this house, when one morning, Mama saw a snake slithering on the bedroom floor. She screamed, grabbed a hockey stick and thwacked the snake limp, when she sighted another beneath the bed, one on the table and another coiled around the lamp… Horrified, her eyes swept across the room, and wherever she looked, there were snakes! The young parents spent the next hour thwacking and hitting and killing the snakes with slippers and sticks while Neymat, cradling baby Noor in her lap, watched goggle-eyed from atop the bed. The snakes, though, kept pouring in. Until Papa deposited Mama and the girls with a neighbour and went in search of a snake charmer.

A week later, another snake charmer showed up and guiltily confessed: Balwant had pointed out the house and instructed him to find a nest of snakes in the vicinity. He had located it for her in the main gutter behind the new house. And sure enough, when he broke the gutter's concrete casing, it revealed a nest of snakes: fifty baby snakes coiled one on top of another—all those had later sneaked into the new house!

But, the newly penitent snake charmer admitted, his pet cobra, the biggest draw of his show, was refusing to drink milk. It was a terrible omen, and before things got worse, he remembered his evil deed, relented and came running to make amends.

Balwant Pua's voice brought Anant back. 'Thinking, are you? What is there to think? Chandigarh is a fine city and you will travel in my car. Besides, your poor weak aunt will be grateful for your help.'

'Oh, Pua!' Anant smiled mischievously at his aunt. 'You and weak!'

From behind her thick bifocals, Balwant Pua gazed at him. 'You have a habit of joking, Anant-uh. But with no son to help, this worldly business is tough handling.' Her perpetually grim mouth stiffened further. 'Those with sons are fortunate.'

'Hmm…' Anant's head was bowed as he considered her statement and she watched him from the corner of her eyes. Now her nephew looked up and grinned at her brightly. 'Happens, Pua, happens all the time in this unfair world: some get sons, while others riches…'

Behind the kitchen door, Anant saw his mother's shoulders relax. Balwant Pua grabbed her purse, made a tremendous show of heaving herself upright, barked out a gruff 'All right!' and minced away.

BAKSH

THE LAST WALK

Across the Sutlej, Baksh could see moonlight glinting off metal. The elaborate fence had been erected in the 1980s to stem the influx of arms and trained Sikh militants into an insurgent Punjab. The fence zigzagged over the Indo–Pak border, swallowing fertile land, while in marshy riverine areas it forfeited its iron march to patrol boats. Farmers lined up in front of the fence every sunrise and sunset to access their farms through padlocked steel gates built into it at intervals. But Baksh had known the fields when they were untrammelled and trouble-free. When walking through them on a balmy winter day, trailing a hand through the golden crop of corn, he had realized that this was what he wanted to do: till his soil, nourish it with water and sweat, sow the bounteous seeds of this hardy country, reap an honest harvest.

1954

'The air is like wine.' Bitta stood in the middle of the green fields, eyes half-closed as he inhaled deeply, his chest swelling beneath his red kurta. 'Go on,' he urged Baksh with a toss of his head.

Baksh closed his eyes and took a deep breath. Bumblebees hummed, the recurring creak of a Persian wheel floated forth, and a faint warm fragrance enveloped him. It was the aroma of a garden on winter mornings, the dewy clean arboreal air toasted on honey-rays of a mild sun.

'Main koi jhooth boliya si?' Bitta wore his trademark knowing look. With a flourish of his right hand he continued, 'There *is* no time more beautiful than winter in the Punjab: flat lands dressed up like a bride, the air so heady you can get drunk on it, and all the vegetables you could want—cauliflower, carrot, radish—and mustard, of course!' Looking at the watercolour sky, Bitta went on, 'The rains should be upon us any day now.' Then he stooped to examine the chilli fields. 'About time—the moisture will do us good.'

Baksh watched his cousin. Bitta was a farmer at heart and approached the fields with the same passion, joyous celebration, pride and care with which he set about all the other things he loved. Baksh enjoyed his cousin's company and the robustness that had not dimmed despite the terrible times they had witnessed. Jinder Paji, though, did not share Baksh's enthusiasm. 'It's because he never thinks,' he would comment dryly. 'That compartment of his brain is empty—permanently stunted.'

To which Bitta, never one to feel slighted, would respond: 'If thinking converts a man to this,' and he would jab a finger at the air in front of Jinder Paji, slouched carelessly in his favourite cane armchair, 'then rab di saun, I am better off a rustic.' He would slap his thigh for emphasis. 'Aa-ho!'

'What say, Baksh,' Bitta said now, as if he had read his mind. 'We need to drag your very-serious not-much-older brother here someday. All the time, he has his nose buried in those books—and he does not even have any exams to sit for. He is MA pass now—time to shut the Dikkan, and Shake-off-the-pear, and see the real world!'

Baksh shrugged. 'You know what he says when you tell him that…'

'Aaho! That he has seen the *real* world, and not taken to it much.' Bitta spread his florid palms. 'But this is life, you know. We all have to move on. Wasn't Lahore beloved of us all? Didn't we all lose when we fled? But life… life doesn't stop, Baksh.' He placed both hands on his young cousin's shoulders, nearly level with his own. 'And if he thinks, sitting on a bed surrounded by imaginary English lands, he can make it go away, he's wrong.'

Jinder had always been a bit of a loner. In the past five years, however, he had turned to his books and writing for companionship. He would lie curled up in bed for hours, marooned on an island of English classics, reading by the yellow-orange light of the table lamp, or staring at the ceiling, his hands resting in a steeple on his chest. Or, in a sudden burst of energy, he would dash off a letter to the editor, *The Tribune*—words strung together in a never-ending scrawl, soaring loops dwarfing the cursive script—stuff it into an envelope and send the servant off to the post office at a sprint, his work suspended midway.

Maji tried to rouse her son out of the stupor. 'What answers do you keep searching for, puttar? Answers don't come if you sit and wait for them. They fall into place as you live your life… Then, they will surprise you with what they have to say.'

Jinder would nod absent-mindedly, stumble out of the room to sit beside Maji in the yard for a while, watch listlessly as she chopped vegetables or recounted some news from the neighbourhood, then tumble back into his room again.

Bapuji, reluctant to censure, would quietly comment, 'How like a severed kite he flails about.'

The cousins walked towards a well that stood next to the wheat field. A jujube tree, laden heavy with unripe greenish berries, formed a canopy overhead. Baksh pulled out a couple of young radishes, snapped their leafy tops, and rinsed them in a rivulet of water that bubbled into the fields. They sat on the springy grass and munched on the succulent vegetable. A flock of white geese flew across the sky, the wings gently undulating as they neared the end of their migratory expedition from Siberia.

Bitta demolished the radish and briskly rubbed his upper arms. 'I am glad you are taking interest in your fields. Jinder is lost in some dreamy world, but things are changing, Baksh...' He looked at Baksh, nodding his head and working on the last morsels in his mouth. 'Jinder needs to wake up... Maasarji will need to figure out what to do with this new act that the gaurment is planning.'

'Which act?'

'Some act to redistribute our lands. Saale! Sauri de!' Bitta spat, depositing a spittle of unchewed radish on the soil. 'As if driving the Punjabis out of their homes wasn't enough—now they want to make the remaining ones landless! Madras or somewhere they have already put the act in place. The plan is to put a ceiling on the landholding of each zamindar. Some paltry thirty to forty acres is all they will allow each farmer. Imagine!' Bitta tilted his chin at the gently swaying sweep of green. '*Imagine!* The land that *our* forefathers and fathers have tilled with their blood and sweat—now the gaurment wants to give away. Like it belongs to *their* fathers!'

'Can they *do* that... I mean, is there no law or...'

'*They* are the law now: the Gaurment of Azaad Hindustan. And they will decide what is right for us, or wrong. Nave hakim te naviyan gallan.'

'New masters, new laws... Hmm... So, what will they do with the land they take away?'

'Give it to other displaced needy farmers. Is it our fault, I say, that we barely escaped getting pushed into Pakistan? Now we have to pay jurmana? Compensation for their political blunders.'

Baksh had seldom seen his cousin this angry.

Bitta snorted and started to vigorously twirl the end of a moustache. 'Give my land away! I say I will give my land to whomever *I* want to—who are you to decide?' He was questioning an imaginary Nehru now, who had supplanted the bamboo scarecrow and stood issuing edicts with out-flung arms.

Bitta turned towards Baksh. 'And that is why you need Jinder—now, now more than ever before.'

'Jinder Paji?' Where did he fit into this equation? If anything, Baksh knew, his idealistic elder brother was most likely to agree to a scheme to rebuild Punjab—whatever the personal cost.

'Aaho Jinder,' Bitta wagged an index finger energetically. 'You see, Jinder is intelligent—when he decides to use his brain so,' and Bitta paved a road with his right hand. 'He is the best read of all of us and he speaks gitter-mitter Angreji like the Angrej. In college, he would argue and hold discussions with the white teachers like they were speaking his own tongue.'

Bitta's mouth opened sufficiently in awe, before he remembered the point of his argument and continued, 'So,

Jinder will be able to help us figure out this kanooni dau-pech, what do they say, legal nut-bolt, hunh?'

Baksh nodded. Jinder Paji was sharp, plus he had a honeyed tongue. But who would convince him and how?

Bitta stood up, dusting loose soil off his kurta. 'Let's see whether we can work on Jinder. We will not give up so easily— there are always ways, and we will find them.'

❧

For a year now, Baksh had been teaching himself the art of farming. It was October, the time for sowing wheat, the main winter crop, and the days were long as he supervised. Consequently, Baksh had taken to sleeping in the fields for a while. At the day's end, exhausted, happy, he was content to lie in a cot and watch the starry night. Another month and the winter mist would begin to roll in, which would render sleeping in the open impossible.

One such night, as Baksh lay in the open, he felt warm. The thick quilt was pulled over his head. Somebody was snuggling next to him. Who the… A hand closed over his mouth, soft, firm. It paused, waiting, as the breath fell on him in short husky draughts. Then it trailed down, pushing aside the kurta neck and resting over his chest. It moved with a deliberate smoothness, fingers stroking the hairs, palm massaging the exposed skin. He exhaled sharply and a mouth closed on his.

The hand was down now, caressing, gripping, moving him to fullness. His legs trembled, he pulled the woman closer in a tight embrace. She placed an index finger on his lips, then slowly proceeded to disentangle herself. As he watched, she removed her shirt with practised ease, without disturbing the canopy of the quilt, and brought her chest to his face. There was nothing to see in the dark, but he smelt her: the aroma of rotis fresh from the tandoor.

She guided his face towards a snug valley. Next she moved it to one mound, then the other, in a firm slow motion, until he latched his mouth around a taut nipple. He drew on it, first unsure, but as her head swung back and she grasped him by the shoulders, he drew harder on the lump of salted jaggery. Her chest heaved now, the breath hurried, and she moaned. The air inside the quilt was sweet, sticky, hot.

She tugged at a drawstring and made to remove her salwar. He gasped at the sudden withdrawal of warmth, his hands groping in reflex. She led them to her back, where beads of perspiration had gathered. As his fingers explored the new velvety terrain, she straddled him roughly, parting the lungi. Shock, a frisson of excitement, wonder and exhilaration washed over him, tugging him onwards.

He felt his life force concentrate into one fierce, jubilant instant. He erupted. The rider had scaled the highest peak; she paused, the body stretched like a taut bow. Then she imploded, heaved, and shuddered in rapture.

When Baksh awoke the next morning, the woman was gone. So was his lungi! He looked at the ground beneath the cot, but no. She must have taken it. Why? To tease him? Something to remember him by? A souvenir of a conquest?

There was no way of getting out of the bed, nor did he feel like it. He stretched out beneath the quilt, yawning, his head resting on his clasped hands. He felt as new as the bright autumn day. Within him, giddily rippled languor, confidence, knowledge. Like someone had handed him the keys to a treasure trove. There was strength in his limbs, a song in his heart, and not a speck of doubt within, for he knew. He knew he had gifts to give. And there were rewards to receive...

Who *was* the woman? After all, there were many who worked in the fields: Bodh Singh's family, Bitta's tenant farmers on the adjoining land, women from Rakhri village... It could have been anyone. She had been young—her body was firm—yet experienced. And she certainly knew how to take. How did she know where to find him? Well, not too difficult: people passed by this way all through the day. And he had been visiting the farm almost daily for the last one year. Enough time for someone to observe him...

Not up to wrestling with questions any longer, he settled into a languid wait for Bitta to come in search of him. The veteran recoiled when he heard of the adventure.

'Sauri de! What are you telling me!' And he lifted the quilt to check for himself the veracity of Baksh's story. After which he rolled his eyes and asked for the details. 'You didn't see her face! Oye, razai vich hi kam chak ta! Was she rich with the malai still in her, or had the cream been taken off?'

As Baksh recounted the incident, his eyes alight with roguish discovery, Bitta listened, punctuating the narration with sighs, exclamations and lusty abuse that traced the mystery woman's salacious family history. Then he whistled his admiration, shaking his head in disbelief. 'You are a true chhupa-rustam, Baksh! Hain?'

The victor sat up in the cot, shrugging and grinning at the awed look on his cousin's face. 'I can't believe it myself. If not for the lungi, and the feeling in my bones, I would dismiss it as a dream.'

'Dream! Lucky bugger.' Bitta thumped him repeatedly on the back.

'But who do you think she was?'

'Oye, you want to eat the mangoes or count the kernels? Though I doubt she will come back again—otherwise her approach may have been less like an all-out assault!' Bitta rubbed both hands and bit his lower lip, then lowered his head and whispered, 'You are lucky… the first time I tried it, I kept putting it in the navel.'

He chortled, and their hands locked in mid-air.

It was 1957. They sat in Jinder's room. Time to wet the whiskers a bit, Bitta had suggested. Baksh, Bitta, Jinder and Shammi were playing a game of rummy, the stakes low, as was the custom in the initial stages of the game: rupees ten each. As the game progressed, the daredevils, or winners, upped the stakes; losers and the weak-hearted progressively dropped out.

'Lehna!' Shammi yelled. 'Fetch some more Scotch.'

The servant, stationed at the door for the explicit purpose of refilling the plates of savouries and replenishing the drinks, hurriedly got up from his haunches.

'Oye, Shammi!' Baksh watched him amazed. They were on their first drinks and the whisky bottle stood almost empty on the peg table nearest Shammi. 'How many have you downed already?'

The person in question was the only son of Mata's eldest son and a couple of years older than Baksh. But he was reputed to have had his first drink—gulpfuls of country liquor—when he was barely being suckled on milk. From the arms of his inebriated father, Shammi had toppled into a cauldron of home-brewed liquor and splashed around in the desi until a retainer rescued him. Thankfully, the potion had cooled sufficiently so as to not scald the child. But it did ignite some peculiar longings.

Shammi claimed that that singular encounter had permanently altered his body's composition: it had ensured that molasses now coursed through his person as ubiquitously as water or blood. It contributed to his fearsome reputation: the highest consumer of desi in Guru-Har-Sahai, his village, where every backyard invariably housed a makeshift brewery. He liked his brew neat, shorn of diluting elements such as ice or soda, preferably lukewarm, otherwise room temperature would suffice.

Noticing the eyes on him, Shammi shrugged, a careless smile on his lips, the topknot loose on a lolling head. 'Practice! Practice!' he said to no one in particular.

'Yes!' Jinder jerked a dismissive hand at him. 'If only Sardars like you could practise at something else.'

Shammi was enrolled in the same college as Baksh, except that he was still trying to pass the first year after three failed attempts. He was also the unofficial head of the students' union.

'Oye, Mamaji! Why do you get so angry? It scares me!' Shammi pretended to cower on the bed where he reclined, a glass resting on one raised knee. 'What will I practise at? Reading, writing? That even my *father* never did!'

'Banda bann, banda!' admonished Jinder, the pennant of his turban quivering sternly.

'Lo! What is to be said? First, the great Mughals told us: read Urdu, then you will become a man. Then the goras came and said: read English, and you will become a man.' Shammi let out a loud burp. 'And now, the latest instruction from the Nehru Sarkar is: learn Hindi, and you will become a man!' Shammi paused and surveyed his audience with bleary eyes: 'Will someone tell me: are they all talking of the *same* man? And if yes, how many times over do they plan to make him a man?'

'You learn Punjabi only—that should be enough!' Bitta slapped Shammi's back from his position on the bed beside him.

'Why? Am I not good enough for your H-h-hindi?'

Bitta looked guiltily away.

'And why do I need to *learn* Punjabi? It is my mother tongue—it rolls off my lips naturally. Unlike some Arya Samajis who will disown it for Hindi.'

Baksh stretched forward in his chair and waved an arm between them. 'Oye, why this sudden aggression, Shammi? What does Arya Samaj have to do with our Bitta?'

Lehna stepped over the threshold, deposited a bottle of Johnny Walker Black Label on the round table and stood waiting for instructions. Baksh waved him away and he hunkered down by the door, lungi hitched around the knees.

Shammi opened the bottle, topped the Scotch in the glass with a Patiala peg, all the while eyeing Bitta like an adversary. 'Ask him,' he nodded to Baksh. 'Ask him.'

'Ask him what?'

'What his mother tongue is.'

'Your needless quibbling is interrupting the game, Shammi,' Jinder's leg shook with impatience. 'I suggest you concentrate on your drink while we play.'

'Jis thaal vich khande ne, us vich mori karde ne.' Shammi refused to relinquish the spotlight.

'What is he talking about, Bitta?' Baksh asked. 'Do you know?'

A constipated look had appeared on Bitta's face. He placed his cards on the wooden table and started to examine the floor.

Shammi watched, a mocking smile playing on his lips. 'Let me be more specific. Ask him: in the 1951 census, what language did he say was his mother tongue—when the gaurment afsars went from house to house asking that question?'

All eyes probed Bitta now.

'Hindi.' He shrugged.

Baksh looked puzzled, Jinder distraught, while Shammi gloated with glazed eyes, announcing, 'I told you these Arya Samajis cannot be trusted.'

'Why Bitta?' Baksh's voice caught. He was perplexed. Bitta's mother and Maji were sisters; while Maji had been married into a Sikh family, Bitta's mother had been given in wedding to a Hindu house. It was common enough practice in Punjab, just as it was customary for Hindu families to give one son over to the Sikh faith. However, in the wake of the Partition, the customary blurring of lines between Hinduism and Sikhism was being forsaken. But Bitta—half Hindu, half Sikh—had coasted along without any serious religious affliction.

'Trading one's mother tongue is like trading one's mother.' Shammi's head bobbed in an exaggerated display of vocalized wisdom.

'*Shamm-i-i! Dekh tun!*' Bitta's index finger pointed at his provocateur.

Lehna, habituated to their frequent arguments, raucous laughter and hearty abusing, was peeping in from his perch by the threshold, intrigued by the sudden activity.

'Sure, I am watching! Show me what you have to show!'

'Shammi, for God's sake, shut up!' Baksh held out a placatory hand to his drunken nephew.

'But why did you feel the need to do that?' Jinder queried, his voice soft. 'Report a different language as your mother tongue?'

Bitta shook his head and said, 'My father thought it best that we cite Hindi as our mother tongue. If we said Punjabi, the Akalis would have enough cause to demand a Punjabi state from the gaurment.'

'So, what's wrong with that?' Baksh frowned. 'After all, so many other states—Andhra Pradesh, Maharashtra—have been formed on the basis of language.'

'But the Akalis won't stop at a Punjabi state—their aim is for a Sikh state. Then where will the Hindus go?'

'But! But… from where did you get this rubbish into your head?' Baksh's hands were lifted in appeal. 'Everyone who speaks Punjabi is a Punjabi. Not an Akali. This misinformation is being spread by the Arya Samajis. Will Hindi make you more Hindu?'

'Perhaps…'

'But what is wrong with a Sikh state?' Shammi jibed. 'After all, didn't *respected* Shri Chacha Nehru promise just such a state to the *brave Sikhs* in 1946? Or do you think'—Shammi leaned towards Bitta as if about to divulge a secret—'it was usual political trickery? Nehru wanted the Sikh numbers with him because Jinnah and his Muslim Leaguers were buggering his sleep?'

Bitta drew a deep breath, regarded Shammi intently, then looked away.

Baksh shifted his chair close to Bitta. 'When you waive your right to the Punjabi language, you play right into the hands of sectarian politicians like the Akali Tara Singh and Jagat Narain, the Arya Samaji. Then what will we all be left with: Punjabi *Sikh* state and Punjabi *Hindu* state? And since people are never satisfied, they will keep dividing till each man is assured of his representation: Khatri state, Brahman state, Arora state, Chamar state... And finally, to each man his own individual state!'

'Back to the Vedas!' Shammi said with a high-pitched laugh, rocking on his knees, lurching close to Bitta. 'The world wants to move forward, while they can only think of going back a thousand years.'

'Quiet, Shammi.' Jinder glared at the sozzled combatant. 'If you can't speak a decent word, then be silent.'

Shammi proceeded to tumble against the bed's backrest and swallow a glassful of whisky.

'The Arya Samajis are misguided, Bitta.' Jinder resumed. 'The question is not of Hindu–Sikh; it is of the spoken language of the region. That is the basis for formation of new states in India. If all Punjabi Hindus deny their mother tongue, what will they become? Not Kashmiri Hindus. Not UP Hindus either. Because without your own tongue, you will be afloat in a multilinguistic India.'

'But the Akalis seem to think differently,' Bitta protested. 'Their agenda is clearly political.'

'Yes! Yes!' Jinder moved to the edge of his chair. 'Political. Po-li-ti-cal. It is not Hindu versus Sikh. It is Arya Samaj versus Akalis. So, let *them* fight *their* battles. Why should we get involved?'

'You are right, Jinder. But many people don't think like you.'

'Well, then they only need to look back ten years: one Partition should be enough in a lifetime—for everyone.'

After that, the game proceeded in a desultory manner and was called off when a slouching Shammi started to snore. Bitta declined dinner and headed homewards; Jinder proceeded to the courtyard where, his hands steepled on his chest, he contemplated the night sky; and Baksh picked at his meal and wondered whether religion was a fluid that circulated through the human body—it was certainly stronger than blood.

DAY 5: NOOR

'Cleanliness is next to Godliness': The words in red regarded them from a white-painted tin board affixed to the entrance gate. Beneath, irregular sprays streaked the red-bricked column. The quest for open-air urinals was a pan-Indian one, the spirit to improvise uniting all Indian men. The shrubbery adjacent to the gate was leafless, struck barren by an excess of urea. A faint stench hovered in the air. Neymat and Noor hurried into the municipality office set in the bowels of a scenic park. Once inside the ancient British building, Noor, having held her breath thus far, exhaled. They looked around. A colonnaded corridor branched out into single-room offices. Atop each wood doorframe, a slim panel announced the department: Education, Accounts, Engineering, Health. Walking down the corridor they studied the panels. Below 'Health Department' were listed:

1. Sanitation
2. Sewerage
3. Birth-Death Record

With Birth-Death ranking below Sanitation and Sewerage, it was no wonder that the clerk could afford a routine disregard for distraught relatives of those deceased.

Inside the arched doorway, a table faced the entrance, its surface uneven with piles of files and loose sheets held down by a glass paperweight with little air bubbles trapped within. At the right corner, a wooden trihedral nameplate said: 'Shri L.M. Gupta'. A swivel armchair behind the table, its maroon backrest draped with a white cotton towel, was vacant.

'Hmm…' Neymat glanced at Noor. 'Wonder where he's gone…'

'I will enquire outside—'

'Hanji? Looking for something, are you?' A man in khaki pants and an untucked khaki shirt asked them from his perch on a stool by the door. He had been missing when they had walked in.

'The clerk, who issues death certificates,' Noor ventured.

'Oh, he's gone out.'

'And when will he be back?'

'Don't know—didn't say. Anything you need?' He tore open a packet of chewing tobacco, tapped its contents into his gaping mouth and commenced chomping. Then he aimed the empty pouch at a large earthen pot beside the pillar nearest him. The foil nestled in the creepers' entrails as the peon idly scanned the corridor. 'Death certificate, eh? Guptaji is light machine-gun. Shri LMG needs grease. Don't say I didn't warn beforehand. How many have lost their lives in the quest for the death certificate. Tch, tch!' He settled back on his stool. 'You can wait there,' he said, pointing at the chairs across Shri Gupta's table.

'Meharbani.' They sat down in the chairs, raised their eyebrows at each other, and Noor ran a forefinger across her throat in a mock demonstration of a beheading. A tube-light, slung from the ceiling on parallel chains, lit the narrow room. Cobwebs trailed the chains, some swayed occasionally.

'Guptaji…' A voice hailed from behind. They turned and saw someone in the doorway. 'He isn't here?' he asked them.

'No. We are also waiting,' Neymat said.

He nodded and turned back to the corridor. The peon seemed to have disappeared again. Noor studied the maroon armchair, its backrest pulled very low. Did Shri Gupta suffer from a lumbar problem?

'Doctor Gill?' A voice enquired. Neymat's head turned in response. It was the same man.

'Yes?' Neymat looked puzzled.

The man was lean, dressed in double-pleated baggy pants, a striped shirt tucked into the waistband. His hair was thick and black, the wavy mass held in place with some shiny pomade.

'You are Doctor Gill from Jammu Civil Hospital?'

'I worked there some years back.'

'Yes-yes. You are the one.' Jabbing an index finger, he hurried forward. 'Sorry for being this curious, Doctorsaab, but I thought I had remembered you correctly.' When Neymat nodded hesitantly, he dragged the peon's stool over the threshold and sat down. 'Obviously you do not remember—so many patients you must see every day. But I remember you. You were very kind to my nephew. He was badly injured in the train accident, remember? All the victims were brought to the Civil Hospital? You treated him… Then, when he recovered, you got him the job of manning the water cooler that the Rotary set up in the hospital. Serving cold water to people—the fountain outside the hospital canteen?'

'Yes. Yes… the young boy from Kupwara.'

'Hanji. Yes-yes.' He rubbed his hands, pleased at Neymat's recollection. 'Ahmed, his name.'

Neymat introduced Noor and recounted the incident. Ahmed had been about fifteen years old and badly wounded; the doctors thought at one point that his legs would need to be amputated. But he had recovered—he was a gritty boy. The job offer had been entirely fortuitous. They were stationed in Jammu Cantonment at that time. The chief medical officer was a friend of Sunny's commanding officer, and had decided to oblige.

'What brings you here?' the man asked.

'We need a death certificate.'

'Is that so?' His face became appropriately sombre. 'If you don't mind my asking, whose?'

'Our father.'

'Hmmm…' He bit his lip thoughtfully. 'Perhaps I can help. You leave the details of the case with me.' He pulled a sheet from the absent clerk's table, plucked a ballpoint pen from his shirt pocket and handed both to them. 'Here, write down the name of the deceased and date and location of death. The rest I will handle.' As Noor started to jot down the details, Neymat asked how he would manage to get the job done.

'Siddi ungal naal ghyyo nahin nikalda. There are ways of bypassing LMG. You leave that to me.' Then, checking the calendar on the wall, he said, 'One week from now you please collect the certificate.'

Neymat nodded and smiled her gratitude. 'Ahmed is doing well?' she enquired.

The man's face flushed. He lowered it and nodded before grabbing the paper and saying a hurried goodbye.

The peon, meanwhile, had returned and had one ear cocked to their conversation. Now, with an offended look, he made to retrieve his stool and retook his perch outside the door. As

Neymat and Noor stepped out of the room, he announced, 'Gone over to the other side.'

As they looked at him perplexed, the peon offered, 'Ahmed, the boy you were talking about, Suleiman's nephew. Apparently, the army picked him up for interrogation when he went visiting some relatives in Kupwara. Suleiman says he was tortured and left to die on the snowy slopes. They did not hear of him for a year until he sent a message that he had become a soldier of Allah in the service of the servant of Allah.'

'Servant of Allah? Who is that?' Noor queried.

The peon slid forward now, 'Why, everyone knows. The most famous one! Who brought the mighty Amreeki army to its knees as they went looking for him in the caves of Afghanistan. Where they are still looking. And when these Amreeki get frustrated, they go down to a crowded bazaar and open fire on public.' Then he crossed his forearms, touched the earlobes with his fingertips and shook his head ruefully. 'Tauba! Tauba! What times we live in!'

৯৫

'So much garlic, Mama?' Noor observed the steel bowl filling up with peeled garlic pods.

'Neymat wants to grind some and store in the fridge.' Preet stopped peeling. 'Speeds up the cooking. Then, this maid is so unreliable…'

The maidservant was frequently on leave—a child was sick, a relative had expired, her husband had fallen from the roof when drunk, the roof had fallen in when a tree collapsed against it… Noor returned from the kitchen with a chopping board and knife and drew a chair close to the folding bed on which Preet sat. After piling several pods on the board, she set about her task with novitiate care.

Preet brushed a stray hair away from her forehead; a sliver of garlic skin hung behind. 'Has Anant returned?'

'Na. He's taken Pasha for a long walk.'

Preet nodded and returned to the peeling. 'Pasha is insecure now—about anyone leaving the house... Animals have great intelligence, man can't fathom it.'

They worked in silence. Noor cast a leisurely glance around. The vernal morning air, the chatter of sparrows on the parapet, her mother's brisk hands engaged in a routine household task, the rising mound of garlic shavings—she found it all comforting. Preet handed over the bowl of waxy pods and asked her to fetch some vegetables from the fridge. 'Might as well finish the chopping for lunch.'

As Noor scrubbed the sticky sap off her hands, a picture came to her mind: Papa on the day bed, eating garlic pearls while reading the morning paper. As surely as fermented fumes lured him at dusk, a bulb of garlic was what roused him at dawn... Even his fart was garlicky! Anant, no mean player in the passing-wind section, jested: 'Business proposition, Noor. Just find a way to bottle the gas—one release, and it will zap all bacteria in the vicinity!'

When they had settled down with cauliflower and potatoes, Preet said, 'That night in Chandigarh, I had a dream. Strange dream it was. I thought I heard the front gate open. And Pasha howling—not barking, mind you—a low mournful sound which would not stop. I woke up with a start. Aneja Aunty, who was sleeping next to me, said it was only a dream. But I kept saying: "Why have you opened the gate at this time?" Then she gave me a glass of water. "Three in the morning, Preet," she said, "no time for anyone to be opening gates."'

Three in the morning. Was Mama referring to the night that Papa went for that early walk, his last? Did Mama know that Papa had left home that early? How *did* she know? Had Anant told her? Had she, perhaps, heard the old neighbour's account after all?

'They say when a person is going to die he lives his life all over again. Three hours he walked about… Where all his memories must have taken him… This town… Where he was born, where he lived all his seventy-one years… So many places to say goodbye to.'

She had known! Mama had known all along about Papa's walk. How naïve of her to have assumed otherwise!

'Death also, he met like a friend. Remember, Noor,' Preet touched her forearm, 'how he would say, "So what, if we have differences, at least we can sit and talk." Imagine taking death on a journey of all the places he loved, conversing with it, getting to know it.'

Was that the way it happened? Papa and a shadow, walking, pausing, gazing, remembering, reliving?

'It was not bad… the manner in which he went. He was doing something he always enjoyed… walking at a time that was his favourite… amrit vela, the ambrosial hour; w-w-with all his faculties in-intact.'

Preet's mouth trembled. She sniffled, then brushed her nose. Slowly, she said, 'Mera mujh mein kich nahin, jo kich hai so tera,' before looking the other way.

Noor remembered learning, years ago in a Hindi class, the verse her mother had just quoted: 'Nothing within me, is mine/

Whatever there is, is thine/ When I restore it to thee/ What can it cost me?' It was from the Granth Sahib. A popular shabad, Kabir's verse. Finding her students drowning in the sea of sagacity, the teacher had elaborated: every water source, stream, river, rain, ultimately finds its way to the ocean; similarly, with the atma and parmatma, the human soul finds its way, eventually, to the universal soul. It was profound, hinting at some larger truth, some truth that her mother had found comfort in. For Noor, though, it was beyond grasp, still.

❧

Noor was running a temperature that, despite the ministrations of Neymat, refused to subside. Suspecting viral fever, Neymat had sent her to the family doctor for a second opinion. Dr LTS ran his clinic from the ground floor of his sprawling, largely unoccupied haveli in the old bazaar. A friend of the family, he had seen all the children through their growing-up years. In the front room, a throng of patients sat, squatted, stood waiting amidst a gallimaufry of medicinal odours, sticky sweat and passed wind.

Noor consulted the compounder, then walked to the open door of the doctor's chamber. In an attempt to catch his eye, she peered around the frame.

LTS. Noor smiled, despite her fever. The initials were doubly incongruous. The portly doctor had the smooth unlined face of a Laughing Buddha, and his patients, confounded by a name that was solely initials, had garbled it such that it sounded like two English lasses standing side by side: Elle-Tess. Peasants from neighbouring villages simply called him Bugga Daktar, the fair doctor. The doctor himself was reluctant to divulge the secret but old-time associates were in the know: London Tor Singh. The lion who would destroy London!

His grandfather had fled home at an early age and become a Nihang Sikh, the traditional Sikh warrior. He had taken upon himself the name Dilli Tor Singh. However, the lion who would destroy Delhi, and therefore the Mughals, had been forcibly brought back by his irate folks. To humour him, they let the name stick. His son, in turn, was named Shamsheer Singh: the Sword Lion. A revolutionary, he affectionately named his child, born in the dying days of the Empire, in the fond memory of his grandfather's martial predilections.

Now, the doctor turned from the examination table to scrub his hands at the sink. 'Biba?' He caught Noor's gaze. Wiping his hands on a towel, he approached her, the smooth forehead momentarily puckered, for he had visited the house two days back. 'Who's unwell?' Upon learning, he popped a thermometer in her mouth.

'Hmm... Low-grade fever,' Dr LTS muttered. 'Are you boiling your drinking water? You children travel all over the world. How will the water of Ferozepur suit you now?' He grinned.

Noor said she played it safe by drinking mineral water.

'Boil it nevertheless,' the doctor suggested.

'Boil *mineral* water?'

'Oh Biba, the empty bottles are regularly collected by urchins and refilled—from taps and bore wells. So boil. Understood?'

Noor recalled the rag-pickers on Bombay platforms who, in the true spirit of recycling, gathered discarded mineral water bottles, then refilled, resealed and resold those. Probably to the same passengers who had discarded the bottles on the inbound journey on their return leg!

As Noor waited for the compounder to dole pills out in a paper pouch, Dr LTS approached her with a manila envelope. Noor studied the print—Stephen Diagnostic Laboratory—on the face, and looked up.

'One of your papa's reports.'

'What report?'

'Routine test. Dr Arora was away, so your papa came to me. He wanted to be in tip-top condition. Really...' Dr LTS shook his head, 'he was as excited as a bridegroom off to see his bride!'

Noor's forehead furrowed. She smiled weakly at her father's old friend and asked, 'Off to where?'

'Lahore, ahoy!' Dr LTS smiled. 'He wanted to visit the old city before he died, he said. One last time.'

BAKSH

THE LAST WALK

Baksh stirred from his reverie. He remembered why he had left home. The pain seemed to have settled into a dull throb, but he wondered if he should see the doctor. He trudged down the riverbank and took the main road. As he approached the gurudwara he heard sounds from within the complex: patter of feet, a lid shutting, low voices. The priest would be awake—Baksh looked at his watch: 3.45—time for cleansing the temple and morning ablutions before he began the recitation of Japji. A young boy—thirteen or fourteen years old, dressed in a dastar and rumpled kurta-pajama—stood at the gate, a steel bucket in his hand. Sighting Baksh, alone on the deserted road, he asked, a quizzical look in his eyes, 'Sardarji? Did you want something?'

It was not that long back when Baksh was a similar age. And had worn the same naïve, open look. Did he want something?

He wanted his life back all over again. And he wanted a magical slate, the kind that children used nowadays: whatever they scribbled, once the flap was lifted, voila! Clean and fresh for use again. He wanted to hold the rain in his palms, before it fell to earth and muddied with the dust. He wanted to run through the lane, his feet following the music of the malang as he lustily sang a ballad, and join the band of admirers swaying to the Sufi troubadour. He wanted to look around him, see things, and not be saddled by his memories of them...

Baksh shook his head at the boy and resumed his walk to Dr Arora's clinic. On reaching, he found the door locked.

A brass Harrison padlock hung from the bolt, the streetlight shone on the nameplate fitted to the upper right half of the double door, the old wood painted a startling blue. Dr S.S. Arora, MBBS, was apparently not at home. Even his Gurmukhi alter ego, Daktar Ass Ass Arora.

Where could he have gone? The last time Baksh had visited his clinic, three–four weeks back, the doctor had not mentioned any travel plans. It was not even school vacations... What could have cropped up so suddenly that the doctor, with his entire family, including an ailing mother, had to lock the place and depart?

What now?

He stood there, vacantly scanning the whitewashed exterior wall beyond which stood the doctor's two-room clinic. In the first room, a compounder-clerk allotted queue numbers to patients variously slumped on wooden benches, dispensed pills in paper pouches and potions in amber-hued bottles and collected cash.

Regulars like Advocate Bhalla were allowed the privilege of jumping the queue, and waved into the second room where the doctor saw patients. The torso of a skeleton stood in a corner on a pedestal, the curved rib cage gathering dust. A chart enquiring 'How do you feel today?' hung from the right wall, next to the door, at an easy glancing distance from the patient's seat. Smileys illustrated a range of human emotions: anxious, happy, dejected...

Dr Arora, balding pate, earthy wit, had the bustle of a man who had decided to make money, having relinquished the dream of becoming a 'great doctor'. His practice was flourishing, thriving on a rural clientele suitably awed by a doctor who could pronounce diagnosis in earthy Punjabi, coloured by choice abuses. A cirrhosis patient, his liver ruined by country liquor, impertinent enough to query 'Daktarji, X-ray shows what?' went back with the following diagnosis: 'A litre of desi and a kilo of namkeen, pehnchod!'

With the townsfolk, though, the doctor's demeanour was placid, like a teacher who gives up on his students once they enter college. They know their fate is in their hands.

The last time Baksh had come here, Dr Arora had hopped from 'equable' to 'grim' on the 'How do you feel today?' chart: 'It does not look good.' The 'not' underlined by the intense ten-second gaze from behind the slim rectangular reading glasses.

'The wound is not healing, despite the antibiotics…'

'It's your weight, Bhallasaab—you have to control it to control your diabetes. Otherwise…' He exhaled long and shrugged mildly.

Baksh knew—he was sitting astride the overweight–diabetic– hypertensive–cardiac go-round that had begun to spin wildly. It could slow down, if he wanted it to. If. If he could find it within himself to sit tight and hold still while the momentum petered off. Then learn to nurse one drink through the evening, an entire evening.

Peeta hain ummeed mein jeene ki… A good drink was guaranteed to cast the world into a fine kaleidoscope: fragments of dreams, shards of bitter love, shavings of hostility, scraps of disappointment, all tumbling together in a comforting blur. But doctors, regrettably, had one-track minds. 'A drink packs too many calories, leading to o-b-e-s-i-t-y, d-i-a-b-e-t-e-s and high blood pressure. Excess drinking could lead to hypoglycaemia that will have you running in the night for the box of sweets in the fridge.' And the circle was looped back.

True, very true. And like most truths, lacking in imagination. Tring. Trrrriiing.

Baksh started. A milk vendor was expressing his annoyance at the unexpected presence of pedestrian traffic in the middle of the road so early in the morning. Baksh moved towards the kerb as the bicycle wobbled by on the brick-paved road, the large iron canisters strung from the carrier rattling evenly. Otherwise, the world still lay quiet.

What other doctor could he turn to at this hour? He touched his chest, gently probing the upper left half with his fingers. There was a dull pain, or was it the memory of the earlier pain? He did not feel any distinct discomfort—just a sort of heaviness... Perhaps, it had receded. For good.

He looked down the lane. Past the chakki where Preet got wheat milled for flour, every quarter. Past the nai who had been a regular fixture in the children's growing-up years, especially accident-prone Noor's: a bandaged knee one month, bruised shin another time, fractured thumbnail... Past a few old houses in various stages of disrepair and quick-fix propping and a mechanic's shop heralded by an old cycle tyre looped from the branches of a jamun tree in front, was the intersection, to the left of which was the crumbling portal called Baghdadi Gate.

In childhood, he had learnt that if he stood at the gate and walked straight ahead—rather, flew straight overhead—he could reach Lahore, Kabul, and skimming over the Hindukush, eventually alight in Samarkand, the city from which Timur straddled his empire, one leg planted in India, the other in Turkey.

Half a kilometre away from the once-imperial gate stood the old haveli Bapuji had built and Baksh had grown up in. Baksh started to walk down the lane, memory leading him on.

1958

Bapuji drew on his ornamented hookah. Gud-gud-gud. The smoke bubbling through water gurgled amidst the reflective gathering. Mindar, Lehna Singh's son, had sprinkled water to settle the courtyard dust and cool the air in preparation for the evening's sit-out. It was a sweltering summer day—the whirring pedestal fan mounted on a corner table barely stirred the air baked by a conscientious sun. Baksh had finished a bath after a hot day at the farm when salt, not sweat, lined the brow and settled in the folds of skin.

'You think the government is serious about this land ceiling?' Bapuji enquired.

Baksh shrugged. 'Bitta is pretty certain, and usually he is in the know.'

Balwant spoke up from the bed where she sat beside Bapuji. 'The ceiling for land holding is fixed at thirty acres. And we have roughly five hundred acres to worry about.'

Her expression was bland, but with Balwant, Baksh knew, one could not be sure. The diminutive frame belied the resolve that lurked within. It had enabled her to quit her husband's house within a couple of years of marriage, only because she could not stand the smell of dung from the cowshed which was the locus of the family's dairy business. Not a single item of her dowry had she left behind at the milkman's; she had, in fact, milked him of the jewellery and silk dresses of the shagan and wedding ceremonies. Upon her return to her parents' house, she had reinstated herself as the first among equals, courtesy her status of being the firstborn.

Balwant's eyes were focused on the ivory inlay of the centre table as she spoke. 'Best to sell it off… the excess land… before the act is implemented.'

'To whom?' Baksh raised his eyebrows. 'All big landlords are settling the problem of their own land… and the small ones don't have the money to buy. Besides,' he frowned, 'it's our land. We have tilled it for years—how can we just sell it? And even if we do, what will we do with all that money?'

'There is enough that can be done with money…' Balwant offered to no one in particular. 'If you know how—'

'Your construction plans again?' Baksh jeered.

'Only a fool can't see the wealth in the building business. The government is setting up a new city, Chandigarh. Land is going a-begging there. Those who buy plots of that barren soil today and put up buildings… houses, shops… will be the Sardars of tomorrow.'

To what extent was Balwant's boyfriend behind all her thinking? Were these *her* ideas she was mouthing, or the machinations of that worthless philanderer? Balwant was in a relationship with a much-married much-older father-of-four. She claimed they had married, but since it was illegal for a man to have two wives, her status as a kept woman was an open secret. And Bapuji… surely he understood what his daughter was up to? Strangely, he continued to be a silent spectator, his reticence increasingly dressed up as assent through deft manoeuvres by Balwant. Baksh laughed, a forced high laugh, and shook his head.

Balwant waved a hand at him. 'Mark my words! Write them down, so you don't forget.'

'What is all this kech-kech! Are you children? Squabbling like fighting cocks!' Everyone looked at Jinder, slumped as usual in his round-backed cane chair. He stayed silent so often these days that people tended to forget he was around.

'Well... Do *you* have any grand plans?'

'No.'

'Then?' Balwant's head was tilted at a belligerent angle, hands resting on her waist.

'Then what? Will shouting provide a solution faster?' Jinder shook a dismissive foot.

'So let's all sit around,' Balwant addressed the rest of the group solicitously, 'and wait till writersaab comes up with an answer.'

'We could confer with some good lawyer. Take Bitta,' Baksh offered, trying to keep the exasperation out of his voice, 'he is seeking advice of this top-shot from Patiala—someone whose father worked for the maharaja himself. These people are well-versed in such legal wrangling. After all, how many Sardars have willingly ever given up their land? What they avoided through bloodshed earlier, now they will avert through legal warfare.'

Balwant stayed silent, Jinder remained disinterested, Bapuji continued with his smoking. The fragrance of wet earth mingled with tobacco floated around the silent gathering.

Finally, Balwant spoke, her expression prim. 'I have an idea. I have discussed it with Bapuji already.'

Bapuji drew long and hard on his hookah, intently examining the paisley work on its rounded base. 'See, what she has to say...' he mumbled.

Balwant shifted her posture, smoothening the creases in her lap. 'I think it is best that we split the land—'

'That's nothing new,' Baksh broke in. 'That much math we know. If we were to split it, in accordance with the government act, four ways—Bapuji and the *three* children,' he paused—after all in any other household a daughter inheriting land would be blasphemy—'we still end up with three hundred and fifty acres of lost property.'

Balwant affected a sigh, of one whose wisdom was superior to that of the gathering. 'I suggest we divide the land amongst us, and Bodh Singh's sons—' Baksh let out an astonished 'Whaaat!' while Jinder stirred enough to cast a sideways glance of interest, but Balwant continued, raising her voice above the rumbling din. 'That way with a thirteen-way split we can keep four hundred acres. The rest we can sell—*and I even have a buyer.*'

So *this* was Balwant's paramour's plan! He was stringing along the love-struck divorced daughter of the prosperous Bhalla clan: fucks for the daughter, stratagems for the father's acres! Buyer! Feckless fucker! Roping *their* tenant, Bodh Singh, into *his* plan. No doubt, setting himself up as *the buyer*.

'Are you mad? *Mad?*' Baksh felt like saying something outrageous, something to rattle the smugness out of Balwant. 'Anyway, what do *you* know of these things? Stick to things suited to womenfolk… maybe, maybe you could learn to cook for a start…'

Balwant snorted and tossed her head. 'Keep this advice for your future wife. And raise your voice at her. Cook, my foot!'

From the cocoon of his massive cane chair, Jinder said, 'Why this sudden concern for the welfare of Bodh Singh's family?' His voice was even, betraying no emotion.

Balwant turned towards him in relief. 'Am I speaking Pashtu or what?' Waving a hand, she continued, 'No concern-shuncern. Only, he is convenient. The eight of them, Bodh and seven sons, can be shown on paper as the beneficiaries of land allotment. In practice, things remain as always. Our land, for us to own and Bodh Singh to labour.'

Baksh attempted to rein in his frustration. 'You think, Bodh Singh's sons will not *claim* ownership of the land after being declared its *legal* owners?'

'Tch,' uttered Balwant in exasperation. 'Paper does not change reality. Bodh Singh's family are tenants on our land. Have been. And will remain.'

'Things have been changing, in case you haven't noticed. Tomorrow, what prevents one of them from claiming the land as his?'

'We are Guruans, the descendants of the Sikh gurus. Do you think anyone will dare to usurp our property?'

Baksh shook his head, bewildered at the nonsense she harboured, of her own thinking, or induced by that boyfriend of hers. Abandoning the pretence of reasonableness, he steered right into her. 'Of late, Guruans have not behaved in keeping with their high traditions, pehn…'

A flush crept on Balwant's wheatish cheeks.

'It may work,' Jinder offered with a careless wave of the hand. 'Maybe we can think about it.'

They sat there in uneasy silence, avoiding each other's eyes, one looking for alternatives, another looking to checkmate.

'Well,' Balwant broke the silence, 'the result is clear: two versus one—Jinder and I on one side, Baksh on the other. Still, we will wait for Bapuji to cast his vote. Then we will know.'

❧

After Bapuji had cast his vote, the option of pursuing farming had been closed to Baksh. What caused Bapuji to align with Balwant and Jinder he could only speculate about. Was it excessive faith in Bodh Singh and his progeny? Or blinkers as far as his daughter's wild ways were concerned? Perhaps a weakness for opium, especially when made readily available by an unscrupulous daughter... or just old age and a spirit at odds with an increasingly unusual world?

Baksh tried his hand at joining the army, but failed the exam. The weight, height and chest-width criteria he met, or exceeded. The physical test—a run of a mile, push-ups, scaling a high wall with jute ropes—proved his nemesis.

When he returned home with bruised hands, aching legs and a 'Reject', Bitta tried consoling him with useless facts. 'Give the other communities a chance, baee. Sikhs have always made up the lion's share in the armed forces!'

Increasingly, law began to seem like a viable occupation, worthy of studious pursuit: the country was rapidly indigenizing its legal framework, new laws were being formulated, and enterprising people were forever on the lookout for legal loopholes. Add to that the Punjabi's ravenous appetite for disputes and settling those in courts. A legacy of their forefathers, aggression was always an option, a very viable option for a Punjabi. Zan, zewar, zameen: woman, gold, land—these made up the acknowledged triumvirate of trouble. A lawyer, at least in the Punjab, was guaranteed never to run out of work.

The newly constructed city of Chandigarh awed Baksh during his first visit when he arrived, with Bitta, to participate in the intercollegiate hockey championship. There, Baksh found the fog of the past few years lifting. His vocational meandering had neared its end: Bachelor of Law at the University of Punjab, Chandigarh.

Baksh had never before experienced anything that was this *modern*.

No Mughal appurtenances of domes, no colonial high-arched ceilings, no dust or crowd or chaos of a Punjabi township. Instead, clean lines, abundant green spaces, neat roads, trimmed hedges, symmetrical flower beds and crisp fresh mountain air. This departure from the past wowed Baksh. The city seemed to have casually shrugged off any design to blend in with the historic plains on which it stood. It was forging a style entirely its own. And looking ahead.

Chandigarh descended straight from the edge of the Shivaliks into Baksh's heart. His recent resolve to make his own way resonated with the rhythms of the Frenchman's planned city.

The girls' hockey team was rehearsing its moves under the keen eye of a coach in one of the two hockey fields. Onlookers—mostly men—watched from the boundary line. Dressed in salwar-kameez and white fleet shoes, the players moved energetically across the ground. One end of the field was busy training for penalty shoots. At the other, the coach watched a group of four work their dribble and passes.

A girl caught Baksh's eye. While the others were moving the ball by short quick taps, keeping it close to their body, this girl turned the stick back and forth over the ball, using the stick's regular position and the reverse to dribble. She was dexterous, not once did the ball leave the stick.

The ribboned plaited loops of her hair swung in joyful arcs as she surged forward, the chunni slung like a sash from one shoulder and knotted above a slender hip. The swift lithe motion reminded Baksh of young treetops caught in a breeze. Her forearms gripping the hockey shaft were fair, slim, toned, giving a hint of the body that moved in fluid arcs down the green grass.

The coach proceeded to tackle her: with his stick in the left hand, he lunged at the ball in an attempt to steal it from her. In one swift move, she placed the head of the stick behind and a bit under the ball and shovelled it off the ground, aiming for the D. There was no goalie to prevent the goal, but it was a copybook execution of a scoop.

Baksh was impressed. 'Who is that girl, Bitta?' He assumed his friend too had been watching the girl.

'Which one?' Bitta's eyes, however, were fixed on the penalty shot drill at the near end.

'O yaar. You are missing the real action.' Baksh swivelled his friend's head towards the other end. 'This one dribbles better than some of our players. Watch!'

Bitta observed the coach and the girl dribble and tackle, and muttered, through puckered lips, 'Not bad, hanh. For a girl.'

'Eyes or buttons? What *girl*? She's a good *player*, period.'

'That's a spirited defence, I say! Any relation of yours?'

Baksh brushed a moustache end upwards, eyes dreamy, 'Aaho! I will tell you when the time is right.'

'Any hockey players here?'

The coach had walked up to the boundary line. He looked searchingly at the spectators. A few hands went up, Baksh and Bitta included.

'Where do you play?' he shot in their direction.

Baksh's response—after he had applied enough pressure on Bitta's arm to ensure his silence—that he was there to participate in the intercollegiate cup seemed to satisfy the coach. 'Good!' He motioned to Baksh with a quick flick of his fingers. 'You don't mind helping with some practice, right?'

Nodding in the coach's direction, Baksh sang softly to Bitta, 'Lotter-eee!'

'Saala! What kismat!' Bitta massaged a sore spot on his left arm.

The coach planned to man the goal; he wanted Baksh to provide the defence and the girl with the plaits to attack. 'She is my best centre forward,' he said to Baksh. 'But,' and now he turned to the girl, 'I need to see how good you are with unexpected defence.'

She started at centre half; Baksh was the fullback entrusted to defend the goal. In the trademark swift style that Baksh had witnessed earlier, she started to dribble down the field. He jabbed repeatedly at the ball, left, right, to make her lose possession as she alternated briskly between the two sides of the stick. They traversed the distance to the goal area with him marking her closely.

Now he had her covered. There was no space for her to manoeuvre the ball in an attempt at the goal. Finding it difficult to move, she lobbed the ball a couple of yards away. Caught unawares, Baksh lost guard of the opponent, and watched the flying ball land to their right. Smart play, he silently acknowledged. Could be dangerous, though, the way she had lifted it, barely missing the level that would disallow the move.

He was beside her in a second, ready for the next round of defence. As Baksh hovered near the ball, she looked straight into his eyes. Bright, keen, a hint of mischief as they regarded him. In the instant that Baksh held that glance, she turned the stick, pointed the blade to the right, and pushed it in the direction of the goal. It struck the right goalpost. The goalkeeping coach made a jump to defend, leaving a gap in the left corner. She ran forward and flicked it in. Goal!

The coach got up, dusting himself. 'That was good!' Turning to Baksh, he asked, 'What happened? You were doing a good job until…'

Baksh shrugged, irritated at the momentary loss of concentration. The girl, holding the hockey stick in both hands, smiled at him. The lips curved upwards to the left in a most fetching manner. A tingling set off within him.

Later, Bitta commented slyly, 'Baksh, what happened, yaar? You forgot the basic rule of the game: eye on the ball, mind on the goal. Always!'

DAY 6: ANANT

Noor sat on the beam of the rooftop terrace, a concrete bar a foot high, and watched the stars emerge from their daytime slumber. Silly, but she could not get it out of her mind: what the woman from the old house had said the other day. In all probability, it was a clumsy attempt at intrigue, a spicing up of a humdrum existence. Delivered with the infantile unconcern of the very old.

Irritated with the mosquito whizzing around her ear, Noor swung her head. If it was all hogwash, why had Mama believed her? And why mention the detail about Papa massaging his left side? Wouldn't it be rather ingenious of a decaying mind to concoct such particularity? Executed artfully as an afterthought?

'Quo vadis?'

At the familiar salutation, Noor smiled and turned to watch Anant approach, his right hand cocking an imaginary gun at her. Bardolatry, Latin-phrase fetish, love of English classics—those were some bridges between them. Besides, they connected on an intuitive plane, their funny bones attuned to each other as they nudged, winked, sputtered through hands clasped over mouths or laughed outright. Neymat called them a 'pair of sillies'. They could go on endlessly with a nonsensical joke, weaving one after another into it, until their continual guffawing prompted Neymat to command: 'Enough!' Also, both of them were—to a certain extent—angst-ridden. His salve was poetry, hers career.

Noticing the jeans, Noor lifted her brows. Normally, given the heat, Anant was content to spend an entire day in his Levi's shorts, preferably shirtless. 'Going somewhere?'

'Bazaar.' Where else, implied the accompanying groan as he started to stroll.

'Do you know how long Papa's last walk lasted?' Noor asked. The strains of a Shabad drifted from the Jail Gurudwara opposite the house.

Softly, Anant said, 'Very long.'

'No. I mean how many hours.'

'Endless. He left home and never came back.'

Noor's hands were slicing the evening air with rapidity. 'No-no. Do you even know how early he—'

'Three. He left home at three. That's when the rickshawala saw him.'

'Three a.m...'

Noor kept repeating the three syllables to herself as she tried to get hold of a single thread to tie together what Anant had divulged and what the old woman had recalled. 'And he is certain of the time because he looked at his wristwatch... Then he...'

Anant watched Noor spacewalk. He had been there before, he knew what it was like to be in a deep pool and not know how to swim. Clutching the wall, he had braced himself until his feet found the bottom: post-death routine that swamped all perception, left no time to actively ponder on the rickshaw puller's revelation.

'Why was he out so early?'

'The pains must have started…'

Anant studied the seven bright stars in the sky and connected them mentally. Sapt Rishi. Seven Saints. Neymat had pointed the pattern out to him the first time. Neymat was unusually perceptive, she noticed ordinary things, the kind others ignored. Standing near the balcony railing on late evenings, she would remark on the faint fragrance wafting from the garden. 'Raat ki rani,' she would say and smile. Queen of the night: the nondescript bush that transformed into a perfumery every evening. Or she would remark on someone's slender fingers, when all Anant remembered was having met a forgettable face. Then there were times when she would finish serving tea to one of Mama's colleagues, step into the bedroom and grin at them. 'POC,' she would say, nodding towards the living area. With interest, they would investigate when the visitor walked away, his trouser hitched up high. POC: Pant On Chest—Neymat's coinage and eminent addition to their argot.

'W-why do you think that?'

He remained silent for a while. What could he say?

'Maybe he couldn't sleep… after all, he was alone at home and may have decided to go out. He did go for walks at times at four in the morning when…' Anant looked at her. 'The bucket and mug were upturned on the bathroom floor.'

'What bucket? Which bathroom?'

'The bucket in the main bathroom. And Papa had a gash on his forehead… didn't you notice?'

'A bruise, yes. So?'

'So, he most likely stumbled and fell in the bathroom.'

'Meaning?'

Anant puffed his cheeks and blew air out. 'He must have felt palpitations. Discomfort. Stiffness. Then when he went to the toilet, the ache must have surged. Most likely, some shooting pain had radiated through him. He fell, knocking the bucket over, and hurt himself.'

'But he might have slipped accidentally... you know, fallen because he had drunk too much.'

'He had not had a drink that night.'

'That still doesn't—'

'Noor.' Anant gripped his sister's flailing hands. 'Listen. Do not speak. Okay?'

Noor nodded mutely.

'Pasha's bowl was full. You know how the dog is—perennially hungry. Then why would his bowl contain uneaten chicken?'

Papa clutching the air, falling in the bathroom, slumping on the tiled floor—the images flashed through Noor's mind. One part processed those pictures, zooming in, zooming out, the sequence all jumbled. Another registered Anant's speech.

'Because he tricked Pasha when leaving the house. He had to use the meat as a ruse. Maybe Pasha was not letting him leave.'

'Why?'

'Who knows?' Anant shrugged, releasing her hands. 'Maybe there is some truth in what they say... a dog's premonitory sense or whatever. But the fact is that he must have left home to seek help.'

'Then why would he be sitting at the haveli steps an hour later? Why not call Jinder Tayaji? Why not see a doctor?'

'How would I know?'

Anant resumed his study of the stars. What was the point of all this? Why had Noor brought it up? The rickshawala was fibbing. Now this Buddhi Bebe! Suffering from senile dementia, likely. Her feet dangled above the grave, that was how old she was! Claiming to have seen Papa at the haveli steps…

Haveli steps… Didn't the road from the house to the haveli go via the bazaar—

Abruptly Anant got up. 'It never struck me earlier. It never struck me…' He hurried off in the direction of the stairs.

'Ant! Ant!' Noor called after him.

Swivelling, he looked at her. 'Maybe he *had* gone in search of a doctor. Dr Arora's clinic is in the bazaar. And the rickshawala saw him heading towards the bazaar…'

'But… where are you going?'

'To meet Dr Arora.' He bounded down the steps.

⁕

In the evening, Gulli arrived to pay his condolences. Seated opposite Anant in the living room, Gulli patted his hand. 'I got to know only today morning… was away for a wedding. I bumped into one of Bodh Singh's sons at the wholesale market. He told me…' Gulli looked at the floor, then wiped his eyes with his kurta. 'For us, Bhallasaab was like a father…'

Anant knew what Gulli meant. His father, Mindar, had been less Papa's servant, more Man Friday. Just as his grandfather, Lehna, had been to Bapuji. Mindar had spent his life with them and, one night, died in his sleep in this very house.

'Bhallasaab used to think a lot. People like us, small brain God gave us, don't need to exercise it much. We eat, sleep, work, and life passes.'

'Come now, Gulli! You were quite colourful in your days.'

Gulli of the denim jacket, red bell-bottom pants, long

sideburns, who had eloped with a married woman! Escaping to Ferozepur, he reluctantly plied the rickshaw Mindar had bequeathed to him. However, the arduous work and uncertain pay had him join a wedding band. The perks were a new set of clothes and complimentary engorgement on Mughlai food.

'How is Naresh doing?' Anant enquired.

At the mention of his son's name, Gulli brightened up. 'Naresh has become a party worker now,' he informed with pride. 'Only seventeen, but he is entrusted with much responsibility— sits in the Race Course Road office of the BJP. For how long he looked for work here in Ferozepur, hain? And in Dilli, as soon as he reached, he got work. No wonder it is the capital city... enough opportunities for employment. He hasn't visited for some months now... very busy. But young boys should stay busy, na? Idle mind is a devil's home, hain?'

Anant nodded. *Busy*, yes, he thought to himself, watching Gulli's obvious pride. The poor man need never know what sort of *worker* his son was. Even Anant would not have known had Naresh not walked into Neymat's home one day, his head bleeding from a severe wound, his saffron bandanna spotted with red. In exchange for the free treatment, he had divulged the true nature of his work: as an organizer for the BJP MLA from Chandni Chowk, he gathered crowds for political rallies, speeches, strikes, protest fasts, and orchestrated riots in aid of the party's agenda.

'In this world,' Gulli was saying, his voice permanently hoarse from yodelling folk songs at marriage ceremonies, 'thinking only makes you sadder. Then sorrow has to be drowned, hain? So, you drink.' Twirling a finger in the air, he said, 'It's all a chakarvyuh.'

'There you are right, Gulli.' Anant marvelled at the rustic logic that equated the circle of life to a chakravyuh, a maze in which one is forever lost.

'This Bodh Singh's family is complete kameeni. Deceit runs in their blood, hain…' Gulli shook his head in dismay.

'Why? What happened now?'

'Oh, they won't let a dead man rest in peace.' He coughed, then cleared his throat. 'Only a scum talks ill of one who is gone.'

'Speak clearly, Gulli.' Anant's voice was edgy.

Mistrust ran deep where the ex-tenant-current-landlord and his posse of army-inspired-and-labelled progeny—Jarnail, Laftain, Major, Subedar—was concerned. When the sons exceeded Bodh Singh's knowledge of military designations, he switched to another Punjabi favourite: English-word monikers. His youngest sons were called Baybee and Littall. It could be a bit disconcerting when you went to meet 'Little' and encountered a strapping sardar who, while you sipped tea, gulped a jerry can of milk—full-fat, unboiled, warm and smelling of hay—straight from the cow barn.

Gulli glanced over his shoulder. Noticing the empty hallway, he leaned forward and whispered: 'In the market this morning… very strange thing he told me.'

Anant's head bobbed.

'I didn't understand it much, but… most likely some new story they have concocted…' Gulli looked at Anant closely now. 'Bodh Singh's son said Bhallasaab was walking in the fields that day. The day he had his hartatack.'

'Rakhri fields?' Anant's eyes had narrowed as he too hunched forward, his hands clasped together.

'Un-hunh. Rakhri farm.'

'But that's very far… on foot…'

'That is what!' Gulli stuck a hand out, cast another look around, and continued: 'I also didn't understand. Rakhri is five–six kilometres away. We always took a car to the fields, hain? Then how could Bhallasaab walk so far? That too, so early…'

'Bodh Singh's son… where *was* he at that time?'

'In the fields. Said he was checking on the crops. He had left the water on in the night. Claims he called out but got no answer—lo!' Gulli looked away from Anant to the recently mounted photograph of Papa on the wall and sighed. 'We know of Bodh Singh's treachery, don't we? Can one straighten a dog's tail?'

Anant crunched his knuckles. 'Time? Did he mention what time it was, Gulli?'

'Hmm … He didn't mention any time really … But he was certain he could see clearly. Probably dawn. If he is to be believed.'

'Five-ish, han?'

Gulli clasped his hands together, then flicked them outwards. 'God only knows what is truth, what is not.'

BAKSH

THE LAST WALK

Baksh realized he had come to a halt. His first encounter with Preet had seized him and, now, years later, the recollection of that meeting was afflicting him in the same way! With a wry smile he reflected how similar first love was to the first drop of rain: full of promise, heedless of the inevitable muddying to follow. A new city and a girl to fall in love with—both at the same time! Amazing good fortune, Baksh remembered thinking at the time. If only he had known then what he knew now.

There is nothing like too much of a good thing. Or a bad thing, for that matter. As he had learnt, whatever the shape of the Kismat-curve, in the end, it all evened out. For some the curve exhibited a fat tail, for others a protuberant middle. While some travelled the course of life in a fairly straight line, others plunged and soared with startling consistency; a few meandered, some raced, many sputtered. What united the diverse curves at the end was the mean luck: sum of good and bad averaged over a lifetime.

While in Chandigarh the godsends had seemed to pile up, in time the misfortunes had also arrived in a heap.

An involuntary sigh escaped Baksh at the memory of those balmy days in Chandigarh, when he had been mesmerized by a girl who had none of the fey charm of a female. Instead, she was unafraid to lock her eyes with an opponent and take him on. The broad high forehead and aquiline nose were of a typical Punjabi beauty. Yet, she wielded a hockey stick better than many male players. She moved with the grace of a gazelle and the pride of a lioness. Her mouth hinted at an alluvium-like richness and he wondered what it would be like to explore its generous expanse, particularly the left corner, tilted in smile.

Preet Kaur Sidhu, Jat Sikh from Malwa, the same region Baksh hailed from, the cradle of Sikhism. She came from a people deeply rooted in their soil, hardy farmers who had a proud history of tilling their land and gamely defending it against successive invaders. He was a Khatri, descended from the same caste as the ten Sikh gurus. His family traced their lineage direct to the third guru himself. With the increasing tyranny of the Mughal Empire, as the complexion of the Sikh faith had changed—pacifist Nanak to militant Gobind—Jat farmers had led the rise in Sikh power. In a reversal of roles, the Jat farmer had fought more battles for his homeland than the Khatri, the traditional warrior class. In the end, Malwa was about the only point of similarity between them.

As happens in life, in the short run, a clash of opposites triggers drama, interest, excitement. Life, however, wasn't a hundred-metre dash. And a marathon called for a separate set of skills: a willingness to compromise and the ability to constantly rebalance. But the free-spirited Jat, who disdained the privileged castes of Brahmins and Khatris, was a worker and warrior who followed his own set of rules. And true Jat that Preet was, compromise did not come easily to her.

Lost in thought, Baksh had arrived close to the haveli. As he walked down the lane, he sighted the nail-studded wooden gate of the old house, its handsome facade at odds with the generally crumbling exterior of the bungalow. When Bapuji had built the two-storey residence around a middle courtyard, he had intended it to be capacious enough to house a joint family. Yet Bapuji and Maji had grown old alone in the haveli. Baksh had been the first one to build a separate house for his family, barely three kilometres away. It was a short distance, yet the divide it represented had proved unbridgeable.

1965

The haveli resounded with lusty singing, accompanied by periodic 'hoyes' from Vir's comrades, as vigorous clapping, sharp whistles and a raucous chorus filled the air. Vir Singh Sidhu had arrived early, carrying gifts for each member of the family—even Mindar had received a woollen blanket. For Preet, the fond brother had carried a gold set.

'Balle! O, balle shera balle!'

The Dholi started to beat the drum, an impromptu circle began to sway, the arms lifted in languid moves as the Bhangra commenced. It was Lohri. Bodh Singh and his sons had delivered the winter crop. The fields stood lush with vibrant green stalks of wheat. At home, Preet had graduated with a teacher's diploma, thus making it a doubly joyous Lohri.

The bonfire had been set up in the courtyard, ringed by cane armchairs and stools. The male gathering munched on puffed rice, sesame seed-coated jaggery and roasted groundnuts;

some swilled whisky, others held up their hands to the leaping flames, then transferred the warmth to their limbs. Jokes, songs, anecdotes were being bandied, the atmosphere of bonhomie unmarred by the chilly night air.

'Baksh,' spoke Shammi, raising his voice in order to be heard above the din, 'the gathering is incomplete without the "enterprise man". What's keeping him?'

Enterprise man: Baksh had given Bitta that moniker when Bitta had first advised him on the intricacies of making love to a woman with a pithy precept—to enter, prise open—having had his first sexual encounter at the age of twelve with an amorous young aunt on a summer night, even as he lay on a string bed next to his aunt and uncle.

Jinder cast a look at Shammi, one that slid down his stately nose. 'Some people have work to do.'

Shammi stooped, his whisky glass embraced in both hands. 'So be it, Mamaji.' Turning back to Baksh he persisted, 'What's the amerjansy?'

Before Baksh could answer, Jinder replied, 'But what am I saying? Sloganeering is also work. Utilizes energy, time, plus money from one's pocket! News is that salt consumption in some households has gone up… what with the frequency of gargles to soothe sore throats!'

Shammi was attempting to be the local flag-bearer of the Akali Dal, which had positioned itself as the rightful representative of Sikh interests in politics. His tongue worked some morsel wedged deep between his molars as he eyed Jinder. Then he rubbed his scanty beard and turned to Baksh.

Suppressing a smile, Baksh said, 'Is meeting some engineer at Bhakra.'

'At the new dam? Angling for a contract still?' Shammi snorted. 'Two legs, and Bitta has planted them in so many places!'

The singing wound down and without the exuberant lyrics, the dancers slowed down too. Vir Singh, who had provided two songs in a row, rested the twin flutes of his algoze atop a table and rotated his shoulders. Then he picked up his glass and took a long swig.

'Oye Vir Singh-a! Why stop?' Shammi swayed forward, his glass held aloft. 'I have barely wetted my whiskers yet.'

'Aaho Sardara! Let's have some more,' came another voice.

'After all, Jat is risky after whisky.'

Vir Singh grinned. By Punjabi standards, he was short. A naturally round face with plump cheeks lent him a jolly air. Which the rest of his body made up for. Beneath the large blanket-shawl he draped was the physique of a medium-weight wrestler. Also hidden underneath was the brown leather holster at his waist.

Thereafter, Vir put up a show. Fingers flitting over the pair of flutes, shoulders jigging merrily, he winked and sang and played the algoze with abandon, fully aware of the riot the Jat had set off in the Khatri household.

For months afterwards, Preet received marriage proposals for her younger brother. Maybe it had been the festive atmosphere, Vir Singh's dazzling display, or his virility coupled with humility, but all suitors seemed to have overlooked the intensity which underlined his pleasant demeanour.

While delighted, Preet ruefully turned each one down. Vir Singh's injunction on the matter was clear: he was caught up in some unfinished business.

Vir was younger than Preet by three years. 'My Vir,' she said, when she referred to him. Homophone 'Vir': in Punjabi it stood for both brother and brave.

She often recounted a childhood incident. In the midst of a game of hide and seek, Vir had playfully thumped her on the back before decamping to hide. An hour passed and he decided to show himself, figuring that Preet had not discovered his hideout. He found her slumped where he had left her, knocked unconscious by the force of his friendly fist.

Vir was a legatee. What had been bequeathed to him, he carried in the muscle-trained strength of his body and slung around a shoulder. Tales abounded of his skilled shooting: a clean shot at a swinging apple was a cinch. A light sleeper, his loaded revolver was cocked before his eyes opened wide at any unexpected twitter. Inscribed on his right palm was an elder brother's murder, committed when he was unborn. To defend with revenge was part of his destiny. Born to a legacy of landed feud, ever-alertness was essential to survival.

Therefore, he arrived unannounced—his attendance at family gatherings could not be counted on. The enemy and he were caught in a perennial spin, one which held the possibility of reversing direction at any point in time. He travelled with armed accomplices; there was strength in numbers. As time went by, he started to arrive in the cover of dark. Daylight became another enemy.

Radio Pakistan was the seminary for the '65 war between India and Pakistan. An unlikely ally, it came unasked to the aid of Sant Fateh Singh who was leading the renewed demand for a Punjabi state. Pakistan, the envious younger brother of Hindustan, sensed an opportunity to splash water into boiling oil. Radio Pakistan served as the sprinkler. In a series of broadcasts, it promised the Sikhs support for driving the Hindus out of the Sikhs' homeland.

Thus providing Shammi with a catapult.

After several years of paying the first-year annual admission fees solely to retain his post of leader of the students' union, Shammi had graduated to being a morcha-organizing Akali loyalist.

At the height of Tara Singh's agitation for a Punjabi state, Shammi had led his band of protestors through the streets of Ferozepur, urging the loincloth-clad Punjabi Hindus to migrate across the Jamuna. 'Dhoti, topi, Jumna paar' was the rallying cry. Even though the Punjabi Hindu mostly wore pajamas. He was arrested. But 'courting-arrest', that launch vehicle for leaders pre-independence, had become passé by then. Shammi remained unrecognized.

Until Pakistan crossed the Chhamb–Jaurian border, entered Jammu and, like a street crier, shouted 'War!'

A politician by instinct, he sensed the direction in which the wind was blowing. Shammi temporarily forgot his differences with the Delhi Sarkar; the Akalis had declared unqualified support to the central government.

'It is a question of our community,' he said, assigning the defence of Punjab, therefore India, exclusively to the Sikh Regiment. It helped that the Indian Army, in its offensive against Lahore, was gathered at Ferozepur's Hussainiwala border. He joined as a volunteer driver for trucks carrying provisions to the army camp.

He was not alone.

Preet was pregnant with their first child, but insisted on serving in the langar. A servant carried supplies to the makeshift community kitchen where civil troops were engaged in their own battle: massing lentil sandbags, bayoneting mounds of flour, tossing thick wholewheat discs, tanking dal and milk, reconnoitring for rations, marching food across to the border check post—for when was war ever won on an empty stomach?

Shammi's take-off came when he overheard a brisk exchange between two army officers as his truck was being unloaded: a C-130 Hercules had dropped Pakistani paratroopers into Indian territory to capture airfields and destroy aircrafts. But the plan had gone haywire—in the dark of the night, the troopers had lost their bearing.

Shammi seized the moment. A few insidious probes later, he drove a hundred miles to Halwara airbase with five or six men. There he took the sarpanch into confidence and organized hunting parties to track down the infidels.

News spread. Zealous peasants slashed the standing crop in places. Angry mobs nabbed a few troopers hiding in the cornfields. Enraged, they slapped and thumped one with their leather juttis until he died. The other jumped into a well and was pounded with stones and drowned.

Shammi's party rounded up one alive. A true showman, he put the captive, a Captain Durrani, in his open-top truck and rode through the streets of Halwara all the way to Ferozepur. Like pollen, news had scattered across the length of the route. Irate folks lined the road, hurled juttis and abuses, showered angry fists, spat and remonstrated with jabbing fingers. The captors rode with their sooty victim—en route his face had been blackened by a furious mother of a soldier—to Hussainiwala, where they handed the catch over to a colonel, surrounded by his hooting command.

The following day, Shammi debuted on the political stage via a front-page picture in *The Tribune*.

❧

Baksh stretched his legs on the low table and awaited the arrival of tea. The dreamy autumn Sunday, plump with the comfort of a winter sun's rays, had cast a mellow drift: numerous rounds of rummy in Jinder's room, buttressed by sips, savouries and prattle.

'Tea?' Preet had raised her brows and held the expression for some time.

'Yes, tea.' He avoided looking at her directly—expecting a tongue-lashing for his daytime tipple—busying himself with priming his moustache in the triptych mirror. 'My usual.'

Preet deposited a tray on the marble-topped centre table. On a lace-trimmed napkin sat a round teapot, white with a sprinkling of red rosebuds, a covered sugar bowl, a two-handled milk pot, two cups with saucers. It was a fine English Bone China set that Baksh had bought during their honeymoon in Chandigarh from a shop that carried 'By appointment to Her Majesty' goods. However, the set lacked a matching tea strainer. So Preet had found an elegant silver two-piece set to complement her husband's English tea set.

'Sat Sri Akal, pehn.' Shammi's leather jutti squeaked its newness as he approached from the staircase. 'Can I trouble you as well?'

With a nod of her head Preet indicated the two cups.

Peering closely at the tray, Shammi said, 'Angreji cha.' Straightening his back, he continued, 'This weak tea is Baksh's idiosyncrasy. I will settle for regular tea if you don't mind, pehn.'

Preet went towards the kitchen.

'This time,' Shammi said, smoothing his kurta over his crossed legs, 'we have the Congress by its balls. Chacha Nehru dispatched to his heavenly abode by the Chini bhai, there is no stopping us now.'

Over his teacup, Baksh peered at Shammi. 'From forming a Punjabi state or Akali state?'

'Obviously the former. Where Punjabi is the spoken and official language. Then who governs is immaterial.'

'You have mastered the art of Looking London Talking Tokyo!'

Shammi smacked his lips. 'A public servant gets called many names. Let cross-eyed be added to that.'

Preet appeared with two glasses of strong milky tea. She offered one to Shammi, then sat down and proceeded to sip from the other. 'You really think we will get a state of our own?'

'Not to worry, pehn,' Shammi sipped appreciatively. 'This time a Punjabi state is a given. After the jaw-breaker of an answer that we have delivered to the Mussalmans in Pakistan.' He snorted before slurping his tea. Thereafter, he broke into a high-pitched jingle.

'Mera mahi chail chabeela, hai ni karnail ni, jernail ni.'

Shammi was burlesquing Noor Jehan, the once-Indian beauty, who had migrated to Pakistan and whose song had become Radio Pakistan's signature tune during the war. So repeatedly was it broadcast that it looked set to replace the

Quami Tarana, the national anthem. The singer had even been taken to the front to entertain and motivate the jawans of the Pakistani Army.

'My lively lover is a colonel, a general,' Shammi guffawed. 'In twenty-two days we reduced him to a foot soldier!' In the next slurp he finished his tea. 'One thing is certain,' Shammi said, working his thin moustache into an upright crescent, 'now the Bahmani Indira Gandhi has to fall in line. Sikhs have made the highest contribution to the defence. The time has come. One state. One language. A Punjabi Punjab.'

'And Akali-Shahi!' Jinder rambled into the courtyard, fingers picking at lint on an elbow. Without looking up, he added, 'Tyranny of the Akalis… isn't that your plan?'

'Sit, Mamaji.' Shammi patted the chair next to him, a sensitive headmaster urging a rowdy child. 'Let's sit and talk.'

Jinder eyed him briefly and continued with his slow perambulation, a to-and-fro behind Shammi's back, even as his speech fired rapidly. 'People like you have to colour everything with religion. So many other officers, soldiers, fought the war, and you can only see the Sikh contribution. There were those Keelor brothers. Pilots. Shot down Sabres. Greene. Leader of the 23 Squadron at Pathankot. Christian. Neb. Rathore. Do these names sound Sikh to you?'

'But the credit for halting the Pakistan offensive goes to General Harbaksh Singh, there is no doubt about that. He also led the operations in Kashmir and therefore controlled the entire war.'

Jinder paused. '*Lieutenant*-General.'

'Aaho. Same thing.' Shammi spread his palms. 'Jarnail is Jarnail, not foot soldier! Overall command he had.'

Arms across his chest, his lean frame inclined backwards, fingers of the left hand beating an impatient tattoo on the right elbow, Jinder blew air out of his nostrils. 'Rustics.' The one-word delivery was flat and even, meant to convey an everyday fact. Then he resumed his walk.

His lips pursed, Shammi turned in his chair, and rested an elbow on the back. 'Why call names, Mamaji?'

'Names?' Jinder looked genuinely perplexed. He halted. 'Names?' Stroking his beard that, unrestrained, spilled outward in a patrician curve, he said, 'What is the word for an illiterate, who can't speak a word of English?' He returned to the investigation of his pullover's lint. Flicking some of the same, he added in a weary voice, 'And people such as these will now manage the state government for us.'

'Now you are labelling my entire party rustic?'

'Rustics all.' Jinder swept an arm. 'Village preachers. Granthis. Matric-fail. Sant this and Master that. Demagogues!'

Shammi puffed his chest, then settled back into his chair.

'Since when has prejudice become sufficient qualification to run a state?'

A vigorous itch had suddenly sprung up in Shammi's hands. 'Conversing with his navel the entire day…' he muttered.

His voice, though low, was designed to be heard. Preet's nasal puff was a snuffed giggle, an uncomfortable Baksh adjusted his turban that a second ago had been fine. Close to two decades, but his older brother had not relinquished his life of silent contemplation, head sunk low on his chest as if in perennial quest of ant trails—on the floor, on his pant legs, on his shirtfront.

'Omphaloskepsis.'

Jinder's dry response rustled like static in the autumn air.

'Big words in gitter-mitter Angreji!'

'Om-pha-lo-skep-sis.'

Shammi snorted. 'Parelsis. Pepsis. Mainu ki?'

'What you call conversing with the navel is a form of meditation. It is the technique that ancient Greeks used to aid thought. Like Indian saints do—'

'Lo!' Abruptly Shammi stood up, flinging his hands. 'Sant Fateh Singh, Sant Jinder Singh. Saints both.' Massaging his chin, he looked directly at Jinder. 'Big difference though, Mama.'

'Yes,' Jinder returned the look. 'The absence or presence of intellect.'

'Oh Mama...' Shammi's hand urged a move-on. 'Some people make do with common sense—that way, at least, they can handle a female.'

Preet got busy with the tea things, the effort producing a Fine-Bone-China rattle. Shammi seemed unsure whether to sit down or continue standing. Jinder was still, contemplating the lint anew. Baksh, hands clasped behind his head, watched his elder brother.

Shammi had certainly delivered a blow by referring to the lady teacher responsible for Jinder resigning from his last job, his third in as many years. Over tea in the staff room, Padmaja, a Maharashtrian colleague at the college, had initiated conversation with Jinder on a couple of occasions. Imputing romantic notions, Jinder panicked and quit within two months of joining. 'Woman and I... where is the meeting point?' Jinder had shrugged in explanation.

Jinder, meanwhile, had finished a detailed survey of the fuzz. He lifted his head and slowly opened his mouth, then closed it again and nodded. 'In a party where whiskers are the determinant of fortune, you may want to do something about the cactus-fuzz.'

Shammi revved up at the spot. He shuffled, raised a hand towards his uncle to query, took a step forward, then decided against it. Jinder lifted the fingers of his right hand in a barely perceptible flick. Takhliya. Dismissal.

To the perceptive, a hint will suffice. And Shammi was grooming himself for political office. He started to rock on his feet, thumb and index finger probing his scanty facial hair.

❧

It was his fourth year of practising as a lawyer, and Baksh had been to Chandigarh for two days for an appeal hearing that his senior partner could not attend. On his return, Preet rustled him inside their bedroom where three-year-old Neymat was sleeping and started to speak rapidly. Her voice, initially hushed to avoid waking up the child, grew more excited with her narration.

A woman had descended on the haveli's threshold with her four children and started to harangue Bapuji, his progeny, then progressed to the Bhalla clan, eventually weaving the entire guru lineage into her lament. A piqued neighbourhood, responding to the hail as if it were a monsoon shower, sprouted on rooftops, behind perimeter walls, atop steps.

Bit by bit, lucidity darted through the loud orchestra of breast-beating, intermittent wailing, children's sniffling: the woman's husband, may he suffer labour pains, she cursed, had absconded with another woman. Leaving her with four—and she smacked the children serially—hungry mouths to feed. The whore who had ensnared him resided in the haveli. 'Big mansion on the outside, but inside, a randikhana!' she declared to the elevated onlookers as she spun an arm held aloft.

Balwant had left early that morning, ostensibly to oversee some land in Chandigarh.

'Had to happen someday,' Preet concluded. 'Bapuji's leniency and Balwant's wantonness.'

Following that, she enrolled Neymat in the Convent School—their discipline was admirable. Then she looked around and located a piece of land for constructing an independent house. It was in a new development, fairly isolated, and therefore going cheap. 'People will come in some time,' Preet predicted. 'The town is expanding. And families are breaking.'

Baksh strummed the idea of Chandigarh. Might as well shift to the 'city beautiful', if they were going to move out.

Extending a palm, Preet said, 'Show me the money.' Then, smiling, she shook her head. 'Best we move to this place first. When your practice takes off, and there is more money at hand, we can move to Chandigarh. Plus, this early in my job, where will I get a transfer?'

DAY 7: ANANT

Jinder Tayaji arrived in the morning, a copy of *The Tribune* tucked under his arm. Annoyed that they had *all* missed it, he briskly underlined a portion of the newsprint with his index finger.

In the nondescript Regional Briefs section, under Ferozepur, ran a two-line announcement: '*Harbaksh Singh Bhalla, Advocate, Punjab & Haryana High Court, passed away on April 20.* The Ferozepur Bar Association, of which he was a senior member, mourned his loss.'

Twiddling the various rings on his fingers, Tayaji clucked distractedly, 'They didn't print the photo.'

After Anant had read the obituary he took the newspaper to the terrace where he wished to read it in seclusion. What interested him was the column to the left of the obituary. Once again he read it.

Taliban's Long March into Indian Punjab?

'Soft' US adding to growing Taliban clout in Pakistan and beyond

New Delhi, April 26: As the Taliban captures more districts in Afghanistan's Uruzgan and Kandahar provinces, India's concerns are rising exponentially because these developments have serious security implications for the country. But while the growth of the Taliban has been a phenomenon that Indian leaders have railed against for the past few years, there is now a related concern, that the US, in its declared support for Pakistan's embattled president Pervez Musharraf, has taken its eyes off the ball.

As Pakistani author Saif Sardar writes, 'The new generation of militants are all Pakistani and represent a revolt against the government's support for the US. Their jihad is aimed not just at "infidels occupying Afghanistan", but also the "infidels" who are ruling and running Pakistan.' The Talibanization of Pakistan will not be halted by keeping Musharraf in power, say Pakistan observers. In fact, the army's traditional tango with jihadi groups has meant that in the post 9/11 phase, Talibanization has had a free ride in Pakistan.

New Delhi refuses to get into the west-inspired soul-searching about support to Musharraf or Pakistani democracy. Pakistan's policies, it is commonly understood, are controlled by the military-intelligence complex that runs Pakistan.

Pakistani analyst V. Raman said, 'India is watching the present developments in Pakistan to see that democracy succeeds there. At the same time, there has been an aggravation of the jihadi threats from Pakistani territory directed against India in the sensitive border state of Punjab where extremist elements appear to be reopening a terror front.'

Anant put the paper aside and cracked his knuckles. *Reopening a terror front...* Papa's sudden passing and the events of that day had disoriented him and he had not even paid much attention. Now, he tried to recall what the fat policeman had divulged on the night of Papa's cremation...

The police was keeping an eye on Bhallasaab, he said. They had noticed heightened activity of some militants in the border region of Ferozepur. One particular militant who had been spotted was an ex-client of Harbaksh Singh Bhalla. The lawyer had defended his case, got him acquitted, after which the militant had lost no time in crossing over. The Iran–Pakistan–India gas pipeline was scheduled to reach Ferozepur from Lahore within the next few months. And terrorists were looking for an opportunity to cause a major disruption.

Admittedly, the policeman was well-acquainted with Papa, having worked closely with him on the case of Vir Mamu, Mama's brother. Yet, could a policeman be trusted to tell the truth, and *nothing* but the truth?

Hitching up his shorts, Anant walked the length of the terrace. In the distance, a black kite sailed in the sky. Someone had decided to use the not-yet-searing morning to indulge in a spot of kite-flying. Anant watched the kite—it was a Gudda, a fighter kite—as it skimmed and swooped in pretend offensives in the clear blue sky.

He felt a pang. He had not flown a kite in a while. As a child he had accompanied Papa to the fields on the day of Basant, the kite-flying festival. The Sutlej marked the periphery of their fields and was a natural border between India and Pakistan. Papa would hoist his kite and compete with the Pakistani flyers. Occasionally, he would let a kite go and watch it sail in the sky across the border. The first time he witnessed it, a baffled Anant questioned him. With a slow, gentle smile, Papa said, 'Why begrudge a kite its freedom? To go where men can't?'

BAKSH

Baksh stood in front of the haveli's gate. He scanned the lane—not a soul. Jinder would be asleep as well, not that Baksh intended to meet him—their last interaction had been prickly. He decided to rest on the steps. Brushing his hands on his pants, he remembered what Shammi, observing the chubby reddish palms, had once jokingly said, 'These hands are not meant for farming!' He had exhibited then, as he would later, a trace of the clairvoyant streak inherited from Mata, his grandmother.

The farms had forsaken him, or he had abdicated them. Either way, the paltry acres he had inherited through Bapuji's will had mostly been sold.

The last good acres of land from the fertile Rakhri plains he had disposed of to finance Noor's MS in aeronautical engineering in the US. His daughter had gained admission in the same college as Neil Armstrong—how could he deny her a chance to study there?

Noor was clearly a gifted child. The first year at school, the teacher promoted her to the next class within three months. There is nothing more for me to teach, she shrugged. Ditto, for the next.

Consequently, at the age of six, Noor studied in the same class as children eight or nine years old.

'Aye kee, Bhallasaab? You need to keep the acres for your son,' some colleagues had advised.

'My children are my investment, each one of them,' he had replied.

They were an investment, but not in terms of a venture on which returns were to be made. Which Punjabi father expected to reap returns on his daughters? He was a proud Sikh, following in the tradition of the gurus who had proclaimed that daughters were princesses, and given them the appellation of 'Kaur'. No, his children were an investment, because they were all he had to show for himself and his life.

As a result, only a couple of acres of his inheritance were left, in a sandy tract where cacti shrubbery grew. And then there was Noor's nonchalant statement that he had done nothing special; as a father, he had merely performed his duty.

The duty of a father. The duties *of a father.*

He had exhausted a life trying to fulfil those. Yet, in this world of perpetual give and take, where love was tempered with expectation, he had consistently fallen short of the mark set for him by his children.

'Why is it that when it comes to me, you never have any money?'

'Why can't you afford the fees of the private college... other fathers can, fathers of children not half as bright as I am...'

However, his children always evoked the admiration and envy of friends and relatives: while their sons and daughters struggled to clear PMT, PET and other assorted entrance exams, he had fathered two doctors and one engineer-MBA. It was a matter of pride for both Preet and him that the children were academically gifted. But they also took it for granted, considering it a compensation of sorts for the general unhappiness of their life.

How had the poet said it… 'Kabhi kisi ko mukammal jahaan nahin miltaa/ Kahin zameen to kahin aasman nahin miltaa…'

He would not deny that there was comfort in his children doing well. It was what he had always wanted for them. What he had envisioned when he had quit the haveli to ensure that Balwant's shadow did not touch his children. However, Baksh himself had found it difficult to escape his sister's tentacles.

Something tickled Baksh—a wet tingle—and he looked down. A pup was licking his foot. It stopped as he looked at it, then started to wag its tail. Baksh smiled and bent down to stroke its head. The pup responded with a brisker wagging of its tail.

He looked around. The walk had tired him. He yawned and stretched his arms—the left shoulder barely moved. It felt numb. He massaged it roughly, then balled his right hand into a fist and thumped softly at the insensate upper arm. On his right, beside the outer walls of the haveli, was parked a cycle rickshaw. A black braid, meant to ward off the evil eye, trailed from its rear. Baksh smiled wryly: a black-braided rickshaw had once whisked him out of the jaws of approaching enemy tanks…

1971

Preet was out watering the fledgling neem hedge when she sighted it. A hand clasped around her slack jaw, she eyed the object hesitantly, then bent forward for an examination. There was no doubt in her mind what it was: tucked within the shrubbery lay an earthen lamp, a yellow and red thread like a carelessly draped muffler around its brown coat, the outfit completed with a vermilion mark and a few scattered grains of rice.

She drew back, comprehension sailed through her and burst forth as a snort. Depositing the water hose in the soil bed, she marched back into the house.

Baksh, snatched away from his morning paper and a second round of Darjeeling tea, contemplated the object of his wife's concern. 'Why do you presume it is black magic?'

'The mauli... the mauli! Don't you see? The yellow and red thread! Then those rice grains, the lamp... all signs of a toona. All these are used to cast a spell...'

'Spell? Why would anybody want to cast a spell on us?'

Preet clenched her hands together. 'Ill-wishers unhappy with the fact that we have managed to build a home for ourselves. This is a symbol of their envy. Otherwise, tell me, how is it that a dressed-up lamp has suddenly appeared,' Preet gestured with an arm, 'in this isolated stretch.'

Baksh glanced around. Besides the two neighbours, a cinema hall a plot away and another residence to their left, their two-room house with a front lawn stood in the midst of flattened rubble. Admittedly, the morning's discovery posed a question—what accounted for the presence of the oil lamp, shiny and unused?

'Cleverly left in the bush so someone from the house will unknowingly step over it...' Preet thrust her lower lip out. 'Harm is sure to befall that way.'

Baksh lifted a puzzled hand.

'Don't be so innocent, ji.' Preet admonished with a flick of her open palm. 'Who in the family is a devotee of Jata Sadhu? For the past six months, no Sunday has been complete without a visit to the fakir with dreadlocks. Mound of lice.' Preet shivered. 'Even bringing some back home from that charlatan. In any case, no pundit in the entire town has been spared a consultation—'

'You know she is insecure. Two children, husband does not—'

'Husband?' Preet crossed her arms across her chest and drew herself up to her full height.

'Whatever.'

'We all know that man won't divorce his wife... his sons from the first woman have sworn to chop his head off if he does. As a concession, they have allowed him this indulgence. Insecure, wah! Whose fault was it? Nobody asked her to leave one husband and seek out a paramour...'

'Achha! Enough.'

'Aaho. Like Bapuji-Maji you have also drawn a veil over your eyes... refusing to see what is apparent to all. Mainu ki!' Preet looked away. Then remembering where it all began, she said, 'But when this woman crosses my path, trying to harm my family, I will not sit quiet.'

'Again the same thing. What proof do you have that Balwant is behind this?'

'Isn't she the one who poisoned Maji's ears, turning her against my London job? Implying that I would fall for an Angrej,' Preet spat out. 'A thief will see thievery in others. The thing is, she could not stomach anybody else getting ahead. She is envious of us, but she knows I have my brother behind me... so she looks for underhand ways to get at us.'

'Still no proof.' Baksh angled his foot towards the earthen lamp. 'Maji never mentioned that Balwant was behind her advice.'

'Hai! Tauba!' Preet pulled him back. 'It is unwise to touch it without neutralizing the spell first.'

Baksh grinned. 'You seem to know a lot about this business of black magic.'

'Okay, make fun of me. But when people in the family start to do crazy things, one has to take safeguards.'

'What crazy things?'

'*Seven* copies of her horoscope Balwant has, each made by a different pandit. And each brought out for deliberation on a particular weekday. Like a newly wedded woman considers which piece of jewellery to adorn herself with. Consulting ojhas for illnesses, real or imaginary. Why, she even made Bapuji sell off the buffalo because it birthed in the month of Maghar.'

'All right, so she is irrational at times. But she is also wise. Her wisdom—'

'Her wisdom we have all seen. Coaxing a trail of ants back into her room.'

Baksh rolled his shoulders. How difficult it was to complete a conversation with Preet! Even when she was right, he felt compelled to object. Though he had to admit that the ant incident was doubtless an example of Balwant's increasing eccentricity. On sighting ants carrying a grain of food out of her quarters, she had spent an afternoon instructing a servant to reverse the trail through the use of candy—the departing ants augured a heavy loss, she felt.

'Bapuji trusts her because her plan for the division of land worked. On paper Bodh Singh and sons became owners, but in reality the land stayed within the house. While others lost—'

'Let it be,' Preet shook her head resignedly. 'If I say something, you take umbrage. But,' she held up an index finger, 'just you watch that old fogey Bodh Singh—ik din naani yaad dila devega! Has any farmer ever given up soil freely gifted to him? In a country where people shed rivers of blood for their piece of land?' Preet raised her eyes heavenwards, closed them briefly and continued softly, 'Waheguru, have mercy.' Thereupon, with her right foot she flung the beribboned lamp aside, scattering the grains and mauli about. 'Now the jamadar will have no qualms about removing it.'

Baksh fell ill a few days later. Disregarding the symptoms, he persisted with his work at court until he was unable to get out of bed, his body sizzling like a halwai's griddle. He sank into long stretches of delirium, barely aware of Dr LTS's troubled ministrations and Mindar's countless applications of wet muslin wipes.

When he came out of it, a week later, Bitta informed him that Preet had fasted the entire time, subsisting on water and boiled potato, and recited the Gurbani whenever she could find the time away from children and housework.

That illness, following so closely on the discovery of the lamp, cemented Balwant's status as a witch in Preet's mind. Baksh himself could not shake off the apparent attempt at black magic—why else would he have taken to bed so suddenly? And why would he have secretly urged Bitta to get his will drawn up, signed it during the patches of lucidity and handed it to his best friend for safekeeping?

Mukti Bahini, they called themselves: Liberation Force. For the liberation of East Pakistan from West. The Pakistani pair, like Chang and Eng, the Siamese twins, was conjoined from birth by thick tissue: eleven hundred miles of India. Growing-up pains, separate spoken languages and the domination of one saw the other demanding separation. Before General Tikka, in-charge of the Eastern Command, could drain its lifeblood entirely, East Pakistan, with the aid of the Indian tissue, took a surgeon's scalpel to the union. And the General was left overseeing the hacking.

Once again Radio Pakistan attacked the airwaves, even as Pakistan Air Force attacked airfields in north India. Lusty, belligerent songs urged the Pakistani soldiers to be relentless in their campaign against the infidels: 'Rakh jigra tey ho ja hun tagra/ deyo ragra aena noon deyo ragra!'

Pakistan opened war on India's eastern and western fronts simultaneously. In its intent to capture large portions of Indian territory in the west, it attacked the entire northwestern border: from the hills of Jammu Kashmir, across the plains of Punjab, to the deserts of Rajasthan. With its hawkish Chinese ally keeping watch from above, it assumed that Indian incursions into the eastern twin would be curtailed.

Ferozepur, Fazilka, Dera Baba Nanak, Shakargarh—the bloody battlegrounds of Punjab once again found themselves riddled by war.

At Hussainiwala, the Border Security Force was celebrating its Raising Day. In the midst of the Bada Khana, the grand dinner, they could hear the raucous beating of dhols and loud merrymaking. A wedding procession, no doubt, was passing along the other side of the border. It was the season for weddings, after all.

Only when the Pakistani infantry breached their positions did the hapless BSF realize that the marriage party had been a decoy: the groom had come riding on a Patton tank that threatened to thunder across the Hussainiwala Bridge straight into the city of Ferozepur...

As the winter evening abruptly morphed into night, a wail rent the air. Gaining in intensity, it penetrated the cold with its persistent moan. Preet, seated on a cot, paused in the act of chopping vegetables for dinner. A warning siren! Rabba, she realized, war!

Unscrambling her crossed legs, she hastened to the bedroom where five-year-old Neymat sat with her homework, head cocked at the unusual sound.

Preet took down a suitcase as Neymat cradled baby Noor. She snatched clothes from the almirah shelves—the children's, hers, Baksh's. Where *was* Baksh? He had gone to the market for his evening round and groceries. From the Godrej safe, she grabbed the Ravalgaon sweet box—it contained her jewellery and cash. What if he had strayed off to a friend's place?

The lights went out.

She groped around in the dark. And remembered: no candles were to be lit. A dark December night readied for war and everything went blind.

In the market, Baksh was feeling a Kashmiri apple in his palm as the grocer prattled on about the unique properties of the petite rosy variety, when the siren began. The bazaar froze for a nanosecond. Then the retailer rocketed from his haunches, the pedestrians bolted, vehicles attempted to escape the bonds of gravity. The blackout followed, succeeded by scrapes, scuffles, scurries.

సౌ

Baksh, Preet and the two girls stumbled through the unlit streets even as combat aircrafts of the Pakistan Air Force drilled overhead. Adult eyes attempted to slice a way through the cacophonous dark: an insanely steady whirring, punctuated by a rat-a-tat, an ascending drone as a plane approached, then an eruption like a gargantuan water balloon had dived to earth.

Their plan was to reach the government school where the commissioner, Baksh had vaguely gathered, had arranged some trucks for transport. Rumours had spilled forth in the city streets like leaking water from a ruptured municipal pipe: the Pakistanis had rolled across the bridge and entered the cantonment area. Sadar Bazaar was ablaze. A couple of tanks were lumbering down the Mall Road.

Baksh clutched a suitcase in his right hand; Neymat, hands gripping his left arm, ran apace. Preet cradled the infant Noor and shuffled along. At each approaching drone Baksh hissed, 'Down.' They crouched in the dust until an explosion, followed by flames, announced that the plane had shelled artillery and gone on. Any minute *they* could be victims of the incineration, the pair of adults knew that. A randomly dropped shell could finish them. So they ploughed and sniffled through the cold night, in a land rendered unfamiliar by the suspension of normalcy. Until a gutter snared Baksh, tripping him. The suitcase buffeted his fall, Neymat landed with a thud and started to yowl. While Baksh helped Neymat up, patting her head, Preet attempted to quieten the frightened child. They had barely gone a few metres when Neymat said, 'My slipper! My slipper!'

It was a pink raw silk slipper, silver paisleys embroidered on it, sewn with glass beads. Since her Vir Mamu had gifted it a month back, Neymat had been unusually attached to the jutti. Preet started to admonish her, but Neymat would have none of it. Baksh retraced his steps and plunged his hand through the gutter. It was a slow-flowing drain and he came up with it finally, a much muddied affair, definitely not fit to be worn. Neymat, though, was insistent. With an end of her chunni, Preet wiped the grime and Neymat clutched the slipper in both hands.

When they finally tumbled into the grounds of the government school, the trucks had departed.

Or were never there in the first place.

Balwant came to the rescue. In a groaning Ambassador car that had passengers seated two layers deep. The ground-floor tenant of her new two-storey house had proved providential. His pharmaceutical company had provided him with an office car for sales travels. The executive, with his wife and two sons, offered a passage to Balwant and three-year-old Lovely. Thereupon, she took a detour to the haveli, picked up Maji-Bapuji, then stopped en route at Baksh's.

The car stood there, but no space was available. Finally, the driver spread-eagled atop suitcases in the dickey, the tenant took the wheel, creating space for Preet to squeeze in. Neymat sat on her lap, legs wedged amongst other passenger limbs. And Noor was cradled on top of her, held in place by the car roof and Preet's arms held aloft.

There was no place for Baksh, though. He urged them on. The car was headed to Golewal, thirty-five kilometres away, where the pharma man had relatives. That would put sufficient distance between them and the enemy tanks. After a night's rest, Balwant and Preet, with the children, were to proceed to Jinder's place in car, truck, trolley, tonga—anything that would get them to safety at Chandigarh. There, Jinder, working with the Central Scientific Instruments Organization, had a two-room second-storey flat, courtesy his organization's housing policy. It would be adequate for the bunch fleeing from Ferozepur.

Baksh sat on the steps of the front veranda, studying the deepening night. The stentorian orchestra was still playing. He had not sighted any tanks. Thus far. How was he to get out? Preet and the children would reach Golewal by midnight latest. That was after accounting for the decamping traffic on the road. Normally, the distance could be covered in under an hour. He glanced at his HMT watch. Green glowing hands showed 9.15.

Something ran past the hedge bordering the garden from the Mall Road. He narrowed his eyes and peered. A figure stood at the gate, attempting to open the latch. The gate swung open; the person let it slide away and strike the neem hedge, then started to hurry down the brick-paved path. A bobbing turla, scrape of jutti, tehmat clutched in one hand...

'Mindar!' Baksh shouted.

'Baksh!' Relief brought forth the sobriquet that Mindar seldom used, always mindful of his position. Mindar leapt over the red bricks that bordered the walkway, crossed the lawn swiftly and was by his side. 'God is kind!' he said, laying a hand on Baksh's shoulder. His breathing was shallow. He blew air out of puffed cheeks, then licked his lips. Then he proceeded to wipe his face with the loose end of his turban. Despite the cold, he was sweating.

'Mindar, what are you doing here?' Baksh scrutinized his old associate. Mindar had been away on leave to his village. He was not expected for another week.

'I heard about the tanks. Came hurrying.'

'Came hurrying? In the direction of the onslaught?'

'Kammo and the kids are safe. What will Pakistan army do with a back-of-beyond hamlet...'

'But why have you rushed back into danger's mouth?'

'Hain Baksh!' Mindar stood with one hand at his waist, the other cupped around his mouth. 'How could I leave you all at such a time?'

Baksh swallowed, then slowly nodded. That Mindar was loyal, he had never doubted. That his loyalty would one day be tested, he had never had reason to consider. And now, his steadfastness shone forth. Much in the manner of the Harsingar—that rough-leafed nondescript tree that grew across the Punjab. When it blossomed, its star-shaped white and orange flowers lasted just one night. But, what a night: the fragrance carrying far into the wintry air and a dewy petal carpet the following morning.

Such was the nature of some things—only when time called did they reveal their finest. And into Baksh's mind came Lehna and a flooded day, and a feeling of immense gratitude enveloped him. He rested a hand on Mindar's shoulder, then proceeded to inform him of the events of the preceding hours. 'We have to think of a way to get out of here,' he finished.

Mindar stood there, head bent in thought, his lungi hitched at the rear and held in place with his left palm. 'Rickshaw!' he spoke suddenly, slapping one hand onto the other. His eyes shone at Baksh. 'Rickshaw.'

'Rickshaw?'

'Aaho. Let's pedal our way out of this place!'

During the daytime, with Baksh away at the courts, Mindar pulled a cycle rickshaw. His vehicle was parked in the lane behind the house. By all accounts, it should still be there, sitting under the tarpaulin cover that Mindar had draped over it before leaving for his village a week back.

Baksh shrugged a shoulder. 'You know I have never pulled a rickshaw.'

'O, we shall see.' Mindar pulled off his shoulder scarf, then wound it tightly about his head. 'Himmate mardan, maddate khuda. Besides, I may be able to pull it all the way...'

Baksh scratched his beard and smiled. 'As good a time to learn as any.' He thumped Mindar on the back.

Mindar and Baksh decided to stay away from the main road. It would be the shortest route out of Ferozepur, but it was the one properly tarred road in the entire town—the enemy tanks would most probably come crunching down that one. Mindar pedalled and Baksh attempted navigation. But Mindar was the rickshaw puller and knew the lanes well.

They fell silent as Mindar attempted to settle into a pedalling rhythm. In the blanket of dark, the eye could barely see a couple of metres ahead. With luck, they would avoid any major pothole or obstruction. If a tyre was punctured, or—

Clink-clink.

It was a faint sound, but had managed to cut through the surrounding growl. There, it came again—a click-ting, a thin sound so out of place in the deafening ambience that Mindar stopped pedalling, Baksh leaned forward and the vehicle glided slowly on.

Once again, it sounded.

A gun being cocked? A lance hitting the ground? A soldier's helmet... Baksh speculated silently.

A churail trailing them? Looking for a body to possess—they were easy prey. There, that sound... anklets on feet that would be facing backwards... Mindar's mind conjured up visions.

He applied brakes and the rickshaw slid to a halt.

Click-ting… Click-ting… Click-ting…

It died down.

Abruptly, Mindar turned around and giggled. He smacked his forehead, angled the rickshaw, then descended. 'Parandi!' he said as he went to the rear of the rickshaw.

A couple of minutes later, he had untangled the thick black thread braid with bells at the base. Like other drivers, he hung it from his vehicle to ward off the evil eye. Depositing it in the dust, he mounted the rickshaw again.

From Mall Road, they turned into the government school grounds. Cutting diagonally through it, they reached the lane that led to the Old Railway Colony. It was a tree-lined alley bordered by sprawling colonial bungalows on one side and an unruly stretch of green on the other. Beyond the patch sat the tenements of junior railway employees facing the other side—the rail tracks.

Once again, they stuck to the side of the road, the tyres crunching on loose gravel, mashing tall grass. From somewhere ahead, a low rumble sounded. Mindar slowed down. In the dark, they could make out the frame of a vehicle. As it came closer, they realized that it was a jeep. The rear doors were open, two people on each side astride a low plank that probably ran atop the floor of the vehicle's backseat providing additional seating. Others balanced in the doorframe, holding on to the rooftop carrier on which amorphous shapes hinted at huddled figures and lumpy luggage. The two parties eyed each other silently as they moved on.

They reached the railway crossing. The shutter was down, but a narrow dirt trail ran parallel to the tracks. Mindar had often used it as a shortcut when a passenger was impatient enough to not wait for the train to pass. It was an uneven stretch and Baksh proceeded to walk as Mindar pedalled with vigour.

The traffic on this stretch was denser. A scooter grunted past, groaning under the weight of multiple passengers. A bicycle, an old woman balanced on the handlebar, a younger one, with two children in her embrace, atop the carrier, the rider bent double like a racing cyclist, while a dog, presumably the family's, trotted behind. It was as if all vehicles had broken into a rash, erupting with people and baggage from open-jawed dickeys, rolled-down windows, rooftop carriers.

As the droning darkness attempted to pinion them, Baksh found a strange respite in the PAF Jugnu aircrafts' periodic flares.

On the Golewal stretch, Baksh decided to ply the rickshaw. In his hands, it became an unruly horse that threatened to careen interminably. Some struggles later, Baksh got the hang of it: pedalling a cycle rickshaw was like pedalling a bicycle—one with an unwieldy parcel hitched to its carrier. Thence, he started a slow zigzag treadle down the highway.

It was not long before he had settled into a rhythm and his mind was off the pedals. With their exit from Ferozepur, the fear of the Pakistani Army had begun to loosen its hold. They could still get them as they came riding out of Ferozepur, but surely the Grand Trunk road to Ludhiana would interest them more?

Was the house still intact? Would it be when they returned? When would they return? Surely the war would stop one day. But what if the Pakistanis captured Ferozepur and made it part of their territory? Even if it became disputed land, all would be lost. They would become refugees...

Homeless, landless, moneyless—they would have to start all over again. The good thing was that both Preet and he were qualified and had relied solely on their combined earnings to build everything. They could do it again.

But what if something else happened? If a shell plonked down on top of their rickshaw? What would that death be like? Would life be snuffed out in an instant? Or would they feel their flesh burn? And as the body singed, would they smell the putrid flesh, hear the crackle of their skin… Waheguru! A swift death, if that was what was willed.

But death would mean… no more Preet or the girls. No more Bapuji-Maji, Balwant, Jinder, Mindar… What if he were never to see his family again? Preet would survive—she was strong. He had faith in her ability to look after herself and their daughters. But his girls…

Neymat. It meant blessing. For what else would one call one's first child? And in so many ways she lived up to her name! A proper little mother's helper, she knew one lentil from another, and minding her younger sister seemed to come naturally to her. When he returned from work, she fetched him a glass of water, unasked. Gentle by nature, her loving disposition endeared her to everyone. Even Balwant was exceptionally fond of her, frequently dressing her in her prized kundan set. Bapuji, who liked to eat his peas-pulao in solitude every Sunday, would call out to Neymat to join him.

And Noor? She took eighteen hours coming on a sultry August afternoon. With the sun blazing overhead, what else were they to call her but Noor? They had not even celebrated her first birthday yet…

His daughters—would they recall their father if he was to go missing from their lives forever? Maybe Neymat, she was older, but Noor? Would they have any memories of their Papa as they grew up? What would they grow up to be?

A pain seized him, it clutched his heart, almost wringing the life out of him. It choked him. Baksh gripped the handlebars of the rickshaw and heaved himself up from the leather saddle. Then, he poured all his strength into his limbs and sallied forward.

'Baksh!' Mindar's voice rose. 'Slow! We can't afford a breakdown.'

'Aaho, Mindar. Neither can we afford to lag behind.'

❦

When the war ended, they returned home to find it intact. Indian soldiers had, in desperation, blown the steel bridge over the Sutlej, denying the enemy a walkover. In their colony, a fragment of a shell was found in the lane, another in a vacant plot. Ferozepur had survived the shelling with minimal damage, even though burnt-out remnants of the enemy's shells were discovered at various places. Surprised residents debated the cause behind the obviously poor marksmanship of the Pakistani combatants.

The answer emerged soon enough. Who supplied it, no one knew, but soon all had it. A PAF pilot had reported that whenever his plane took to the skies above Ferozepur, a haze seemed to envelop the land beneath. Due to which, he resorted to random firing. The haze was at its most intense near the National Highway stretch. Its epicentre, in fact, seemed to be a humble shrine: the dargah of a Sufi saint, Sher Shah Wali. No surprise then that the dargah's faithful surged in numbers, regardless of minor encumbrances such as religious leanings.

However, the war strengthened Baksh's resolve to quit Ferozepur for the safety of Chandigarh. The time had come to distance himself from the border that had plagued him all his life.

He started part-time work with a senior lawyer in Chandigarh for the first half of the week. Wednesday evening, he caught a bus back to Ferozepur, the journey lasting four to five hours, depending on the driver's appetite for speed.

Work was slow, but that he had expected. What surprised him was the sense of unease that gripped him and wouldn't let go. He never felt himself to be whole, neither in Chandigarh nor in Ferozepur. First, he put it down to the new place, big change, missing home and family, established practice suffering, etc. However, after six months or so, he began to understand.

In Ferozepur, he missed Chandigarh's blue-grey ring of the Shivalik mountains, lungfuls of clean air, roads good enough to eat off, fish and chips at Kwality, the refined gentry... In Chandigarh, he longed for Ferozepur's rickety Sessions Court, the sweet-stale-spiced bazaar, the crumbling haveli with its plank to his childhood, the two-minute nourishing exchanges with people he had known all his life, reflective rickshaw rides, fruitless farm visits that provided sustenance somehow...

He would have to decide between the two, he knew. Simultaneously astride two boats... it was a certain recipe for drowning.

❦

While Baksh had been mulling over his dilemma, his brother-in-law had stayed focused on his goal and accomplished it. Vir Singh Sidhu was interned in Ferozepur Central Jail on the charge of murder. While the charge was grave, the evidence was thin. At the time of the alleged shootout, Vir was at a marriage party. An entire gathering was willing to testify in court. The body of the dead man was found next to his fields. He had apparently been gunned down as he stepped out of the tall sugarcane plantation in the early hours. His usual ring of accomplices had been absent—perhaps he had not anticipated danger in his own lair. By all accounts, it was an audacious murder, akin to entering a tiger's belly in order to slay the beast. Vir Singh had been rounded up primarily because of past acrimony between the two families and the allegations from the victim's family.

The sprawling jail compound was situated on the Mall Road, right opposite their home. Which made it convenient for Preet to carry a tiffin box of warm lunch for her brother every noon after she had returned early from school. And send one with Mindar in the night.

Though Baksh visited his brother-in-law frequently even as he tried to arrange bail and ensure—through the jail warden with whom he had been acquainted over several years of law practice—that Vir was treated well, his wife's daily trip to the jail made him uncomfortable.

'Why can't Mindar deliver at noon too?' Baksh quietly asked. 'Central Jail is not the most appropriate place for women. Criminals of every shade can be found within those four walls.'

Preet, packing rotis in a linen tea towel, did not look up. 'For me, he is my brother. If others regard him as a criminal, so be it.'

A fortnight later, bail was arranged. Vir Singh came home. 'Jail yatra!' He jiggled his brows. 'Now I have joined the league of Nehru and Gandhi.'

As per the tradition of Indian courts, the case would last some years and Vir would be required to travel for hearings, but in the end the verdict could only be one: not guilty. While the motive was clearly vendetta—the victim had years ago gunned down Vir Singh's elder brother—the case against Vir was thin: no witnesses, speculation as evidence, strong defence. Besides, Baksh had built a solid practice as a criminal lawyer of repute.

That he was not particularly keen on the case, he could not voice: for Preet, it was a given that her husband would defend her brother. The fact that it would be an unproductive use of Baksh's time—his fledgling Chandigarh practice would suffer, plus another lawyer could handle the watertight case as well—and bestow notoriety on him, she did not regard as reason enough.

Around the same time, Bodh Singh decided to demonstrate to the Bhalla clan who the real master of their large landholding was. Much as Preet had predicted. Balwant, unbathed, the hennaed hair finger-combed, disturbed Baksh's morning tea as she blew her stale breath into his face and attempted to explain what had occurred.

'Bodh... uh... Singh... um... his sons have signed fresh papers.'

'What papers?'

'They are giving the land to their sons in turn! The new law, gaurment law. Eighteen acres is the limit now, hain, for each landowner. So, Bodh Singh's sons are splitting the land further amongst their sons. His grandsons. You understand?'

Baksh remained impassive, the signing away of the farmland had hurt him too grievously for him to summon up a self-righteous 'I told you so'. Besides, the foolish woman had no empathy for the land, only a canny idea of its price.

'You understand what I am saying, don't you?'

'What is there to understand? It is the new Land Ceiling Act with the upper limit fixed at eighteen acres. Bodh Singh is doing exactly what we... *you* did many years back.'

Balwant peered at him, then at Preet seated close by. 'It is not his to give away.'

'It is not?'

Baksh crossed a leg and sat back in his cane chair. 'You had given the land to Bodh Singh and his family. Bapuji signed it away, on your advice. Have you forgotten?'

'But the land is *ours*. Bodh is a tenant. So is his entire family.'

'Does the paper say that? The legal paper?'

'That is why I have come to you, Baksh-uh. We will file a case against them. We will prove that they are committing fraud. That they forged Bapuji's signature. Got him to sign under the influence of hashish. Got—'

'Now you want to declare your father a charsi in the courts?'

'But this is, this is… ' Balwant began to thrash like a rat with its tail caught in a trap. 'Impossible. Baksh, we have to do something. Anything to save our lands.'

'First, we don't have a case. Two, I am busy in Chandigarh half the week.'

Balwant's habitual sly look emerged. 'But you have time for Ferozepur cases. Preet's brother… With Waheguru's blessings… you will be able to get him off the hook, right?'

Preet stood up. 'Keep my brother out of all this,' she said sternly before turning to Baksh to ask him if he needed some fresh tea. When he shook his head, she proceeded to the courtyard to water the plants. In a sunken concrete corner, she affixed the green rubber tubing to the lower of the two taps, unfurled the hose and, with an index finger poised on its mouth, she converted the flow to a spray and started to water the earthen pots.

Balwant meanwhile went back to imploring her brother to fight the case. 'Baksh-uh, don't leave for Chandigarh at this juncture. Now at least they know you are here, so they will be afraid. But if you were to go, their boldness would know no limit.' Her shoulders slumped and she seemed to collapse on the bold floral patterned divan. 'They will thump their chests and declare in the bazaar that they have become masters.'

DAY 8: ANANT

Anant was carting a twelve-pack of one-litre mineral water bottles up the steps and through the porch when Gianiji intercepted him. The Sikh priest had just finished discussing arrangements for the Akhand Path with Mama. The forty-eight-hour non-stop recitation of the Granth Sahib would come to an end on the tenth day with the Bhog ceremony, and friends, family and associates had been invited to join in prayers for the departed soul.

'The loudspeaker... Should I get it or would you prefer to arrange it yourself?' Gianiji asked him now.

'Loudspeaker?' Anant frowned, the carton weighing him down. 'What for?'

'To relay the Gurbani,' Gianiji offered, his face bland.

'*Relay?*' Anant looked around. 'Gianiji, this isn't such a big house...'

'For the other residents, the colony,' Gianiji said, smiling benevolently. 'They should also benefit from the recitation.' The prospect of the Gurbani blaring out to besiege the inhabitants of the colony seemed to fill the priest with animation. With a quick toss of his head, he asked brightly, 'So I shall assume the responsibility.'

'Why not keep it a quiet affair... private?' said Anant quietly.

'But puttar,' Gianiji's voice held the distress of a priest counselling a child fleeing his baptism. 'Why deprive the community of experiencing the peace and blessing of the Gurbani recitation?' As Anant made to speak, he continued, hands gripping the ends of the long indigo stole around his neck. 'After all, everyone is broadcasting his religion from rooftops, be it the Hindus with their nightlong mata-da-jagrata, or the Isais with their Mass.' Leaning forward, he said in an undertone, 'We should not stay behind.'

'How can one surge ahead without a good night's sleep, Gianiji?' Depositing the carton on the floor, Anant straightened up. 'Ordinary folks like us need to rest after a day of hard work. This relish for non-stop recitation,' he snorted, 'is suitable only for those involved in holy business.'

The priest looked like he wanted to protest, but he pursed his mouth in a long thoughtful pause. Then he lifted his shoulders in a ponderous manner, said a grave 'Think about it' and walked off.

Inside the dining area, Anant deposited the carton on the table and wiped the sweat from his forehead. Hurriedly, with the tip of his scooter key, he slashed the tape binding the carton flap and retrieved one bottle. He twisted the lid open and swallowed greedily, letting some water drip down his chin.

Neymat stood in the bedroom doorway watching him.

Anant wiped off the water that had trickled down his neck, a comforting wet-cool on his bristly skin. 'What?' He shrugged.

Neymat marched up to him and held her open palm under his nose. Nestled in it was a red rubber band. 'If you tied your hair, perhaps you would feel less hot.'

'Okay! Okay!' Holding a palm up, Anant ventured, 'In this heat even the great Abdali abandoned his invasions and fled to his mountains. I know I was to get a haircut, but...'

Anant had been heading for the barber's when a fat policeman had flagged him down. It was the same policeman who had come to their house late at night on the day of Papa's cremation. He was sucking a juicy cucumber, his belly slung over his leather belt like a sack of grain, as he waddled over. Lowering his voice conspiratorially, he had launched into another revelation, at the end of which Anant hadn't known what to believe. What made it worse was that he couldn't share the information with anybody. Uncle Bitta had advised lying low and letting it blow over. Noor was sure to hyperventilate if given the details. And Neymatdi was running the household and the kitchen and managing the mourners and getting stressed about his hair...

Anant sighed and said, 'Tomorrow, okay? I'll get a haircut.'

Neymat kept looking at him without saying a word.

'Silent treatment,' Anant remarked. 'Splendid!' His lip curled with anger as he flung a dismissive hand at his sister. 'Just what I need.' He strode off angrily towards the porch. One instant he was appointed *man of the house*. Next, he couldn't even be himself. He was advised to be responsible, then packed off on errands around the sweltering city like he were some mundu. Neymatdi and Noor could sit inside the house and grieve while he had to venture outside and deal with folks like Mela Ram. In the bazaar the grocer had sidled up to him, barely finished shaking his head in some form of commiseration, before thrusting a bill at him: 'Unpaid, Bhallasaab left.'

'Anant-uh!' Preet came hurrying after him. And from beneath the divan, Pasha's sinewy frame emerged. He leapt at Anant's retreating figure.

'Let go, Pasha!' Anant brushed the dog aside brusquely without looking back.

Pasha persisted. He sprang at Anant again. As Anant walked on, Pasha's paws dragged down his back. His blue Pathani kameez ripped.

Anant pounced at Pasha, hitting him with his right hand, the left holding his collar. As the blows rained down, the dog whined at his feet, paws lifted in quivering defence, body twitching on the floor.

'An-ant! What madness is this?' Preet shouted as she rushed forward, her slippers clacking alarmingly. 'Wha-what are you doing? Why punish this dumb creature?'

Anant seemed possessed. He continued with the walloping, the strips of torn shirt dancing with every lunge, sweat shining on his bare back. Pasha remained on the floor, wagging his tail meekly, darting his face for a quick lick, attempting to make amends.

'Enough, Anant! Enough!' Preet put her arm between them. 'Why hurt an innocent animal? He didn't mean to tear your shirt, you know that. He was just trying to prevent you from leaving the house.'

'WHERE WOULD I GO?' Anant shouted before his voice broke. 'Wh-why didn't he try to stop the one who left that day?'

Tears coursed down his cheeks. He held his head in his left hand and sobbed loudly.

❧

Anant had finished recounting Gulli's story to Noor: how Bodh Singh's son had sighted Papa in the fields at dawn on the morning he died. Brother and sister were walking Pasha in the gardens of the Advanced Training Institute, empty after the final term. It was Anant's attempt to make amends with Pasha. Also, he needed some time alone with Noor. Of course, he would have to be selective about what he told her. The idea was to offload, not to end up having to answer questions he himself was struggling with.

Anant's visit to Dr Arora had yielded no answers. The doctor had shifted his practice to Moga, set up a polyclinic with another friend. His compounder, whom Anant traced to his house, said that the doctor had informed every patient verbally of his move. He could not recall if Papa had been one of those. Noor, in turn, had disclosed that Dr LTS had said that Papa had been planning a Lahore visit. Anant did not think it was important. Both Jinder Tayaji and Papa recalled Lahore fondly. And Uncle Bitta's recent trips would only have made it seem viable.

What was clear—from Gulli's visit, the old neighbour's account and the rickshawala's revelation—was that Papa had spent three odd hours roaming his old town before he reached the hospital. What for? Anant had no answer. But talking to Noor would help. It would take some of the weight off his chest. Or, at the very least, ensure that he did not lose his temper like he had only recently.

'The whole thing seems impossible.' Noor hoisted her spectacles on her head and put her palms over her eyes. 'How can a man wracked by cardiac pains be trudging across town? Five–six kilometres?'

'Wracked would be incorrect. Sometimes, the pains start, then the symptoms disappear for a while, only to emerge later.'

'So while he was walking, he was probably not in pain?'

'Maybe not intense pain... discomfort, yes.' After a while he said, 'Angina Pectoris.'

'What?'

'*Angina Pectoris*, it's Latin for "strangling in the chest". That is probably how it started.'

'But why was he walking? Why all over the city? Especially when he had gone in search of a doctor in the first place? Why not just walk to Mission or Civil Hospital... if walking was what he wanted to do?'

'Slow, Noor, slow.'

'What *is* the truth? Will we ever know?'

Anant shrugged. 'There is no way of knowing the truth... knowing what really happened. Don't you see that?' He halted in his tracks and faced her. 'There is no video recording available that will play back for us the last few hours of our father's life. We cannot walk the walk with him... therefore there is no way for us to be certain.'

'So? What are we looking for then?'

A yelp and they saw a woman with a Pomeranian squeeze in through the partially open gates. Anant hurried to Pasha and snapped the leash on. Noor followed him. They proceeded with their walk, the dry peepul leaves crunching beneath their feet.

'The day after Papa's cremation, Kapoor, a lawyer, came calling. You know him?'

'No.'

'He was a junior colleague of Papa's. He died yesterday.'

'What! How?'

'His scooter skidded. Apparently he was passing a construction site where there was gravel around. But then I bumped into the policeman, the officer on Vir Mamu's case, remember?'

'The one who dropped in the night Papa was cremated?'

Anant wagged a knowing head. 'He said there was some suspicion regarding Kapoor's death. An examination of his scooter revealed that the brakes were not functioning!'

Alarmed, Noor asked, 'But why would somebody want to kill him?'

Anant took a look around, sucked his stomach in and then blew out. 'Beats me. But the rumour is that Kapoor was a khabri. A Ferozepur local, a border-area boy, he was apparently inducted into the ranks by the CBI at the height of the Punjab militancy in the eighties. He was a small-time spy but an efficient one... he had provided leads into many cases, eventually leading to the capture of some prominent Sikh militants. It could be one of their comrades or some disgruntled family member or...'

'Or what?' Noor's voice was faint.

'Or the ISI.'

'*ISI*? The Inter Services Intelligence of *Pakistan*?' Noor's face was incredulous.

'Pakistan was Kapoor's territory. And it's an open secret that rogue ISI commanders are trying to hitch up with disgruntled Sikh militants to sabotage the new peace initiatives between India and Pakistan.'

'Hang on!' Noor bit her lip, hands on her hips. 'This is all too confusing. So, even if... say it was rogue ISI men, why kill Kapoor? Why now? I mean, they could always have done it, right?'

'Perhaps *now* was the time. Or, perhaps, Kapoor was on to something that the ISI didn't want Indian intelligence to find out.'

Around them the air pulsed with nature's evensong: busy twitters from the eucalyptus and peepul trees, wings flapping overhead, soft scratching of doggy paws, the smell of freshly scraped earth—all manifest in the blessed quiet of the large garden.

'When Kapoor visited the day after the cremation, he spent quite some time rummaging through Papa's papers. He was looking for something...' Anant nodded thoughtfully. 'I don't know what, but *something*. He had that look in his eyes...'

'What look?' Noor whispered.

'I don't know. Like a... like a madman who believes he is about to win a lottery.'

'What does all this *mean*, Anant? What does Papa have to do with this? What should we *do*?'

Anant stayed quiet, seemingly considering something. Then he placed a hand on Noor's shoulder, a firm but gentle grip. 'We sit tight. When the eyes get used to darkness, they figure a way out.'

BAKSH

THE LAST WALK

Baksh sighed. Possession being nine-tenths of the law, Bodh Singh had become landholder the moment his foolish sister had mooted her idea. Now the haveli looked set to go the same way.

Jinder had settled in the haveli after his retirement. After all, Bapuji had bequeathed it to him in his will. A lifelong bachelor, hiding behind years of loneliness, he suddenly found himself adrift in his erstwhile home. Each door opened into a room, each room had stories to tell, each story conjured memories. However, the principal players had departed the stage or changed roles completely, and Jinder was left confounded.

So he started to people the place.

Forgotten acquaintances began to drop in for the free tipple in the evenings. In a show of gratitude they made him president of the Committee for Hussainiwala Indo–Pak Peace Initiative.

His servant suggested another hand to help with the housework and the increasing load of guests. And taking Jinder's nonchalant wave of hand as assent, proceeded to fetch his wife and two children from his village in Uttar Pradesh: there was a generous Sardar who would let them have a room entirely to themselves. The haveli was now a satellite hamlet to the village of Kuralia in UP. Jinder resided in the master bedroom, the only room left available to him. Or sprawled on a divan in the courtyard, dwarfed by the yellow-green sarees of the women and checked lungis of the men flapping on the clothesline, while a swarm of surprisingly chubby children crawled on the floor. Odd-job men—whitewash men, plumbers, electricians—hung around the house, waiting to stake their claim as soon as the Bade Sardar took to bed, or passed away.

There was still time, Baksh had advised Jinder—time to dispatch the truckload of hangers-on before they qualified to evoke the tenancy laws for legal claim on the haveli. However, Jinder had some excuse to proffer every time. Losing their ancestral lands had clearly not been lesson enough.

The first strains of Japji started to pour forth. At the end of the lane, tucked in the right alcove of Baghdadi Gate, was the gurudwara from which the morning prayers were coming. The area around the temple was well-lit and, compared to the crumbling Baghdadi Gate, the gurudwara appeared to be in good health: fresh paint, shiny gate, elaborate grilles... As a child, Baksh had spent many hours playing hockey in the gurudwara's grounds, biding time until the pershad was served, reclining in the shade of the old mango tree and observing the trail of red ants, filling buckets of water from the hand-pump for the kitchen.

Maji had gifted one of his paintings to the gurudwara when he was fifteen. A painting of Guru Nanak, Mardana seated a few steps away with his rabab, and Bala, dressed in his mendicant's ochre robes, with a flywhisk made of peacock feathers. Bala and Mardana, the two lifelong companions of the Guru: one a low-caste Muslim, the other a Hindu. Nanak, who believed in the unity of mankind and spent a lifetime walking the world so that he could convince others of this simple truth. Would he rue those travels if he were to walk down the roads of Punjab today?

Did the painting still hang inside? It had been many years since he had visited the gurudwara. There was no place for a whisky-swigging Sardar amidst severe-looking godmen in flowing beards, reciting the scripture stridently from behind a palanquin surrounded by shiny brass vases topped with plastic roses, its velvet canopy decorated with silver sequins.

The few times Preet asked him to accompany her to a gurudwara—Baisakhi, the birth anniversary of a guru, a pilgrimage to the shrine of Baba Buddha to pray for the gift of a son—he would offer some flimsy excuse. Not that it deterred Preet from visiting. As a Jat Sikh, Preet took her role as protector-preserver of the Sikh faith very seriously. Maybe it was genetic—her forefathers having saved the faith from the tyranny of the Afghans and Mughals—or, perhaps, she was compensating for the foolish romantic notion that had made her fall for Baksh, a Khatri Sikh. The fact that the Sikh gurus were Khatris had probably spurred her love—it was only after marriage that she had discovered the laxity with which her husband followed his faith. So Preet made up for it by praying daily and visiting a gurudwara once a week. And it was not long before her zeal looked set to consume her—and the family...

1977

'A lot of construction happening,' Shammi said, casting a backward glance.

Baksh and he were seated in the balcony of the first floor that Baksh had recently added to his house. Shammi had come in from the rain, an unexpectedly heavy January shower, and hesitantly agreed to Baksh's offer of a whisky. A prominent Akali leader, he preferred not to be seen in the company of spirits. Baksh, though, knew him better. 'Who's watching you here?' he waved aside Shammi's hesitation as he poured a drink. 'No reporter. No priests.'

Shammi smoothed his untied beard, patting it like it was a pet dog. A dedicated approach to Unani medicine had rewarded him with ample hair growth. On consultation, the Unani Hakim of Qasur—across the border but with a branch in nearby Faridkot, Faizan Dawakhana—had identified 'patchy growth' as the culprit behind the scanty hair. Amla oil, prepared by boiling dry amla in coconut oil, was the hair tonic prescribed. A night treatment of liquorice paste—mulethi ground in milk with saffron—was also advised.

A diligent Shammi applied it over the bald patches before going to bed every night—it covered the lower half of his face entirely. His wife had taken weeks to adjust to the sight. Shammi, however, couldn't have asked for more. As per the Akali fashion, he could now leave his beard untied. Its cascade, though still unable to compete with the best, had surged him into the Akali top league.

'How many rooms are you planning?'

Baksh shrugged. 'Depends on the money at hand.'

Shammi gave a half-grin.

Lately, his visage had acquired a curious tragicomic dimension: pinched eyes, knit brows, a perennially neutral smile. As a result, an onlooker could never accurately read his face.

'Thought I would rent out the lower floor… that way I have another income stream.'

'Looks very neat, hain, the layout. And those tiles.'

'Got the idea from Chandigarh—it's quite the rage nowadays. But you tell me, how's the passive resistance going?'

Shammi waved a hand. 'Only time will tell. The Amerjansy has shamed the Bahmani in the world's eyes. Yet, she persists. Very clever woman, this Indira Gandhi! It helps that she is such a badmaash janani. The court ruling went against the shameless woman, and she decided to suspend the fundamental rights of all citizens! Where was the justification for Amerjansy, I ask?'

'You are right. But in Zail Singh, she has found an able lieutenant in Punjab, hmm?'

Shammi spat, depositing whisky-laced spittle on the brick floor. 'Jholi-chuk!' Snorting, he added. 'Toady of Indira. Ramgarhia wants to be a Gursikh!'

In the general elections of 1972, the Akali party had lost to Indira Gandhi's 'Garibi Hatao' campaign. Four years down the line, poverty had shown no signs of being eradicated—the only thing in danger of extinction seemed to be freedom, as prime minister Indira Gandhi had declared a state of Emergency in India. With derision Shammi had dismissed Zail Singh as a lower-caste Sikh, but he was playing the Akalis at their game. An ex-priest, he used to read scriptures in a Sikh temple before Indira's son Sanjay spotted his potential and picked him up.

Baksh shrugged. 'Chief minister Zail Singh will breathe only when he's proven that he is more Sikh than you Akalis, therefore closer to the Sikh public.'

'The Congress calls itself secooler. Then it goes about organizing bicentenary celebrations, hain—Ranjit Singh Maharaj, Guru Tegh Bahadur's martyrdom. Oye, people call *us* Akalis communal. At least our colours are visible to all. No deception. And this Bahmani… Ram and chhura both within her cloak, secooler on her lips.'

'Two-pronged approach: retain the Hindu vote, woo the Sikhs as well.'

Shammi squared his shoulders. Sitting up, he poured himself a large peg, not bothering to dilute it with either ice or water. 'Khair,' he declared, 'we shall see. She cannot appeal to the public better than us.'

'I wouldn't be so sure. Sometimes, the same tired message from the lips of a new messenger can sound fresh to the public.'

'Oye, it's only because of this Amerjansy, I tell you.' Shammi slapped his thigh, the whisky in his glass sloshing. 'People have sealed their mouths. Except for us Akalis. At least we are opposing such misuse of power. Say anything and, next moment, you are in jail. Such terror Nehru's daughter has spread.'

Baksh acknowledged this with a sage nod.

'Renaming roads, even if after the gurus, organizing prayer recitals, courting Sikh holy men of various taksals… does this make Zail a better Sikh? Hain?'

Baksh popped a couple of salted peanuts into his mouth and asked in an innocent tone, 'It does not?'

Shammi let out a dismissive cluck.

Baksh chuckled. 'The villagers who collected the droppings of the guru's stallion certainly seem to be convinced.' Zail Singh had paraded a couple of horses down a highway lined with incredulous villagers who believed they were being graced by the presence of the progeny of the tenth guru's stallion.

'Foolish peasants. Imagine! Believing that a string of horses were descended from the stallion of the last guru! Such a storm of lies Zail has created and they have swallowed them whole.

What to do when people have such credulity. Anyone can make a fool of them.'

Brushing grains of salt from his hands, Baksh settled back with his drink. 'And the traditional Akali vote bank? Is that made of some other people?'

❦

It was 1979 and Bitta and Baksh were driving down the Chandigarh–Ferozepur highway. Bitta said he enjoyed driving—it gave him time to ruminate, which he seldom got to do otherwise. He was always on the run: overseeing the farms, directing his fleet of two threshers and three combine harvesters which he loaned during harvest season, managing his flourishing contract business. From the initial days of supplying cement during the construction of the massive Bhakra dam, he had added an entire range of building materials to his supply portfolio.

'There is something about these straight roads,' Bitta observed, pointing at the two-lane macadam highway. 'Helps the mind meander and focus at the same time.' Turning to Baksh seated in the passenger seat, he added, 'You would know.'

'Hmmm…' Baksh glanced at the fields stretching on either side. 'Work brings me to Chandigarh every now and then. Though I don't get a Contessa ride every time…'

'Useful car it is. Spacious. And the AC works well.'

'You have always been fond of regal vehicles.'

'Baee, my philosophy is simple you know, Baksh. Dab ke vah, te raj ke kha.'

Baksh nodded in acknowledgment as a pond came into view. Buffalo heads were visible above the grey-green surface. A child rolled a bicycle tyre along the edge, following its wobbly progress. Bitta had been consistent in his credo: Till with vigour, eat with relish. In turn, he had reaped rich dividends. Fortune had also favoured him. Baksh could not recall a single instance when Bitta had worked for something and not got it.

Inadvertently, he compared his situation with his cousin's. They had started from the same point, but now, Bitta was rich, Baksh was well-to-do; Bitta's marriage had brought him prestige and connections, his, notoriety and fetters...

It could not be denied, though, that the seemingly simple Bitta—Jinder's 'Ignoramus'—had steered his life with acumen: marrying right, retaining his property through foresight, identifying opportunities for advancement, then seeing them through. Meanwhile, Jinder, the family intellectual, earned in salary what Bitta paid one of his many employees. No wonder Bitta was the 'enterprise man'!

Baksh's own choices, though, had exhibited a peculiar knack for turning belly-up. Because they were *his* choices, he knew that ultimately he was responsible, but he did ponder the role of kismat that had swept away many of his attempts like chaff, while the world's labours had fructified in heaps of golden grain...

A farm trolley, bloated with rice husk, was crawling up on them. Sumo wrestler bellies were slung from each iron sidewall and Bitta proceeded to the edge of the road for a safe berth.

'Other than that, what skill do I have?' Bitta asked Baksh.

When Baksh frowned his incomprehension, Bitta clucked. 'Land and landlordy, besides this, what do I know?' He followed it with a familiar self-deprecatory chuckle. 'But at least—' He honked at a cyclist who abruptly sprang onto the road from an opening in the bordering field. 'Son-of-a-donkey has to die under my vehicle only...'

Bitta loosened his shoulders, adjusted the rear-view mirror and turned to look at Baksh. 'At least, rustics like me knew what life had to offer and how to use its offering. But nowadays, young adults think differently. Their head is in the clouds.'

'Why, what happened?'

'My wife's sister's eldest son, you remember? The tall boy everyone claims looks like Sunil Dutt? Well, he fancies that he can become a phillum star. Last couple of years he had gone on and on about how he just needed his father to sponsor him, get him started with Chopra-Vopra... some Hindi phillum director... and he would, undoubtedly, be the next Dharminder. Lo, kar lo gal! His father, like any sensible parent, refused. And you know what that ullu da pattha did? Ran away to Bombay. In the family Mercedes. With a couple of lakhs which he stole from the family safe. The car broke down and was abandoned near Jaipur. Finally, the police tracked him down in Bombay, but he begged to stay on. His father said okay, when the money runs out, he will return.'

'Right.'

'Aaho. Now latsaab is back after six months. Affects the mannerisms of phillum stars. Claims he will soon be seen across cinema halls... some picture with Bachchan... *Kala-Safed Pathar*, something. Hain.'

Bitta briskly scratched his tied beard. 'His delighted mother isn't sure whether she should preen, but the father soon figured out it was a thirty-second shot in a three-hour movie, playing the sidekick's sidekick! Foolish woman, he told his wife, it would probably get snipped by the film editor.'

Bitta laughed and Baksh joined in. 'Where do these boys get such ideas?'

'Oh, it is all these NRI cousins of his. They bring him videocassettes from UK. All day he watches those in his darkened bedroom with other dissolute friends. Says he is learning to do stunt-scenes.' Bitta leaned towards Baksh. 'Blue movies,' he said. Drawing back, he assessed the road behind, then added, 'I think he does drugs as well. At least his friends do... most of them are heavy-lidded'—Bitta's eyelids sank dramatically—'and answer in monosyllables.'

Baksh replied with raised brows. He had increasingly heard of drug use among young boys—one of the ways in which the family's increased disposable income was being spent, besides TV, fridge, phone, washing machine.

Bitta stopped the car by the roadside. 'Going to see a cheetah off,' he said, with a devilish grin before trotting off into the fields.

Baksh ran a finger against the wooden dashboard, tuned the knobs of the built-in music system, then sighed and rested his palms against the grey leather of the seat.

Thanks to the Green Revolution, the farms of Punjab had seen an enormous increase in yield and living standards had improved drastically. Sons, whom their families had managed to send to the Middle East or Canada, were sending money back home: double-storeyed bungalows were no more a rarity in the countryside. His rural clientele even had more money to fight court cases—petty scuffles often erupted and went out of control under the influence of liquor.

Bitta walked back, rubbing his hands against his trouser legs, leisurely scratching his groin as he surveyed the road in both directions. Satisfied, he got into the driver's seat, adjusted the neck cushion and turned the key. 'Anyway, I decided to err on the side of caution,' he said, resuming his narrative. 'So, I divulged my suspicions to my sister-in-law. Now she's planning to visit some saint in Damdami Taksal, some Bhindranwale… to seek his counsel.'

Baksh shrugged. 'Such are the times.'

❦

Preet had been simmering for a while by the time Baksh returned from court. Her breath came in short rasps, her eyes were wet with, presumably, onion tears, for she was chopping those seated on the divan in the front veranda, and she wiped her nose against her sleeve frequently. She offered him tea. It was when she placed the glass in front of him that Baksh realized that there was trouble ahead.

'Who is this Bansal?' she asked, having returned to her seat. Though her voice was soft, Baksh could feel the whiplash beneath her words.

So, Bansal had visited. Hmm… that was fast. He had not expected him for a couple of…

'Bansal. Mr and Mrs and two children were here.' Preet's eyes flashed. Her index finger circled overhead, the kitchen knife gripped in the fist. 'Touring the house, they were. Said Bhallasaab told them to.' Preet mimicked an ingratiating smile. 'Baniyani, her daring you see, told me she had fallen in love with the house. Would pay whatever price Bhallasaab set for sale.'

Baksh lifted a dismissive hand. 'O, I just thought they could look it over. Bansal is Bitta's friend. Is planning to shift to Ferozepur. And is searching for a place—'

'So my house is the only one left in the entire town for the sneaky baniya to set his eyes upon?'

'Oh, let it be. I just thought if we decide to shift to Chandigarh some day, let me get an estimate of the value of our house—'

'Shift to Chandigarh! Shift to Chandigarh. This lament I have been hearing since we got married. Twenty years on, and still you harp on it. When the time was right, you didn't move. Now, by Waheguru's mercy, we have a beautiful two-storey comfortable place, and you want to sell it. Two girls… where will we roam with them? Have you thought?'

'Mitti pao! It was only a recce.'

'Recce! Reck-kee? What's wrong with you? So much money we have spent on this place. Just last month you got all the doors changed. Why? Because you took it into your head that single doors are modern. Those are the fashion in all the Chandigarh houses. So all the double doors were changed. Such good wood, and what did the carpenter give in exchange? But no, you have your fancies and they must be fulfilled. Even if I have to pawn my gold for them.' Abruptly, she started to cry. Through the sniffles, she went on. 'This is what I get. For the paee paee that I put together to build this house. I could also have fulfilled my fancies like other women, bought silk suits, a new gold piece every month… But no, I put my heart and soul into building our home, and this is what I get. Bargain-hunters, buyers, wheeler-dealers… all over my house!'

A long sizing-up glance at Baksh later, Preet gathered her bowl, onion peels and knife and shuffled to the kitchen. This, however, did not signal an end to their sparring. It was only a lull. To gather the heap of previous skirmishes. To draw out the baggage, accumulated assiduously over the years, of past grievances. To burnish scabbed wounds until they shone raw red. To draw blood afresh.

The venue shifted. From the veranda, it moved to the kitchen, where Preet clanked and sniffled and grated, and the adjoining dining area where Baksh sat propped by his Johnny Walker, holding a conversation through mute rejoinders.

Lurking in the midst of Preet's lengthy charge sheet was Exhibit One: Opium. Some months back she had discovered in Baksh's coat pocket several pastilles of afeem, under the deadly haze of which the entire Bhalla clan had lost its efficacy, she alleged. Bapuji, perennially doped, while his daughter made merry, having emasculated the sons through her shenanigans. No wonder that the family that once owned villages was reduced to paltry acres.

Afeem: Yes. Baksh was guilty of that. He had given in to the need for some sedative, something to numb his mind. He had wanted to live in a haze for a few days in order to avoid his thoughts. Thoughts that hammered inside his chest, throbbed in his head, washed his stomach with acid, so that neither whisky nor rum dulled the ache.

Bapuji had died, and Balwant, who was by his bedside, thought it fit to inform him twelve hours later when their father's body was ready for the crematorium. At work in the Sessions Court, his standing as a criminal lawyer of repute drew sniggering acknowledgement: intimacy with a home-grown felon—not every criminal lawyer was privileged to have a murderer for a brother-in-law—was bound to sharpen lawyerly skills.

Preet next offered Exhibit Two: Other Woman. He had something to hide, she knew. Otherwise, why would he be off to the 'city beautiful' every second week? What fire was within him? Not that he had suddenly become very thick with Jinder. Something was afoot, she was not a fool.

Other Woman: No. Preet was not a fool, she was a Masterni—that was the term villagers used for female teachers. However, despite her obviously perceptive intellect, she was mistaken—nothing was afoot, least of all a paramour. And in her heart, Baksh knew, Preet knew. She was too much of a Jatti to stand even the shadow of another woman in her life, leave alone a presence tucked away.

In any case, where was the need? For despite their differences, or perhaps because of it, Preet and he enjoyed a wholesome sex life. By turns, giving and demanding, they did unusually well in bed, unlike in day-to-day life.

It was Preet's way of venting frustration at something she did not understand: his queer fascination with, as she taunted, the *city beautiful*, his need to constantly see it. The city of gentry, where retired IAS folk, academicians, professionals had made their home. Where one could spend an evening watching a play at Tagore Theatre. Where walls weren't streaked with piss, sidewalks weren't littered with dried turds and stairways weren't coloured with paan stains. A civilized place, where Baksh felt he could periodically regain his sanity, forsaken in the dense dusty litigious sprawl of Ferozepur.

They would have gone on in that fashion if Noor had not intervened in the manner of a judge, who, realizing from the rising cacophony that things needed to be brought to order, pounds his mallet with a stern 'Order! Order!'

The girls were sitting on the double bed under their razais, in their bedroom, studying. They had been thus preoccupied since the Mahabharat began a few hours ago. They were habituated to it, the chapters having unfolded with monotonous regularity at various points of time. But Noor had probably reached the point of boredom with the frequent telecast. Or, perhaps, she could not concentrate on her homework. Perhaps, she was still a child, unable to comprehend the trite tragedy of domesticity. Whatever the motive, Noor walked into the dining area, plucked Baksh's Johnny Walker bottle from the sideboard, marched into the kitchen, hoisted it over the sink, then turned it over.

Baksh heard the gurgle-gurgle as the whisky sputtered in the sinkhole. Then he heard the bottle clink in the dustbin. Next, Noor reappeared in the dining room. She glared from Preet to him, then back. Then her face crumpled. It dissolved into tears, and she walked to the front balcony and huddled against the railing.

Noor, he sighed as he watched her slumped back. He had named his second daughter Noor because splendour could not—would not—be hidden. Preet's doctor had informed her in advance that the second child was *also* a daughter—to avoid disappointment later, he had wagged a knowing chin. Some of Preet's friends joined in with gratuitous advice. It was early days, she could afford a safe miscarriage. And there was never any dearth of ways... Strange medical practice it was that aided the disposal of a girl child. So the mother could continue, unhindered, in her quest for a son.

When Preet casually brought up those conversations, Baksh decided to turn her favourite phrase of admonishment on her. 'Beware,' he said, pointing an index finger heavenwards, 'the blue-canopied one! Nothing is hidden from him.'

Thereafter, when the child was born, in part joy, part righteousness, partly because her birth time was twelve noon, he had named her Noor. Admittedly, she was wheatish-complexioned and nowhere near the picture-pretty baby that

Neymat had been. Her smile, though, was an ear-to-ear grin, her eyes wide, and she seldom cried. Later, he never realized when, he started to call her Raja Beta. No particular reason. Maybe it had to do with the fact that the other children called her Double Roti. She was a healthy tomboy. She doted on her Papa. Tiny hands fetched him hot puffed rotis for dinner. Feet pitter-pattered ceaselessly back and forth, for the rate of consumption was greater than the rate of fetching. For dessert, Noor served her exploits-of-the-day.

The few occasions he needed to buck her up he called her Sher Puttar—that comparison with a tiger cub was guaranteed to make her perk up.

❧

Bitta had decided to flee Ferozepur. Partition's churail, the woman who died giving birth to Pakistan, came seeking the body of Punjab. Only this time, the plains were pregnant with strife between cap and turban, shorn hair and topknot. In the land of fault lines, fresh ones were being drawn: Hindu–Muslim, Sikh–Muslim in 1947; Hindu–Sikh in 1982…

'God only knows how long this will last Baksh,' Bitta said as he massaged a furrowed forehead. 'The atmosphere is so tense, what with the rumours of a hit list.'

Bitta's obvious wealth and prosperity had drawn the attention of insurgents who had frequently taken 'protection' money from him. A half-Hindu, they grinned, needed the support of the Khalsa, the pure Sikhs they claimed to be. However, with the increasing lawlessness, even brigands had started mailing ransom notes to the wealthy, Bitta included. Baksh shook his head. 'This hit list is a strange demon. Anybody's face you don't like, just inform Jarnail Singh Bhindranwale, then watch... Sooner or later the man will be eliminated!'

Sant Jarnail Singh Bhindranwale, a commonplace saint from a religious centre in Punjab, first came into prominence when villagers began flocking to his sermons like flies hovering over sweetmeat shops. The nectar on offer was baptism for patits, sinners. Soon he was elevated to Baba, the revered one, who ran de-facto people's courts—settling land disputes, dowry cases, various peasant grievances—in the manner of a Mafioso. An armed retinue ensured the implementation of verdicts delivered. In the immensely popular preacher, the Congress had sighted a potential challenger to the Akali leadership, and begun courting him. Emboldened by the political patronage, the Sant had proclaimed himself the messiah of the Sikh community disgruntled with its leaders: a bullet-charged bandolier strung about his chest, he carried a silver arrow in his hand, like the tenth guru.

'What times are we seeing, Baksh? And we thought the madness had died with Partition.'

Bitta stroked his erstwhile French beard that he had lately started to grow. There was wisdom in disguising oneself as a Sikh, especially during travel. One man's hair-splitting on all matters hairy had sent barbershops and hair salons packing. Hirsuteness had become de rigueur.

Sikh militants called themselves Khalistanis—people of Khalistan, the Land of Truth. The proposed nation fell adjacent to Pakistan, the Land of the Pure. Punjab, the land of five rivers, of constantly shifting alluvium, an Aryan–Persian–Arabic–Mongolian Jalfrezi, marinating for centuries in exotic sauces, was sought to be precisely demarcated into twin capsules of purity and verity.

Bitta's shoulders slumped under some unseen burden. 'Daily there is some new terror unleashed. People being snipped like sugarcane from fields. And the government…'

'They are all in it together. Congress, Akali Dal, Khalse… each is interested in playing us Punjabis like chess pieces.'

'Bhindranwale's men are roaming free, dispensing their brand of justice, and all the Congress government does is to look the other way. Akali leaders like Shammi claim that Bhindranwale is their stave to beat the Opposition. Now that they have appropriated him from his erstwhile Congress masters like Zail Singh and Indira—'

A rasping sound erupted suddenly and Bitta turned hastily in his chair to glance towards the Mall Road. Then he looked at Baksh and sighed. A singsong voice had started to render loudly the exploits of Sikh martyrs. The voice rose feverishly, then broke off into a rambunctious ditty extolling the virtues of a martial race unafraid of sacrifices. It came from the gurudwara located within the jail that stood directly opposite the house.

Bitta glanced at Baksh, raised his eyebrows, then proceeded to examine his sandalled feet.

'That is the music we get to hear nowadays. Earlier the gurudwara used to relay Gurbani, now it is mostly these rustic preachy numbers.' As Bitta nodded in silence, Baksh, slowly rubbing his hands, added, 'Who would have estimated the influence of this rabid illiterate? Even Preet has a few cassettes stored in the sideboard! But Bhindranwale is out of control now… of both the Congress and the Akalis… But you are serious about moving?'

'Aaho, Baksh. Things don't look good here. Either I convert to Sikhism or we move bag and baggage to Chandigarh. At least, the Akalis and their extremist friends cannot run the Union Territory like it is their uncle's house.'

Bitta looked into the distance, examining the traffic, his eyes narrowed. 'It hurts. Having to forsake the place you have always known as home. Once, we were fortunate and survived. Ferozepur was not given to Pakistan... But now, in our own country, it is our turn to flee.'

It struck Baksh then how Bitta's voice had changed: the lilt of shehnai in it had given way to the sad twang of a sitar. Baksh breathed audibly as his left hand played with his kara, moving the steel bracelet up and down the right wrist. Bitta wore a similar bracelet, in the manner of numerous Punjabi Hindus whom Guru Nanak, the founder of the Sikh faith, could count amongst his followers. When the guru died, it was said that his Hindu and Muslim disciples bickered over whether to cremate him or bury him. However, when they lifted the drape that covered his body, they found flowers instead. Apparently, it was a last message for his petty human followers.

The traffic sputtered on. The two friends sat in silent contemplation.

❦

Bitta couldn't have timed his departure better. His accountant was shot dead late one evening in the office and the safe was broken into. The Akalis launched a religious war, a Dharam Yuddh they called it, to ban tobacco in the holy city of Amritsar. Despite the Sikh Gurus banning all narcotics Punjab was a state of tipplers—ranking first in per capita consumption—and peasants routinely chomped on opium pellets and dry opium flowers, the consumption spiking at harvest time. Tobacco, though, was primarily consumed by Hindus and provided the Akalis with a platform on which to rally religious sentiment. The Hindus retaliated with their slogan: 'Cigarette beedi peeyenge, hum shaan se jeeyenge!' The Sant unleashed a reign of terror such that the phrase 'hit list' became another word in the Punjabi language, *hitlis*. One night, a bus travelling from Delhi to Amritsar was hijacked: six Hindu passengers were pulled out and gunned down.

The next morning, as Baksh sat reading the newspaper, Bhindranwale's recorded voice started screeching shrilly in the background. Lately, it had become Preet's early morning brew of choice. Baksh walked to the tape recorder and switched it off.

Preet, kneading flour in the kitchen, frowned at him. 'Why? Why stop my tape—this is no time for ghazals.'

'No. This is the time for odious oratory from the mouth of a murderer!'

'Hain! Now you are calling the Sant a murderer?'

Baksh shook the paper at her. 'What else do you call a man who has the blood of innocents on him?'

'Wah, wah! If Bhindranwale is a criminal then why did the Bahmani Indira want him on her side? She even called him a spiritual leader.'

'She has been using him as a pawn.'

'And now that he refuses to be a pawn, he becomes a criminal?'

'Terrorist—that's what your Sant is.'

Preet, her flour-smeared hands at her waist, strode to the doorway. 'The British called Bhagat Singh a terrorist. So did that make him one? What would you know about heroes and martyrs of Sikh history? You, who don't even know Sukhmani from Rehraas!'

'It doesn't matter.'

'Doesn't *matter*?'

'No. Don't you see? The definition of a terrorist is clear even to those who don't know one Sikh prayer from another.'

Preet waved an exasperated hand at Baksh and withdrew to her kneading. 'The question is of the rights of Sikhs. First, Sikh farmers were deprived of their lands during Partition. Then the Congress split Punjab into three new states, further depriving Sikhs of their share. Then that Bahmani refused to give Chandigarh to Punjab after having taken land from Sikh farmers to build the new city. How come you show no concern for the rights of our people—'

'Right to prepare hit lists and knock off people?'

'Right to protect one's faith.'

'By killing those of other faiths?'

Preet swivelled her head towards Baksh, her hooped earrings swinging. 'Nothing was ever won without shedding blood.'

'What?' Baksh was perplexed. Preet's shifting threads of argument could confound the most astute lawyer. Then, comprehension dawned. 'Khalistan? Khalistan! So that is the trophy to be won! Hmm... And what would you do in a nation like that Masterni Preet?'

As Preet looked on, Baksh's head bobbed. 'Head covered with chunni, forever. A new version of the burqa. No English-medium schools. Punjabi will be the language of instruction—'

'What's wrong with that?'

'Everything.'

'Why?'

Baksh snorted. 'Do I have to remind you that you are an English teacher? Besides, it is a richer language. There is more literature written in it. It connects us to the rest of the world...'

'So you can forget your own?'

'Uff!' Baksh shrugged his irritation. 'If ever there was a state of Khalistan, I would certainly migrate. Besides, such an entity would never last. Because,' he opened his mouth wide, baring his teeth, 'Pakistan would swallow it for dinner one night.'

'Aaho!' Preet assented disparagingly. 'And are we wearing bangles?'

Baksh walked into the kitchen. Preet, having finished kneading the flour into a shiny mound, patted it and covered it with a moist cotton napkin. 'Look,' Baksh said. 'Look,' he urged. Preet gave him a quick, miffed glance. Baksh waved the front page of the newspaper at Preet. The main picture showed a gory sight of bloodied bodies splayed on the ground. 'This bus that the militants hijacked, the innocent passengers they pulled off and shot. Imagine if that bus was carrying Neymat back home? And your daughter was a victim. Imagine?'

Preet pursed her mouth, glared at Baksh and looked away. Neymat, having started her first year at a medical college, was living in a hostel an hour's bus ride away and came home during weekends.

Baksh's eyes narrowed. 'Imagine,' he insisted.

Preet did not answer. Instead, turning her back to him, she started to stack kitchen utensils on the rack, the resulting clinking and clanging drowning any further attempt at conversation.

DAY 9: NOOR

Noor chopped beetroot and watched the juice bleed onto the scarred chopping board. There were circles under Noor's eyes. She had been flopping around aimlessly until Neymat had nudged her towards the chopping while she scrubbed dishes over the kitchen sink. Once again the maid had not turned up.

Noor's way of dealing with uncertainty was to attack the problem as she became completely immersed in concentration over a calculus or physics question, or the differential impact of the various growth drivers of the aviation industry. As a child, Anant was known to frequently sit upright in bed while asleep, urging the fielder to catch the ball before, *by God*, it went over the boundary, while Noor's night-time murmurings alluded to definite integrals and Gaussian surface.

That very same problem-solving ability had led Noor to where she was now: she could wade through an ocean of data, churn it into remarkable candy-coloured charts and draw up probable scenarios—all for a handsome salary. Recently, she had shown Neymat a flowchart on her laptop that mapped the aircraft industry. Dotted with connecting lines and symbols, it looked rather intricate. A perplexed Neymat had commented:

'An entire industry captured in *one* chart. Why, Gray took a thousand pages to illustrate the human anatomy!' Noor had grinned in delight. A consultant's job was to analyse a problem to cellular detail such that no uncertainty remained.

The situation she found herself in now was unusual: with no numbers to slice and dice, and random information, source unreliable, what was she to do? She had dismissed the policeman's disclosure to Anant. Either he possessed a colourful imagination, or his profession had moulded him into a conspiracy theorist. What occupied Noor was the last few hours of Papa's life—hours, it seemed, he had spent walking about the town he was born and grew up in. Where all had he walked? If only there was a way to find out the route he had taken, she might be able to deduce his thoughts as he walked. Those, in turn, would give her some sense of her father's state of mind before he passed away. Once she knew that, Noor hoped, she would find some certainty, some closure, some rest.

However, underneath that deliberate and careful reasoning, Noor was vaguely aware that what she was really seeking was a window. A window through which would unfold how her father had changed in those years since she left home, years in which Noor had grown up and her father had grown old. What Noor was really seeking was to know the father she thought she knew.

So, possessed by a frantic energy, Noor was tussling with *the walk the walk the walk*, but reaching nowhere. That afternoon, she had visited Queen in her home opposite the haveli. The woman had nothing to offer, except a regurgitation of her earlier story and ginger-cardamom tea.

Noor's hands were red from the beetroot sap. She scooped the cubes into a bowl. Next, she rummaged through the vegetable tray for onions and, finding only two, made a mental note to send Anant to the market.

'Done!' Neymat declared, pointing her head to the neatly stacked kitchenware. 'I think we could do with some tea.' As she grated some ginger and added it to the water, Neymat turned to Noor and, in the searching way she had, asked, 'The walk?'

It was well-known in the Bhalla household that Neymat's panacea for all ills was: talk it over. Through the years, she had used it when refereeing her siblings—with considerable success; when mediating between her parents—with mixed results; when diagnosing her patients—with healthy outcomes. Noor suspected Neymat had used it on herself over the past one week, as she sliced and diced and fried, using the quiet time perhaps to meditate on Papa. The fact that he had appreciated her cooking would only have aided the contemplation, as colours and aromas wafted in the kitchen, flipping open the lids to distinct memories, as if they were trapped inside the multiple compartments of a Chinese jewel box.

'The walk?' Neymat enquired again.

Noor nodded.

'The walk is important, but only as a means.'

'A means to what?'

'To those three–four hours that he was awake and alive.' The water started to bubble and Neymat reached for the tea leaves. First, she added the curly Darjeeling tea, then followed it with the stronger CTC. 'Maybe the walk helped him think of his life coherently.'

'Coherently? Meaning?'

'It's tough to make sense of life when we are living it. But what if you got a chance at perspective while you were alive?'

With a spoon, Neymat stirred the contents of the pan. 'The last few times I met Papa it seemed like he was physically there, and yet, not there. Like he was withdrawing himself from the world around him. Perhaps he sensed that his time was near and he had started to close his book of accounts.'

'You mean he was entering renunciation mode? Tyaag? Nirvana?'

Neymat shrugged, then recounted the story of her friend Radha's dad who, one day, handed the keys of his house to Radha and set off for Dayalbagh, Agra. Since his wife had passed away, he decided it was time for him to renounce a householder's life and spend the remainder of his time in meditation and seeking God. Radha said she was surprised, but not upset—it was fairly customary among elderly Hindus.

Noor looked incredulous as Neymat strained the tea.

'I am not saying Papa would have gone off somewhere.' Neymat half-laughed. 'I just had a sense that he was beginning to detach himself…'

Noor picked up the teacup that Neymat slid over and took a grateful sip. For a while, the two sisters rested, their backs against the marble kitchen counter as they sought refuge in a well-loved familiar brew.

After she had finished her tea and rinsed the cup, Neymat spoke of death, and how she came across it frequently—an occupational hazard of being a doctor. From what she had seen, she had learnt that people died pretty much the way they had lived. Mr Khanna, long-time patient, senior executive, always harried, took a minute's pause during a meeting, loosened his tie, rested his head back and never opened his eyes again. Mrs Khote, bedridden for two decades, died in her sleep one night.

Only when her granddaughter came in with the morning cup of tea did the household realize that the matriarch had passed away, with minimum fuss. And General Mathur, the hero of the '71 war and Sunny's ex-commanding officer—he battled death until his entire family, from places like Budapest and Bhutan, had gathered at his bedside for a final farewell.

Neymat tucked a loose strand of hair behind Noor's right ear and looked her younger sister in the eye. 'I like to believe that Papa's walk was a final hearing, where he played both prosecutor and defendant for the life he had lived.'

Very quietly Noor asked, 'So what was the result of that hearing?'

'There are no transcripts available, Noor. And we cannot replay the final hearing unless we know the details of the case. Perhaps,' Neymat sighed, her eyes suddenly brittle, 'that's what the death of a parent does—it forces us to learn the story of their life.'

༄

It was past ten in the evening when Uncle Bitta arrived after a six-hour car ride from Chandigarh. Loath to serve him leftovers, Neymat fried potatoes in cumin to serve them with ajwain parathas.

'What was the Vaak, Biba?' he asked as he removed his paisley-embroidered leather juttis.

As per tradition, Gianiji had begun the Akhand Path ceremony by opening the holy book and randomly picking a couplet that he had then read out. It was the guru's counsel for the day: Vaak.

'Sura to pehchaniye, jo lade din ke het.'

'Kabir.' Uncle Bitta nodded.

'Is that so?' Noor asked. 'I heard it first in a TV serial, *Tamas*. At that time, of course, I didn't relate it to the Granth Sahib.'

'*Serial?*' Uncle Bitta's head recoiled. 'This couplet by Kabir is from the Granth Sahib. And has much resonance in our community.'

'What sort, Uncle?' Noor asked.

'First, the meaning.' The uncle translated the couplet for his convent-educated niece: 'He alone is a spiritual hero who fights in defence of religion. He may be cut apart, piece by piece, but he never leaves the battlefield.' Stroking his beard, Bitta added: 'During the Pindi riots... Partition time... Sikh women and children plunged to their death in wells chanting this verse. It resonated with them deeply.'

Neymat placed a plate on the table. The waft of fried potatoes made Bitta nod in appreciation.

'That was how they showed it in the serial also,' Noor was saying. When he frowned, she added, 'The Partition riots. When I saw it the first time, I was amazed.'

'Amazed? At what?'

'At the atmosphere of terror, the fierce conviction of the faithful, and those terrible, terrible scenes... It was difficult to believe that things were so bad...'

Uncle Bitta cupped his chin. 'You children can write an essay on the Holocaust. But on your own history, you come up short. Why?'

Noor shrugged. 'No Sikh producers in Hollywood?'

Neymat, hands cradling the steel plate on which she had brought a fresh paratha, said, 'Nobody really speaks about it... the Partition. I remember asking Papa about it, about his Lahore days... but he was reluctant to talk.'

Noor perked up. 'Why don't *you* tell us, Uncle?'

'Tell what?'

'Everything… All that you know about Partition, about leaving Lahore, about the city, the mention of which still lights up Jinder Tayaji's eyes, about the riots… About everything!'

'That will take a long while.' Uncle Bitta settled back in his chair. 'I was thinking I'll go rest at Jinder's…' Noticing the brightness in Noor's eyes, he sighed, then cleared his throat. 'Why don't you motivate me with a kettle of green tea? And bring out those Peshawari pine nuts, and we will talk of old times.'

BAKSH

Baksh stretched his legs. The hijacking of the night bus and the subsequent killing of Hindu passengers had been just the beginning. Thereafter, people's lives, and newspaper columns, started to crowd over with phrases such as random killings, premeditated attacks, parcel bombs, police encounters, plane hijacking…

For wily politicians, forever looking for opportunity amidst chaos, 'cross-border infiltration' became the new political bogey to replace the jaded foreign hand. The porous border town of Ferozepur was anointed a 'terrorist hotbed'. And curfews started to ring with the frequency of a school bell.

Baksh saw a light come on in the window of the house opposite where he sat. Shadows played behind the lit curtain at the window. An old woman lived in the house, by herself—Queen, Noor had nicknamed her since her son was named Prince. Her elder son had been rounded up by the police and detained as a terrorist. Later, he was killed in an 'encounter', a neat little ploy devised by the Punjab police, whereby the prisoner was taken to the border in the night, ordered to run, and shot in the back. Next morning, newspapers *reported another successful police operation, police figures on militants killed swelled by one. Then the police had picked up the second son from his engineering college hostel in a midnight raid. Queen had come to him for help, for old times' sake. Her husband, weary from dragging himself from court to police station, had died when his eldest son's mutilated corpse was brought home.*

Baksh, his client list now populated with helpless parents of boys who had been 'picked up', had added Queen to the list. He had been able to plead Prince's case successfully—it helped that the boy was an excellent student with grades to show. In turn, Baksh got mud on his face. It was rumoured that Prince had fled to Pakistan. The police promptly listed him as a Khalistani—they believed that he continued to be alive and active...

Baksh rose and started to walk down the main road. His left leg dragged, his left arm was limp by his side. He really should be reaching a doctor. Instead he had been meandering through Ferozepur and sifting through his life like a woman sifts through lentils for pebbles. Except, Baksh sighed, the memories he had picked up... were those lentil grains or pebbles? To his right, in the distance, a red sandstone pillar loomed. As he approached it, a Patton tank became visible. Captured in the Indo–Pak war of '65, it was an important enough showpiece to have the memorial built around it. Ferozepur, in any case, was a city of war memorials: Barki, Saragarhi, Hussainiwala. Woven into its identity was a fundamental symbiosis of border and war. Four wars, Ferozepur and Baksh had witnessed: '62 Indo–China, '65 Indo–Pak, '71 Indo–Pak, '84 India–Bhindranwale. Yes, the Indian army's fourth war was not with one of its neighbours. It was with someone the Indian state had created and nurtured and his ragtag band of Mar-jiware, the living dead.

The army, of course, didn't call it a war.

'Operation', they labelled it: a swift military manoeuvre designed to 'flush out' extremists, a precise surgical exercise to restore the health of the Golden Temple. Blue Star, they codenamed it: military officialese for an attack on the holiest temple of the Sikhs. Under the command of three generals, nine infantry companies of the Indian army mounted the assault. Vijayanta battle tanks—famed for winning the '71 war which granted Bangladesh its freedom—pumped high-explosive shells with pinpoint accuracy.

Jarnail Singh Bhindranwale set up his command post within the Golden Temple in the Akal Takht, the white-marbled building that had historically stood as a symbol of Sikh resistance against the Mughals and Afghans. His defence ring comprised machine guns at the entrance to the temple, brick and sandbag gun emplacements in its windows and arches, and snipers on the rooftop.

The wily Sant was hoping for a mass uprising in the villages of Punjab. In anticipation, the government put the state under siege: rail, bus, air services were suspended, telephone and telex lines disconnected, the Indo–Pak border sealed, 375 gurudwaras across the state blockaded.

Armoured personnel carrier. Rocket-propelled grenade launchers. Battle tanks. Machine guns. Howell guns. And still, an 'Operation'?

Not surprisingly, the lead players on both sides in this war too were Sikh soldiers, veterans of previous wars.

Lieutenant Colonel Ranjit Singh Dayal drew up the plans for Blue Star. Commanding the attack was Major General Kuldip Singh Brar. The former, an infantry man, was a living legend. During the 1965 war with Pakistan, a frontal assault being impossible, he had climbed the steep mountain towering the Haji

Pir Pass and rolled down on top of the enemy. Thus, he captured the hitherto impregnable pass and severed the route leading through Pakistan Occupied Kashmir into the Indian state of Jammu and Kashmir. Major General Brar was a gallantry award winner of the Bangladesh war.

The commander of Bhindranwale's 'army' was an erstwhile guerrilla commander of the Indian army: Major General Shahbeg Singh. In the 1971 war, he had trained and led the Mukti Bahini guerrillas in a secret capacity, never admitted by India. After Bangladesh, charges were brought against Shahbeg Singh. Dismissed without a court-martial, he had lost even his pension. Disgruntled with the establishment, the guerrilla commander had gleaned a way forward in Bhindranwale's fiery rhetoric. He had overseen the fortification of the Golden Temple, trained the Mar-jiware and masterminded the defence of the temple.

But the soldiers, as always, were merely pawns. It was the monarchy—King Zail Singh, Queen Indira Gandhi and as Bishop, the Akali trinity Badal-Longowal-Tohra—which had been orchestrating the moves all along.

Zail Singh, the erstwhile advocate and mentor of Bhindranwale, had been handed the juiciest bone for being Indira Gandhi's most loyal follower: President of the Republic of India and Supreme Commander of its Armed Forces. Indira: Prime Minister of India. The Durga of the '71 war, the Liberator of Bangladesh, reeling under the backlash of Emergency, transformed into Kali, sticking her tongue out at the Frankenstein she had created, Bhindranwale. When the village preacher morphed into her nemesis, it was time for checkmate. In a televised broadcast, she proclaimed, 'Shed hatred, not blood,' and then proceeded to do the exact opposite. Three dithering, politicking, backstabbing Akali politicians made up the third component of the monarchy.

Badal was an on-off cloudburst, his political fortunes fluctuating like his namesake; Longowal, a religious leader who specialized in launching agitations; Tohra, with overall control of gurudwaras, had allowed Bhindranwale to set up office in the Akal Takht. Envious of one another, they affected leadership of the Sikh community in a perennial game of musical chairs. With the approach of D-day, they became stool pigeons for the Queen, cooing and hooting in last-minute negotiations, eventually barely managing to save their flowing whiskers by surrendering to the army as the assault began.

1984

Baksh and Preet had stopped quarrelling. Instead, in the manner of acquaintances gathered to offer condolences, they heard each other out. There was no question of agreement, of similarity in views—the need was to speak, to hear oneself speak, to find an outlet. Blue Star was the string that threaded the Sikhs together, for once. What gagged them from within—that which needed to be aired—was Blue Star's universal outcome: a wounded pride.

And its diverse dimensions.

For Preet, it was the deliberate desecration of the Golden Temple on the martyrdom day of Guru Arjan Dev, the guru who compiled the Holy Book, who built the temple. The faithful—men, women, children—denied food and water in captivity and, as the military action rolled, allowed to die. Heavy battle tanks crunching the marble parikrama, tearing down each tile inscribed over the years with the name of its devout donor. The Akal Takht reeling in shockwaves of high-impact shelling.

Cigarette-puffing, beer-imbibing army jawans in control of the shrine.

To Baksh's mind though, the defilement had started much earlier. When the administration and police had looked on as arms were smuggled into the holy place. When news had filtered through of the fortification of the Golden Temple, of holes dug into marble walls for placing guns, of sandbags in the windows of the Takht, visible to any pilgrim. When Bhindranwale first converted the Akal Takht into his head office-cum-sleeping quarters.

A shrine whose foundation was laid by a Muslim, Mian Mir, with doors on four sides to welcome all people, had become the sanctuary of a hate-filled terrorist. And ordinary Sikhs, regular people like him, had watched it all happen. Minding their own business, discussing *extremists* over shopping for groceries, pursing their lips while reading the newspaper, even as a madman and a madwoman took their personal rivalry to a public stage. In a strange twist of fate, Baksh had been tainted as the 'militant lawyer': the one to turn to if you were a militant! The fine distinction between *being* a militant and *accused of being* one was lost in the newly black-and-white atmosphere of Punjab.

Once, in a sterling show of Gandhian non-violence, average Sikhs had faced British lathis and jails and given their lives trying to free their gurudwaras from corrupt mahants. Sixty years down the line, in independent India, they were enervated enough to sit and watch those same gurudwaras being corrupted all over again.

 Hit lists, and the middle-class longing for comfort and security, had proved stronger than the white man's blows. Or, maybe the new-age Sikh was a malleable breed, bending in the direction of the wind.

After Operation Blue Star, the entire state sat around, waiting for *something* to happen. Frequent curfews, prolonged summer vacations at educational institutions, shops downing their shutters early, Raja Talkies discontinuing the popular night show—all of it made folks at Ferozepur fidgety.

❦

With the state in a limbo, educational institutions were temporarily closed and Neymat returned home from medical college. Noor, meanwhile, having taken her seventh standard examination, had no worries, not even exam results. Anant, taking short, tottering steps as he started to walk, was the source of joyous relief in an otherwise anxious period. He had arrived a year earlier—his conception had taken both Preet and Baksh by surprise. After two girls, Preet had given up hopes of a son, and was still in shock over a miscarriage when Anant stirred in her womb.

Neymat, preparing for her term exams, postponed courtesy Blue Star, sat at the study desk, reclined on the bed, hunched over the dining table, lay on the living room carpet, and gazed for hours—at a human skull.

Preet had been aghast at the sight of the bony shell as Neymat had casually plucked it from her travelling bag and plonked it down amongst her belongings. 'Rabba!' She had clutched her mouth. 'What's this?'

She wasn't convinced when Neymat told her that it was an essential element of her study-kit as she prepared for her anatomy exam. 'This mountain-heavy book,' she said, pointing to *Gray's Anatomy*, 'doesn't this have diagrams and pictures you can use instead?'

Neymat, suppressing a laugh, had pointed out, 'Not the same as the real thing. And Mama, if these holidays continue, I might have to get other body parts.'

At that, Preet drew in a sharp breath.

'The cranium is not the only part of the human anatomy, you know.' Neymat pulled herself up to her full height, barely five feet, and grinned, enjoying the effect of her prospective skeletal implements. 'In our hostel, for study purposes, every wing is assigned *one* skeleton each.'

In glee, Noor went all loose-limbed and slack-jawed, impersonating a skeleton hung from a ceiling.

Preet gave up.

When not being meditated upon, the skull sat amidst the clutter on the study desk, pens, coloured pencils, stapler popping out of its eye sockets. Noor, exhibiting a macabre delight at this casual association with a human skull, brought her curious friends along for sneak peeks. And rewarded the cranium in turn—for its tremendous show-off value—with a stem of flame-coloured gulmohar flowers, or a dried stalk of barley, the missing teeth in the bared denture serving as slender horizontal vases.

Housebound in a curfew-bound city, Noor wore a perennially bored expression. She spent her time fiddling with the radio, tuning in to BBC World Service and watching Doordarshan's coverage of Blue Star and its aftermath. Then she reported the differences in the two accounts to all. Of course, she also spent time arguing with her mother. 'Uff-oh!' she would counter Preet's retelling of some event, 'how can you be so wrong?'

Preet continued listening to her jingoistic cassettes, albeit with the volume toned down—Neymat *needed* to be able to concentrate if they were keen that she pass. Though Preet pointed out that the Hindi film songs Neymat played on her portable radio did not seem to hamper her studies. Noor sustained a drone alternating between the BBC and DD. And the unfamiliar backdrop of curfew-imposed silence magnified every sound.

Those days, most conversations with Preet ended with a refrain: the Golden Temple had always been a rallying point for Sikhs. Massa Ranghar, the ruler of Amritsar, had desecrated the temple by using it as a dancing hall. He was killed by Mahtab Singh. In 1761, the Afghan invader Ahmad Shah Abdali blew up the temple and filled the sacred tank with refuse. Deep Singh had laid down his life in revenge. So many years of a valiant and proud history, yet Indira never figured out the Sikhs. Khair, now she would. She had signed her death warrant.

One autumn morning, brooding Punjab was jolted out of its limbo. The prime minister's Sikh bodyguards had pumped bullets into her. Then proclaimed their deed, arms raised, as they attempted to surrender to the commandos in Indira Gandhi's garden. Dazed by the surrealism of the unfolding scene—crisp autumn morning, the prime minister falling on her way to a television interview, her saffron saree turning red, a panic-stricken personal assistant—the guards let off another barrage of bullets.

Much as Preet and other Sikhs had foretold, the hurt Sikh pride was avenged. By a Mazhabi Sikh, an untouchable who had converted to Sikhism, a type the dominant Jats and Khatris despised. This, though, was no time to broadcast that inconvenient little detail. It was a time for unity, since in less than six months, the creator, unrepentant throughout, had been dispatched to the same abode as her Frankenstein.

DAY 10, MORNING: ANANT

The tenth day dawned like an overexposed photograph, white heat blurring the contours of everything. Its incandescence lit up sandy grains from the pavement, they glittered like diamonds. Barefoot visitors to the Bhog ceremony hobbled down the concrete like they had corns on their feet.

A day that should have been in a hurry to get over itself for the respite of night, chugged along like a toy train. For it was a typical May day of the Punjab plain. May day. *Mayday Mayday* sounded Noor's heart, the distress call ricocheting mutely within.

Jinder Tayaji was the first to arrive. After bowing to the Granth Sahib, he enquired how Mama was holding up. Then he sat silently in the veranda, contemplating the fidgety thumbs of his interlaced hands.

Suddenly, he looked up. 'You know the secret to a happy life?'

Anant shrugged while Noor glanced at him from where she sat on the daybed combing Arjun's long hair. Neymat had entrusted her with the task—she was occupied with supervising the couple of labourers the contractor had sent. Wooden plank tables were laid out in a U-formation in the garden. The sheets covering them were grubby and Neymat had dispatched someone to fetch fresh ones. Meanwhile, she felt it was prudent to watch over the arrangements.

'Good health and poor memory... that's what a doctor once told me. As I approach eighty, I tend to agree. Nothing like the ability to forget... But your Papa,' Jinder Tayaji paused, 'remembered too much. And health...' He shrugged.

A scraping of feet, and the cook's assistant stood in the doorway with a steel jug. Two hundred people were expected for the prayer ceremony, at the end of which lunch would be served. A cook had been hired for the purpose. His troupe had staked claim over the courtyard below; the clanging of vessels and barked commands periodically floated up. 'Drinking water, Saabji,' the boy spoke in a monotone, holding the empty flask forward. 'Ustaad said to make it cold.'

Noor took the jug and went inside. They heard her wage battle with the stalactites and stalagmites in the old fridge's perennially frozen freezer section. Jinder Tayaji leaned forward and hurriedly asked, 'Have you heard of a man called Prince?' He darted a quick glance in the direction of the dining room from where the sound of ice cubes plonking into water came.

Anant looked unsure: was this the same militant whose case Papa had fought successfully in the eighties? Who, on gaining freedom, had fled to Pakistan? The same militant to whom the fat policeman had alluded when he had flagged Anant in the bazaar...?

Jinder Tayaji hunched forward. 'Two days before your papa died, he visited me. He was distracted. After a couple of whisky pegs, he started to talk. He couldn't be sure, he said, but he thought he had sighted Prince in the wholesale market a week back.' He furrowed his brow. 'Prince, you know?'

Anant's shrug was noncommittal. From the kitchen came the sound of Noor refilling the ice trays.

Jinder Tayaji shot a quick look in the direction of the kitchen. Softly, he said, 'This Prince had been a client of your Papa's many years back. At that time, he was a student of chemical engineering at the Agricultural University in Ludhiana. The police had picked him up in 1990, after his elder brother, implicated in a terrorist attack on a Hindi newspaper's office, was finished off in an encounter. Prince was detained under TADA and his mother had come begging Baksh to take the case—after all, they were old neighbours from the old haveli.' Jinder Tayaji's thumbs ran furious circles around each other. 'This boy, Prince, was finally released after Baksh petitioned the court for two years. But guess what? He ran away to the other side! Said, he was already tainted... now he would live up to the label they had anointed him with. From that day to this, Baksh said, he had never seen him. In the news, we heard of a bomb-maker who was such an expert at mixing chemicals that he could conjure up a bomb in a pantry! The police codenamed him Babbar Bomber, after the terror outfit, Babbar Khalsa, which claimed responsibility for those attacks on cinema halls in Delhi.'

As Jinder Tayaji paused, Anant remembered the brouhaha over the screening of a Hindi film that was deemed offensive for its title, a popular Sikh religious phrase.

'The same group,' Tayaji resumed, 'had assassinated chief minister Beant Singh in 1995, remember? Apparently they are still active underground... From the sketches that the police had released, Baksh felt Babbar Bomber could be Prince.'

The kitchen door swung shut and they could hear Noor's approaching footsteps.

His voice dropping perceptibly, Jinder Tayaji continued, 'Baksh thought he saw Prince that day... he could not be sure; after all, a wholesale market swarms with people! But Baksh said there was one thing that he could not forget about Prince: his shoulders sloped in a peculiar way which made his chest cave in such that when you sat with him it was as if he was huddling with a close friend.'

Noor walked out to the balcony with the condensation-coated jug. The cook's assistant sprang down the steps gratefully.

Jinder Tayaji hissed, 'Baksh saw this man huddled over the counter of an electrical goods shop. By the time he walked up, Prince was gone. So was the shopkeeper.'

A quick pitter-patter sounded and from behind the door Arjun peeped and beckoned to Noor. Pointing to his topknot, he said, 'The thread has come loose... you need to tighten it.' Noor harrumphed and the two retreated indoors.

Jinder Tayaji probed his beard. 'You see, your papa blamed himself for having secured Prince's acquittal. And the insinuations of some of the lawyers—that he was a militant sympathizer—did not help. I dismissed his suspicion saying he was probably mistaken. But he was in a black mood. He retorted, "What would you know, you ineffectual candle-lighter!"'

Jinder Tayaji headed the Committee for Hussainiwala Indo–Pak Peace Initiative. It organized initiatives like candlelight vigil at the Indo–Pak joint check-post every Independence Day. Everyone had been dismissive at first, but people had turned up in large numbers: folk singers who sang love ballads and broke into Bhangra while a drunk dholi madly beat the drum. It was now a regular event, one that had even been captured by a TV crew filming Independence Day celebrations.

Jinder Tayaji shook his head, setting his pennant aflutter. 'And then I said something I never should have.' He puckered his mouth. 'I told him since he knew the right way to do things, he would also know how to rein in the monster he had helped create.'

The next instant Noor reappeared. With a slight smile, she approached the daybed. 'What all have I missed?' She did not notice Anant look guiltily away while Jinder Tayaji started to examine his hands intently. She settled down, her knees drawn up, arms strung loosely around them, and turned to her father's elder brother.

'Tell us more, Tayaji,' she said. 'Of our Papa.'

Anant hitched up his shorts and proceeded indoors. He heard Jinder Tayaji start to tell Noor about the time when Papa and he would bicycle to Rakhri farm to see who could hack a bigger pile of fodder by plying the hand-wheel.

❧

Guests were beginning to troop in. Anant, sporting a neat crew cut and dressed in a recently tailored grey Pathani salwar suit, accepted condolences. Arjun and some neighbourhood boys busied themselves in a soft, slow version of 'Catch-em-catch' in the veranda as they wove around the uncles. The sheets could not be ruffled, they had been warned, and they were to *behave*. The uncles, meanwhile, were discussing the Iran–Pakistan–India gas pipeline—it was the headline news that morning in every newspaper...

The pipeline was to reach Lahore in a month's time, after which it was Ferozepur's turn. And again a suicide bomber had blown himself up—this time as Musharraf's motorcade passed by. Such boldness. The militants are getting desperate. They would do anything to stop this handshake across three countries. Why did the Mussalmans, the English-educated middle class, not speak up against the fundamentalists? After all, if they didn't, who would? Somebody had to denounce the suicide bombings, the glorification of the bearded Saudi... But the Americans also should know better. First, they went into Afghanistan and bombed the country out of shape looking for Osama. And now, have they found Osama? That is true, but it is still no excuse for Muslims to not condemn all this senseless violence. Why is their middle class so powerless? But tell me, where in the Muslim world is a middle class? Right from Saudi Arabia to Pakistan, it is as if the feudal society of the seventh century has catapulted straight into the twenty-first: sheikhs and educated elite at one end, the poor and militant at the other. Sighs. But they are bad for business, these mullahs conniving in their madrassas, pouring nonsense into young heads...

Anant sat crosslegged. His senses were on high alert, his mind staving off grief through a clinical classification of his observations. His training as a doctor was coming handy: to avoid being overwhelmed by the suffering of patients, medical students were tutored to first observe the symptoms. A clinical concentration on symptoms forced focus on the ailment and away from the grief of the ailing patient, helping a doctor to remain objective in his assessment.

Epidermal osmosis: The sweat filtering through faster than the breeze could drain it. Beads of perspiration sprouted on foreheads, ringed upper lips and chins, trickled down the eyes, trailed thighs, streaked the back. Cotton clothes, tinged by sweat, had acquired a deeper hue while synthetics shone in the bronze daylight. People periodically switched their crossed legs and tugged at their shirtfronts to air their clammy bodies.

Milk-white milieu: The living room and veranda floors swathed in new white, old off-white, sheets of Azad Tent House; visitors in cream-alabaster-ivory-coloured clothing, sporting solemn masks as they mimicked the family's sombre mood.

Musical momentum: The vigour of Gianiji's recitation surging with the influx of mourners.

Smell suffusion: Buttery aromas of fried greens and cottage cheese and tempered lentils wafting from the makeshift courtyard kitchen.

Anant glanced around the living room. That was another way to distract himself. The symptomatic classification over, he scrutinized the faces around.

Mehta Uncle was quaint in a large handkerchief tied scarf-like beneath his chin. As the pedestal fan rotated in his direction, the overhanging hanky flap took flight and Uncle looked like a granny about to levitate.

In the front row, right corner, sat Bull, their next-door neighbour. Bull was the English moniker derived from his Hindi surname—Bahl. Setting up house next to him had been a case of 'Aa bahl, mujhe maar', Mama was fond of quoting the proverb. A neighbour wholly lacking in neighbourly virtues. Even that morning, as he offered a ten-rupee note while paying obeisance to the Granth, he hunted for a five-rupee change from the scattered donations, then pocketed it. Even with God, his ledger was balanced to the last paise.

One half of the congregation was women. Queen sat in front, her eyes seemingly stuck on Noor who sat at the other end. Balwant Pua, with her spinster daughter Dimple, sat diametrically opposite Lovely. Dimple had probably decided that the Bhog could provide suitable hunting ground—the matrimonial stakes must be creeping higher with every tick-tock of the biological clock. Her ample self shrink-wrapped in high-waisted jeans, umbrellaed by a frilly top, she reminded him of a dog stuck in a clay oven. She had walked in, swinging her legs as if she were modelling down the runway—only, the jeans were way too tight and some women had gasped audibly. A surreptitious Chinese whisper had then started off in the women's section.

Anant rubbed a thumb against his palm and studied the momentary blanching. Several men in the gathering had been there ten days back, the day he had had to battle with them over his father's body... While some had chosen to stay away and a few sat sullen in the gathering, most seemed to have erased the episode from memory completely. Ten days back, Anant had also stumbled over a rickshawala's disclosure. Since then, he had reeled about, picking his way gingerly through what seemed like a minefield—only, the cue, indication, glimmer had all turned out dud. So would this new revelation by Jinder Tayaji, even if it tied in with what the fat policeman had told him. After all, Papa wasn't even sure... How could you be, if you had not seen a man for almost two decades! Anant swung his head angrily. Like David in *Kidnapped*, he had scaled uneven stairs in darkness, reached the point where the stairs fell away, peeped into the abyss below and, unlike David, taken the plunge. But the abyss had turned out to be a shallow ditch! He lay there now, feeling like a prized fool...

Antim Ardas, the final prayer, was approaching and Anant felt strangely relieved. From the rustle that lapped through the gathering—clearing of throats, smoothening of creases, shuffling of bottoms—he sensed eagerness: numb legs and growling stomachs were anticipating a walk down the corridor to the garden where lunch was laid out. They had mourned for ten days, the official period, and were now ringing in the end. Human existence was rather basic: the dead moved away; the living moved on.

BAKSH

From Barki Memorial Baksh's steps had turned right and brought him to the road that led to his—no, his erstwhile, he reminded himself—fields. Why had he not stopped thinking of those fields as his? After all, except for a couple of years when he was young and naïve, when he had apprenticed as a farmer, the fields had never been his. Bapuji had donated them to Balwant, who, in turn, had lost them to Bodh Singh. So why did it feel like the fields, the land, the farms were a part of him?

Perhaps, that proprietary relationship with land was the inheritance of every Punjabi who, finding himself in the crucible of the constantly shifting alluvium, clung to whatever piece he could claim as his own. And it was this land that brought out their true colours: Balwant could connive for it, Jinder abdicate it, Bitta innovate for it, Preet fight for it, and Vir... Vir had lived and died for it.

1988

The survival guide to being bad was to *always be bad enough*. Either Shammi had forgotten that mantra, or others were more skilled.

Baksh watched him nurse the glass in his hands as he tap-tapped his enormous ruby ring against it. 'Things are not good, Baksh,' he said, at last.

Had Shammi lost weight? His face wore a puckered look. But his girth was fashionably ample, in the manner of people from well-to-do—as defined by a Punjabi—households. He looked his usual prosperous-politician self, just distracted.

Shammi leaned forward. 'Fortification... once again,' he whispered. 'Inside the Golden Temple.' His shoulders twitched and he moved back. He resumed his survey of the glass before taking a long sip. Following that, he sucked his cheeks in, then blew out. 'Jasbir Singh Rode and other militants freed by the government have walked right back into Akal Takht. And just like Bhindranwale, they have started stockpiling weapons. So many factions there are now... Akalis. True Tigers. Sant's Fauj. Sometimes they exchange abuses, other times fisticuffs. Lately, they have started sniping at one another. And all within the gurudwara premises...'

The evening air was nippy, a faint mist hovered around them as they conversed. The absence of traffic due to curfew added to the ominous hush all around. Shammi was a VIP, and therefore had the privilege of travelling around. Chameleon-like, he had survived the turmoil of Operation Blue Star and its aftermath and got himself elected in the brief period when Longowal had won the state election. However, Longowal had been assassinated, the government dismissed, and Shammi had decided to lie low.

His unexpected visit had taken Baksh by surprise though—not once during the difficult days of militancy had the powerful nephew called on Baksh or Jinder. 'Our land specializes in turncoats,' Jinder often snorted. And Jinnah was to be blamed for starting the trend; after all, pork-eating whisky-swigging Saville Row-suited Jinnah had morphed into the sherwani-clad Qaid-e-Azam, Father of the Islamic nation of Pakistan!

Shammi sighed a long sigh and looked up. 'But you are doing good work, hain Baksh? Not too many lawyers taking up cases of militants. And we all know how much of a terrorist these innocent boys are... Picked up by the police from their homes, tortured to sign confessions, and if nobody comes forth to bail them, executed in staged encounters. After all, the police needs to show it is succeeding against the militants...'

The doublespeak irritated Baksh. 'Don't you think,' he said, sliding forward in his faux-leather chair, his voice low, 'the leaders of this state are responsible for the current situation?'

Shammi screwed up his mouth, then started to wag his head. Finally, stroking his beard, he said, 'We had not meant for it to go this way.'

Baksh sipped his whisky and looked away. Of what use was logic ever when debating with a politician?

'At least, I had not,' Shammi added softly. 'But be careful, Baksh... Times are such, you don't know whom to trust...'

Shammi was certainly speaking a different language. What was eating him? Baksh had heard rumours of Shammi getting sidelined in Akali politics. It was common knowledge that a Khatri was seen as a lesser Sikh compared to his Jat brethren who largely made up the Akali party. *Bhapa*—that was how the virulent Jat Bhindranwale had categorized Khatris like Shammi, conveniently forgetting that the ten gurus had come from that same caste!

'Look.' Abruptly, Shammi thrust his hand forward. 'Look at my ring, Baksh.'

Baksh saw the ruby rock in the thick gold casing and raised his brows. What was there to look at? Shammi had worn that ring since he was first elected MLA. It was a precious gem, a symbol of riches.

'Its lustre has dimmed.' Shammi withdrew his hand. 'It has.' He nodded to himself. Looking into Baksh's eyes, he asked, 'Know what that means?'

Baksh shook his head.

'Some loss coming my way. Big loss.'

'Oh come on, Shammi! You are not ill or anything?'

For a while, Shammi stayed silent. Then he took a quick swig, emptied the whisky glass entirely, and pulled himself up.

'It has been a while, hain, since we sat and talked?' He smiled wistfully at Baksh. Turning to go, he wobbled, then stretched his left arm backwards, the hand lifted in parting. Without looking back, he said, 'Ho chukeen Ghalib balaayen sab tamam...' and tottered towards the door.

Baksh watched his retreating form. He remembered the second line of the couplet: 'Ek marge-nagahani aur hai.'

All calamities, Ghalib, have had their say, now one remains—that of death's sudden sway.

❧

The station house officer said that there was no chance of survival. The bullets, six of them, had likely gone through the sternum, rupturing left lung and heart. The gun's mouth had been placed on the left shoulder blade, the firing had been brisk. It was all over in a matter of minutes: the startled driver jerking to a halt, the near-empty bus emptying of its few stunned passengers, the assassin vanishing into the darkness with his lone accomplice, Vir Singh breathing his last.

Baksh and Preet had not known, but Vir had been travelling to Ferozepur. Unannounced, as always. And alone. His associate had taken leave at Zira, the last stop before the bus reached the city, twenty kilometres away. When exactly the assassin, with his accomplice, had boarded the bus was unclear. He had obviously stayed undetected, possibly camouflaged in his voluminous loi, not unusual for the time of the year.

Hardly had the bus turned onto the highway from Zira, when the old foe struck. Vir, the eternally vigilant one, had succumbed to the muggy night air of a shuttered bus—the panes frosted over, a dim bulb glimmering in the front—and destination some minutes away, and fallen asleep. The enemy stalked up to Vir, from beneath his woollen blanket-shawl he withdrew his gun, and…

The shocked driver sent a tremulous conductor to the nearest police station. It was fortunate that the SHO was on duty, that he was personally acquainted with Bhallasaab, the criminal lawyer from District Court, Ferozepur, and that he recognized Vir as the avenging jail-going brother-in-law. With instructions to a couple of his men to remain at the murder scene and ensure no intrusion, the SHO had hurried to inform Bhallasaab and wife.

Preet and Baksh heard the SHO out. The bell had rung so late in the night that Preet was filled with a vague foreboding. And Baksh, unlike regular days, had abstained from his evening tipple. Even before the SHO had reached the end of his narrative, Baksh saw his wife fade away. Legend has it that when Shah Jahan surfaced after a night of mourning the death of his beloved Mumtaz, his hair had turned white. That would have been dramatic, but what was unfolding in front of his eyes was no less so. Preet's face had shrunk, her complexion had turned shades darker, her generous mouth recomposed into a grim line. Instantaneous ageing. And irreversible.

When the SHO had finished recounting, he sat there, clasped hands cradling a plump belly, his gaze fixed on the centre table.

In a matter-of-fact voice, Preet offered: 'A lion should never underestimate an enemy, even when the enemy is a goat.'

'Unemotional' was not a quality Baksh associated with his wife. With that one deadpan delivery he knew: something had changed forever.

The SHO massaged his intertwined hands, each palm alternately with a thumb, and said it would be a *difficult case*. No witnesses would come forth. Even the conductor and driver were unlikely to have taken a legally acceptable good look at the assassin or his accomplice. It was cold, most passengers were huddled beneath their warm clothing, late at night, and the bus was badly lit. And even if they could identify the murderer, would they be willing, considering the great risk involved?

As Baksh sat pondering, Preet spoke quietly. 'There was one witness,' she said. 'One companion with Vir at the time of the shooting. That witness would have no difficulty in identifying the murderer. Nor would there be any fear of taking a stand in the witness box.'

'Hain, Pahbi?' The SHO's bewildered gaze travelled from Baksh to Preet and back.

Baksh knew where Preet was heading. He watched her as she sat erect in the nylon rope chair, her eyes looking at the SHO, yet afar. 'I was my brother's companion,' she said. 'I will be the witness whose testimony will nail the killer.'

Preet's plan was typical of her: bold, uncomplicated, teetering on the razor's edge between courage and foolhardiness.

Preet as Vir's travelling companion for the journey would be indisputable. None of the bus passengers, or even the driver and conductor, could testify with absolute certainty against her presence in the bus. A bus ticket, proof of travel, was easily obtained. A police officer in charge of a case was a powerful entity, especially with the conductor keen to avoid any possible implication.

To the case, she gave her all. It became the all-consuming motive of her life. She was still a mother and a wife, but overriding it all was the sister who had lost a brother.

A brittle sheath wrapped around her iron core as she snapped at the children, abruptly switched off the TV or music system, cooked the usual good meals, but ate the previous day's leftovers, cried silently and prayed infrequently.

The children watched in alarm at first, then got used to their mother's new avatar. The disruption in their lives was minor: meals were still on time, clothes were laundered and ironed, they could sleep their undisturbed sleep and wake up to the alarm clock in order to study.

They tried, though, to get through to their mother, Neymat especially. But what was to be done when someone decided to stay put in the deepest dungeon within a walled fortress surrounded by a moat, the drawbridge pulled up permanently?

❧

In 1990, in the Disturbed Area of Ferozepur District, local leader, ex-minister and popular Akali politician, Shaminder Singh, was found slumped on the steering wheel of his Maruti

1000. A bullet had gone through his right temple. The Punjab Police was trying to determine the cause of the killing and the one responsible for it.

There were differing takes on the murder.

One: Shammi had been travelling with a militant on the run. In an encounter, the army had, as part of its mopping-up operation of remaining militants, killed the fugitive. Shammi, unfortunately, had got caught in the firing line, one more casualty in the endgame as the army attempted to close in on the militants.

Two: True Tigers, who had escaped from the Golden Temple on the eve of Operation Black Thunder in 1988, were hunting down the traitors of the community. Shammi's was yet another name on the hit list.

Shammi's last visit—two years back—and his atypical conversation troubled Baksh. He could not put the niggling thought out of his mind: Shammi had foretold his own death. Mata's clairvoyant streak had skipped a generation and surfaced, again at random, in her grandson.

Baksh turned the things Shammi had said over and over in his mind, whatever he could recall of it. Was there anything *else* Shammi had prognosticated? Baksh's mind regurgitated their last conversation repeatedly, until a stray thought found its way up through the whirlpool: 'Be careful, Baksh, in such times you don't know whom to trust…'

DAY 10, EVENING: ANANT

'Dr Bhalla's Clinic,' Anant said, sketching a rectangular nameplate in the air. 'How does that sound for a ten-bed clinic on the ground floor?'

It had been a popular suggestion from relatives and friends at the Bhog. In fact, a two-in-one suggestion: 'Mrs Bhalla, get him married. Son, daughter-in-law and children—with Waheguru's mercy, they will arrive soon—living with you on the first floor, and Anant's practice on the ground floor.'

'The aunties have your life all figured out, Ant. Watch them line up their oh-so-eligible daughters next,' Noor half-snorted. 'Boy, are you going to be happy!'

'No. I am going to be responsible. Have you forgotten? It's the popular demand.' Anant crunched his knuckles. 'What about you? How long will the client in Rome wait?'

'He won't.' Noor shrugged. 'Another consultant would be on the job already. In the corporate world, at least, one body is easily substituted by another.'

Noor took her spectacles off and rubbed her eyes. Then she proceeded to clean the glasses with the edge of her kameez. 'Ant, what if Papa had—'

'Stop! Go open your laptop. Don't you have any assignment to work on, data to play with? Your mind is not used to being idle… no wonder it's running away with you!' He began to crack his knuckles again.

Noor, taken aback by Anant's vehemence, bit her lip. Pasha, sprawled on the brick floor by their feet, darted his tongue out at a fly whizzing by.

The guests had departed, well-fed; the cook and his minions had been paid, and after lashing their pots and pans, they feasted on food they had cooked and left; the contractor's men had pulled down the tent, gathered the bamboo poles, stacked the chairs and tables, hoisted them all onto a truck, then hunkered down in the garden for the luncheon. Anant, of course, had had no appetite. The well-attended gathering made him want to be alone… But Noor, inquisitive, grieving Noor… how was he to explain to her?

'Stop going down this path, Noor… *if* he had reached the doctor… *if* he had not gone for a walk… *if* he had been more careful of his health… there's no closure to *if.* You go down that track and, ultimately, you will be spinning fur out of a strand of hair.'

Pasha sat up on his hind legs, facing them, his tongue lolling in the heat, expelling blasts of hot breath. 'Uff Pasha!' Anant brushed his face away. Reluctantly, the dog shifted sideways.

Noor saw the nervous twitch in her brother's left eye, the exhaustion on his face, the way his head hung. Softly, she said, 'You are not telling me something.'

For a long while Anant sat quiet. Pasha breathed noisily. Noor waited. Then he divulged what had been on his mind since the day the fat policeman, who had served on Vir Mamu's case, had dropped in after Papa's cremation. The police, he said, had been keeping an eye on Papa. They had been on alert ever since noticing militant activity in the border region. The Iran–Pakistan–India gas pipeline, as scheduled, was to reach Ferozepur from Lahore via Qasur within the next few months. And terrorists were looking for an opportunity to cause a major disruption, anything that would create an atmosphere of mistrust, spread panic amongst the people, delay the pipeline if not halt it altogether.

One particular militant who had been spotted was an ex-client of Papa's. Papa had defended his case, got him acquitted, after which the militant had lost no time in crossing over. What was he doing in the region again and why? Perhaps Papa knew. After all, Harbaksh Singh Bhalla and his family was a potent bunch, the policeman had insinuated. His elder brother, Gajinder Singh, headed some nonsense committee for Indo–Pak peace that organized song and dance at the border every now and then.

'But-but,' Noor protested, but Anant steamrolled through.

Such festivity and gaiety were in bad taste, the police officer had gone on, it was the Line of Control, and on the opposite side was the army that had fought four wars with India! Honestly, these woolly-headed people had no sense of proportion! And then the police had come across a new development: Harbaksh Singh Bhalla had recently applied for a visa to Pakistan. What business was taking the lawyer to Pakistan, hunh? As it is, he had a cousin who journeyed to Pakistan like it was his in-laws' house! Of course, Mr S.S. Bitta was a big-time businessman, with high-level connections, and the police would leave him alone... But there were enough reasons to put Bhallasaab under surveillance.

When Anant finished, Noor's jaw hung as loose as Pasha's. Finally, in a daze, she whispered, 'This is so cray-zee!'

'Kapoor's visit, you remember?' Anant paused, tracing the corners of his mouth with an index finger and thumb. 'He was probably looking for some evidence that would link Papa with this militant.'

'What's *wrong* with them? Papa was not a militant. He was not a militant sympathizer!' Noor had risen, her arms were clenched against her sides, anger and helplessness battling across her visage. 'He could see the good in people that others couldn't. How dare they try to sully his name, how dare they?' Hot tears burst onto Noor's cheeks.

Pasha, perplexed at the sudden activity from Noor, had risen in sympathy. Now, he stood between brother and sister, swinging his face dolefully from one to the other.

Anant gave a limp shrug. 'Perhaps Kapoor was on to something... Remember, he died mysteriously.'

'Oh! Pshaw! Bull!' Noor stamped a foot. 'Even if this Kapoor was killed because he was on to unravelling some conspiracy, it still does *not* prove that Papa was involved with any of it.'

Anant stood up now, hitching his shorts with his thumbs, and looked Noor in the eye. 'I never said he was. The police and intelligence are hounds... they will follow any scent. They are doing what comes to them naturally. Just as Papa did.' Then he tilted his head up. 'That was our father, Noor. He lived his life on his terms. Not the happiest, not the luckiest, not the best life, perhaps. But certainly, lived his way.'

In the distance, the horizon had bleached into greyness. Soon night would be drawing out its star-spangled quilt. The stars would twinkle in the company of one another and perhaps the moon would come out, luminous or crescent or some shape in between, and commence its lonely sojourn through the night sky. In his convictions, Papa had walked alone. He had hoped for understanding from his loved ones and, occasionally, he had got it...

Anant liked to believe that for each person in this world, there was a verse that summed them up entirely, that captured their essence in a few short lines. Glancing upwards, he began to hum softly: 'Jodi tor daak shune keu na ashe tabe ekla chalo re.'

It was as if the baul had wandered from the paddy fields of Bengal into the tall mustard fields of Punjab and, somewhere on the way, misplaced his accent, but his heart was still in his song and he sang now with all the passion of a mystic minstrel, his face lifted to the sky, the voice rising in effortless grace, seeking communion with what lay beyond.

> If they answer not to thy call walk alone,
> If they are afraid and cower mutely facing the wall,
> O thou of evil luck,
> Open thy mind and speak out alone.
>
> If they turn away, and desert you when crossing
>   the wilderness,
> O thou of evil luck,
> Trample the thorns under thy tread,
> And along the blood-lined track travel alone.
>
> If they do not hold up the light when the night is
>   troubled with storm,

O thou of evil luck,
With the thunder flame of pain ignite thy own heart
And let it burn alone.

Anant put an arm around his sister and, wagging his head, said, 'One hell of a dogged guy he was, Noor, our father… one hell of a dogged guy!'

BAKSH

THE LAST WALK

Yes, Baksh nodded to himself, Shammi had indeed inherited Mata's clairvoyant streak. Baksh knew it for a certainty when Shammi's last prediction—you don't know whom to trust—came true. And once again, the porous border of Ferozepur let Baksh down.

Glocal: It was a word Baksh had learnt from Noor. It was a fusion of global and local, she explained; for instance, global brands, local marketing; or global companies, local operations. In a globalizing world, borders disappeared, she said, and her lifestyle illustrated that: while based in India, Noor spent more time in airplanes and foreign countries than in her home country.

Baksh found the notion of glocal, with its wondrous collapse of borders, intriguing. Would it mean that in a future world, the porous border of Ferozepur would crumble upon itself, yielding to an earlier expanse? Would Punjab, the land of fault lines, smoothen over its cracks and throw up a single surface? History did not support such a hypothesis and, while Baksh had listened to Noor's consultant's spiel, he had wondered when the smug theory would fall apart. It did. On an autumn morning, in the world's premier exponent of glocal, the USA. And in its wake, the fissures reappeared and new borders sprang up. And while Noor continued to traipse over the globe, albeit with dampened enthusiasm for glocal, Anant discovered that the land he came from—with its baggage of fault lines and associated appurtenances—would trip him over the new borders of the US he aimed for.

2004

Noor and Anant sat at the dining table while Baksh enjoyed his whisky in the balcony. Through the open French windows their boisterous conversation poured forth.

'Do you know that our neighbour Bull has got a marble *bathtub* installed in his newly renovated bathroom?' Anant snorted.

'But this place gets water for one hour in a day!'

'So why should that be an impediment? You should know: Bull has just illustrated that while he is a citizen of a third-world country, his aspirations are first world.' He shook his head. 'Honestly, I think this economic boom story of India is highly overrated.'

'No, India is where the action is. And the US, in fact, is looking to build its brick business.'

'Brick?'

'B-R-I-C,' Noor supplied. 'Brazil, Russia, India, China... the growth story of this century. That's where the Americans are headed, my dear brother. That is why I say you should reconsider going to the US. By the time you finish your post-graduation from a US university, India would be offering better opportunities. And you should be here, to cash in.'

'Hunh!' Anant snorted. 'Really Noor, you consultants do believe in glossing over ground realities. Just open your ears. What do you hear? The thundering of bloody generators... each house has one, if not two... and there are probably twenty going on right now, spewing their smoke and noise into our eyes and ears. And since morning, we have had no supply of fresh water! The Mall Road, Ferozepur's most prestigious street, is dotted with garbage dumps because the jamadars don't believe it's their duty to do the work for which they get paid. The result: flies and mosquitoes and flu!'

'Correct. Yet,' Noor smiled cheekily, 'India is a land of contradictions, and everything else is correct too! Of course, infrastructure is bad, but there is always a phase lag between economic growth and development. Look at the opportunities that are coming up. I meet young boys and girls who come from villages to do data-entry work at BPOs for which they earn 5,000 rupees a month. Ten years back, the girls would have been married off young and the boys would have choked on fumes in a chemical factory. To get into my office, a fancy concrete and glass high-rise which could have come straight out of Shanghai—New York cannot compete any more on glossy high-rises—I have to navigate my way across a water buffalo and high-jump over several ditches.'

Anant was nodding furiously. 'Then why don't you open your eyes? The fact is you belong to a privileged elite in India right now, those who earn a dollar salary while living in India. Let's look at the present. India is a third-world country. Perhaps, in the future, it'll become first world. But I am interested in the present, and in the present, the finest medical colleges are in the US. And a doctor in the US doesn't have to worry about running water in the bathroom at the end of a long workday!'

Noor shrugged. 'The US is also getting racist...'

'It still continues to be the world's cultural melting pot.'

'Really?' Noor asked. 'Then how is it that every time I land at a US airport, the security personnel still instruct me to step aside, courtesy racial profiling because of my name, and ask: "Are you Islam?" Noor's neck recoiled in mock horror. '*Am I Islam?* Heck no, I am Muhammad, and I transported myself straight from seventh-century Arabia to twenty-first century America... so pardon my poor Bedouin self which just dismounted from my camel at your doors.' Noor shrugged. 'Three years after 9/11, you would expect them to have sorted out Islam, the religion, from Muslims, the followers!'

Et tu, Brute?

If Preet had shared her children's Shakespearean leanings, that was what she would have said. For Anant, her son, heir to her Jat Sikh legacy, had, despite sincere attempts not to, pulled a Brutus on her Caesar.

One weekend, coming home from college—his final year—Anant had descended from his scooter, ascended the steps to their first-floor residence, and appeared: a marble-faced, lawn-mowed apparition. Bereft of a beard and turban, his face looked shrunken in relation to the rest of his six-feet plus gym-built body.

Preet's reflex was a soundless shriek.

Six months earlier, Anant had applied for a tourist visa to the US. The general wisdom was that it was best to visit the US once, get a 'Return' stamped on the passport, thus convincing the sceptical Americans that one had no desire to immigrate permanently. In return, he had got a 'Reject'. No explanation was given but it was generally understood that the embassy staff, clueless about the difference between a Sikh turban and the one sported by Bin Laden's gang, had decided that safety lay in disallowing any bearded-turbaned aspirants into their nation.

Anant, thereafter, figuring his loyalty was more to his aspirations than to the religion he was born into, had decided to discard the offending accoutrements of beard and turban.

Baksh was surprised by his response to his son's act. Was he a hypocrite? In the same class as 'pseudo-secularists'—the epithet flung at people like him, who were perceived not Sikh/Hindu enough by their co-religionists who accused them of untoward sympathy for other religions. Or at those like Jinder, who went to the Hussainiwala border every Independence Day and held a candlelight vigil. Even when the party from the other side did a no-show. Or, when post Operation Blue Star, the head of the committee for gurudwaras in Pakistan arrived for the vigil, lit his candle, then started berating Hindu India's mistreatment of Sikhs, getting so carried away that he snuffed his candle in a huff and was forcibly carried away.

Baksh sighed. Why had Anant's haircut hurt thus?

After all, he was the same son—just turbanless, beardless. Sure, he looked different, but that was like an old man dyeing his hair—they would get used to it. To the sight. Besides, Anant had his heart set on the US, on the Johns Hopkins School of Medicine. At a time when the rest of the world seemed to be eyeing India again, shouldn't Anant reconsider? But then, if the young did not spread their wings and soar, who would? And Anant was right: with a bearded and turbaned visage, would the Americans welcome him or assign him straight to Guantanamo?

Well, the reality of today's world was that the US and the beard were incompatible. If you were a Sikh whose religion ordained unshorn hair, well then, you got grouped with the bad guys. Even Noor had threatened—jokingly, he hoped—to change her name, sick as she was of being pulled up at airports.

So, what *was* his problem? Exactly where did his angst lie?

His mind supplied the answer promptly, only he kept pushing it away: even for a liberal like him, shorn hair equated loss of Sikhi.

What would Anant's identity be? Human being, the voice inside prompted. Was that enough? he asked. Didn't something need to tie us down? Our culture, our faith, our language—were they not our foundations? Bereft of them, how would we soar?

But you trim your beard, the voice in him replied, even when Bapuji did not. Anant had only gone a step further. Each generation made its changes, found its own equilibrium.

Perhaps, *he* was the one out of sync: when he was advocating communal harmony, Hindus and Sikhs were at each others' throats; now that entire Ferozepur, indeed Punjab, was celebrating the impending arrival of the Iran–Pakistan–India gas pipeline, he felt burdened, as if a shadow hung over him. What *was* it? Of course, it would be wonderful to open the Hussainiwala border again—perhaps, Bitta, Jinder and he could take a tonga once again down the sixty-kilometre road from Ferozepur to Lahore? Ever since the prime minister had made public his dream of 'breakfast in Amritsar, lunch in Lahore, dinner in Kabul', Bitta had gone gallivanting over the terrain, crossing the Indus at Attock, rubbing shoulders with Pathans in Sarafa Bazaar, climbing the Bab-e-Khyber to gaze at Afghanistan, ferreting opportunities for trade and commerce. A week back, en route to Pakistan, he had stopped overnight and Baksh and he had discussed the visit and made future plans. 'This Indo–Pak handshake is throwing up many opportunities,' Bitta had said, pumping his hands with relish.

Baksh had lifted his shoulders in a hopeful shrug, then added mischievously, 'What about China? They say China is hot!'

'Aaho,' Bitta had assented, 'China is hot.' As if every Chinaman was running, feet scalding, hair ablaze, pants on fire, his tea boiling. *China is hot! China is hot!* Suddenly China and the Chinese were everywhere: the Diwali firecrackers came from Hangzhou, Guangzhou, or some xyz-zhou, and Suzie Wongs, with their straight-as-a-knife-blade hair, razor-thin eyes and hilly cheekbones, had replaced the milky, *mast* model-like Marias of mother Russia in the prostitution ring. Those slit-like eyes—how could you trust someone if you couldn't look into their eyes? No, the Chinese were not to be trusted, Bitta was adamant, not after what they did to Nehru. Any trade route opened to them would need to be lined with soldiers and cannons!

From his two earlier trips, Bitta had returned with a night's worth of tittle-tattle and a suitcase filled with the booty he had accumulated from his foray: the latest DVD of Bin Laden, picked up from Peshawar's smugglers' bazaar; bags of pistachio, niyoza and green tea over which they watched the scraggly bearded Saudi deliver his omens. And in guttural Pashtun, he had narrated his tall tales of enterprise.

Enterprise was Bitta's middle name, as Baksh had rightly bestowed upon him, and he had spent a lifetime spotting opportunity where others saw wilderness, dacoity, terror, trouble, fever. In the process, Bitta had become a crorepati, long before *Kaun Banega Crorepati* promised to make millionaires out of regular folks. As his business empire grew hydra-headed, Bitta shifted the base of his operations from Ferozepur to Chandigarh to Delhi, leaving factotums behind, whom he frequently tested by sudden drop-ins.

And yet… this unease of Baksh's refused to go away.

Just eight years ago Pakistan had once again wrangled with India. This time, over a barren mountain strip—Kargil—that had no productive use for either country. And now, there was jubilation and much bonhomie because suddenly India was an economic tiger, its economy was surging, and all Pakistan needed to do was clutch at India's coattails and enjoy the ride! What about ISI—the dreaded Inter Services Intelligence—which had reared itself over the years solely on hatred of India? What about the bombs that still went off in the bazaars of Punjab? They were sporadic, yes, but they were increasing in frequency. And the mention of outfits such as Babbar Khalsa and Khalistan Commando Force was beginning to pop up in print again. Even as it was rumoured that Bhindranwale's nephew Rode and other militants were hiding in Pakistan, where they were forging alliances with Islamic Jehadis…

THEN, NOW

Another power cut.

The rooftop terrace seemed the best option to escape the heat. There was no breeze, but it was not stuffy either. Tired from the stress and swelter of the day, the entire family had quickly fallen asleep on stretched-out folding cots.

It started suddenly: tiny grains settling on them—pinpricks on exposed skin—alighting on the bedsheets. Swirls of sandy wind began to dance around the terrace.

'*Haneri!*' Mama was the first one to yell. 'Quick! Let's go down. It looks like a nasty dust storm.'

As she started to jolt Anant and the sleeping Arjun, Neymat began to pull up the bedspreads and bundle them. Noor got busy with folding up the vacated beds. Arjun stood around, bewildered, covering his eyes, squinting at the sudden greyness eddying around them. While Anant stacked the beds in the vacant storeroom, Neymat guided Arjun down the stairs. Others trooped back into the house, trailing sheets, shielding their eyes, stealing glances at the raging storm.

On the first floor, Mama was busy snapping the windows shut and securing the netting doors. It would be stifling, but already a thin grainy layer had settled on floor and furniture.

People staggered into various rooms and fell asleep on available beds: Mama and Neymat in Mama's room, Anant and Arjun in the girls' bedroom, Noor and Pasha in Papa's room.

The house went to sleep again. Only Noor could not. She lay awake—her eyes, once acquainted with the dark, picked out familiar shapes in the room. Her father's wooden almirah, the table piled high with papers and books—she had spent hours poring over these after Anant's disclosure about Kapoor's rummaging, the framed picture of the Golden Temple above the door, the reading lamp hooked onto the wall...

Noor switched it on. The light was bright yellow and she swivelled it down. Sliding forward on the bed, she reached towards the table and picked up a stray book.

The Bhagvad Gita: A Precis. By O.P. Sharma.

Noor flipped through the paperback, sighted her father's signature, riffled through the pages. Then she jigged back on the bed, reclined against the wall, and randomly opened the book.

Arjun, distraught over the death of his son, Abhimanyu, was instructed by Lord Krishna to fetch a pitcher of water from a river flowing nearby. When he returned, Lord Krishna made another request to Arjun: Return to the river and fetch me the same water in the pitcher as you did on the previous trip.

Arjun protested: But the river flows on, Lord—how can it be the same water?

As he looked on, perplexed, Lord Krishna's answer was a smile. Then, understanding dawned on Arjun. Time was like the river: what moved on could not be retrieved.

So, in life. The only thing that did not cease was motion, forward motion.

And into Noor's mind floated a line from a long-forgotten poem: 'For men may come, and men may go, but I go on forever.'

＊

Life had weighed him down. He could feel the weight on his heart and his limbs. The struggle to do what he believed to be right, to summon the strength required to do it, to fight his failings and succumb to them, to lose often and win seldom—it had worn him out.

The other day in the market, when he was buying vegetables, he thought he caught sight of someone he had not seen for a long time... Was it *him*? If so, what was he doing in Ferozepur? Pakistan had failed in its attempt to midwife the nation of Khalistan. But Punjab Police still had a prize on Prince's head—what had brought him to the area again?

In an attempt to dislodge the questions, Baksh shook his head. He just wished to be left alone.

He *was* alone.

Standing in a field of golden wheat. A dark night sky. The cool air. His hands clammy. His forehead wet.

As he moved a hand to wipe it, he realized he was perspiring. Profusely. His shirt was sticking at the front and the back and he could feel the sweat trail down his legs.

But his hand, his left hand—it had not risen beyond waist level.

Then he remembered. He had left home in search of a doctor. Glancing down, he saw the time: two hours later, he was standing in his fields. His ex-fields. Bodh Singh's sons' fields.

Strange, he could not recall walking that entire stretch. His mind had carried him backwards, his feet forward. He looked down—his toes were wet, the sandals moist from brushing against dewy stalks. How long had he been standing there?

As he looked around, he became aware of a pair of eyes, then a shrouded face, crouching in the tall grass at the edge of the field. The eyes did not blink—they seemed to be waiting. As Baksh watched the face, hazy in the dark, the area barely lit by a lone bulb strung some distance away, he felt a decade and a half collapse in front of his eyes. It was the man's chest, the way it caved forward, that had given him away. Baksh had not forgotten the young boy he had met in detention—not after the manner in which he had repaid him. Prince was a grown man now, and he sat very still, like a predator before attacking.

Once before, Baksh had been turned away from these fields. At that time, it was not in his hands and he had been forced to accept it. But now, it was his decision to make. He would not turn his back on his fields this time. No, he would stand his ground. As Baksh stood there, some part of him registered the pain surging through his body. He would not flee his land, so he pushed the pain back into the earth and let it feed the soil that had nourished him.

How long the two pairs of eyes were locked in combat, nobody knew: neither party made even the slightest move. Until the sky looked like it would start to blush. With the slightest rustle and a final look, the man slunk away. Baksh knew where he was headed: through the undergrowth, under the barbed wire, across the flowing Sutlej and into Pakistan.

His entire body was leaden and soaked. The pain was unbearable. It *was* a heart attack. He needed to see a doctor urgently. And here he was, rooted in the middle of nowhere. His chance of survival lay in reaching the road where he could hope to catch some vehicle. He lifted one foot, then the other. Like trudging through the monsoon slush, awkward, but possible. Only, his chest felt like a bag of cement which had hardened.

❧

Quietly, Noor slid the curved latch back on the gate. She took a deep breath and tightened her hold on Pasha's leash. Then she took a step in the direction of the bazaar. Pasha fell into step with her. A flick of her wrist showed the time: 3 a.m.

Noor had not figured out the route of her father's walk—she followed her instinct. Down the Mall Road to the city chowk, past Old Gul's lottery stall, past the Sutlej riverbank, until she paused outside Dr S.S. Arora's ex-clinic—the nameplate, unaccountably, still there. Then past the flour mill and the Nai Dawakhana—a smile inadvertently crept up on her face as she remembered her frequent visits to the herbal doctor—until they reached Baghdadi Gate, turned left into Tarkhana-di-Gali, finally arriving at the haveli. There, Noor sat on the steps. Pasha, sensing she would take a while, stretched out on the floor, resting his face on her sandalled feet. The night was still—not even mosquitoes buzzed—and Noor wondered what Jinder Tayaji would say if he chanced upon her. She sat there for some time and the only movement she caught was behind the curtained window of the house opposite. Perhaps Queen wasn't getting much sleep tonight either, Noor thought.

Then they walked down the lane, past the gurudwara, and proceeded towards the Barki Memorial. Crossing that, they went past GND College until the road narrowed and began to be bordered by fields. Finally, they reached a stretch of pasture, where Noor stepped right into the patch of land. Bundles of straw lay around, stacked in rolls. Wheat had been harvested.

Papa had stood in these fields less than ten days back. Ten days back, wheat would have been standing tall. Ripe kernels would have brushed against him as he walked, golden stalks stroking him, dew drops gliding on his limbs... Noor remembered the infrequent farm visits of her growing-up years, Papa simultaneously happy and wistful as they waded through tall mustard, plucked juicy carrots, chomped them by the tube-well to the gurgle of water and, at the end of the visit, departed with Bodh Singh's customary gift of fresh produce.

Was Papa at peace? Did he find what he was seeking?

When she started back, Noor instinctively took a path that she had accompanied her father on during childhood visits to the farm: cutting across the fields, taking the dirt road past the old bus stop, towards the city chowk.

As she did, Papa walked beside her, willing his feet forward. Sweat glued his striped shirt and turban rim. He was so close Noor could see the drops on his face, she saw them quiver as pain convulsed his skin.

Was he loved? Had he loved well?

He was drenched in sweat as he walked on. Was he walking fast or was he dragging his feet along? He had no idea.

He had decided to take the short cut: cutting across the fields, taking the dirt road past the old bus stop, towards the city chowk. He had a vague recollection of having walked this road with... Noor, was it? But he had met nobody, seen nobody since leaving the fields. Perhaps his decision to take the shortcut had been faulty.

He could not see clearly—or think clearly—as sweat dripped into his eyes, and the twin questions swamped his mind.

Was he loved? Had he loved well?

❧

Next, they were at the chowk. Giani shouted something, then hopped onto his rickshaw and started to pedal towards them. Papa turned to look at Noor. He lifted his right arm to place a hand on her head, his eyes and smile urged her in a familiar gesture, the one he used to reassure her, whether it was in the wings before she stepped on stage for *The Old Woman in The Shoe* in Class 3, or at the hostel gates, after admission into engineering. 'You are my Sher Puttar,' he would say, and Noor would know she would manage, she would do fine on her own. You didn't get to be a tiger cub for nothing.

Noor watched Giani cycle away, carrying her father down the Mall, past number 7, the rickshaw becoming smaller, his back receding, until it misted into the horizon.

❧

Giani's posterior jiggled in mid-air as he pedalled briskly, pushing the rickshaw harder with each step. 'Bas, Bhallasaab, thodi der hore...'

As he drew long hard breaths, Baksh wondered what it was with him and rickshaw pullers: once Mindar had pedalled him out of harm's way, now Giani was attempting the same.

Pain streaked through Baksh's body like lightning, tingling electric charges that unfurled in his chest, gripped his arms, tore through his heart. Struck from within, he keeled over.

'Bhallasaab, Sardar Saab.' A worried Giani glanced backward, the pedalling paused, momentum carrying them forward.

Baksh's head writhed above his knees. Sweat broke afresh on his forehead as he drew in air.

'Bas, Bhallasaab…' Giani resumed his pedalling. 'Almost there…'

It was then, in the darkness before his pain-clouded eyes, that he saw them all. A collage that swayed, the shifting images variously coming into focus before yielding place to another. Bapuji, in his white mulmul kurta-pajama, sucking on the hookah beneath the mango tree in the courtyard; Jinder Paji, riding in a tonga down Lahore's Mall Road; Guru Nanak, singing hymns as Mardana played the rabab; Miansaab, beaming 'Maashala'; Mindar, tehmat hitched, hurrying down the gravel path, calling out his name; Kareem, tugging at a kite on a rooftop; Baba Farid, doing the mystic's dance; Anant, perkily replying 'I am stupid' when asked by Shammi whether he was intelligent like his sisters; Bitta, singing Heer at his wedding; a terrorist, standing in the highway; Pathans, riding down a dusty slope, sending pebbles shooting; bloated bodies, afloat in floodwaters; Preet, hockey stick in hand, tossing him a lopsided smile; Noor, attempting to make her fingers meet, her arms clasped around him; Mirza Ghalib, drinking, alone, the flame of a lone candle making shadows dance in the dim room; Balwant, rescuing them in an Ambassador car, then dumping them by the roadside; Neymat, in a doctor's white coat, stetho slung around the neck; Maji, her face partially veiled with a chunni, challenging a horde.

Waxing and waning, his life passed in front of him, now lit, now dark, now love, now love's burden—the presence of one giving meaning to the other.

Giani, meanwhile, rode down the railway bridge and decided to turn into Amar Hospital. There *was* no time to lose. Mission Hospital, half a kilometre down the road, might prove too far.

'Aa gaye, Bhallasaab...' He sailed into the open driveway. 'Aspataal.'

The cool morning breeze stirred the sweat drops as Baksh raised his head and squinted at the rickshaw puller.

Was he loved? Had he loved well?

Giani walked beside him, shuffling as his extended arms flapped, ready to support in case Bhallasaab, who insisted on walking, lurched. The emergency staff worker had hurried ahead and now stood in the doorway, the netting door held wide open.

The whitewashed hospital corridor, some wooden chairs lined against the walls, stretching ahead of him, opened into an expanse of wheat fields. He could not recall the hospital being situated in the midst of fields, but there they were, as far as the eye could see: golden, waist-high, the stems swaying in a gentle breeze. He could wade through, into the embrace of long tan leaves, the yielding alluvium cradling his feet, his palms skimming the golden awns, feeling the rough caress of plump ripe kernels... the recurring creak of a Persian wheel, the sky, a China-blue-and-white, the breeze of a summer morning and, from somewhere, the aroma of fresh tandoori roti...

Giani's hand was insistent beneath his right elbow, prodding, urging, attempting to steer.

Time to reap the abundant grain of his bounteous fields, to thresh and winnow, to pile it into golden pyramids—then leisure. Baisakhi mela and Bhangra. His toils, his hopes had reached their denouement: it was harvest time.

It did not matter. No question mattered. It was *his* life. And he had *lived* it—the only way he knew.

They made him lie down in the emergency room. Beneath intensely white light. On a steel bed mounted on tall legs that he had needed help to ascend. Someone gave him Disprin, two tablets, while the doctor, who had been telephoned, hurried over. Then they unrolled a tube and put a clamp on his mouth. Giani hovered anxiously, until someone took him aside and whispered conspiratorially. Then he touched his arm and said he was going to fetch Jinder from the haveli.

The people in the room got busy with pulling leads and strapping them to his legs, arms, chest. ECG, he knew from previous cardiac tests.

The doctor's face above him was tensely calm as he worked the blood pressure pump and assessed the reading. Baksh stirred and moaned. The pain, could they do something about the pain?

'Morphine, doctor?' Jinder's voice was asking.

'BP is very low,' floated the reply.

'Dem-er-ol?' Why was Jinder slurring?

Baksh dilated his eyes, trying to focus through the pain swamping him. The doctor glanced at the ECG ticker, lips pursed, as he eyed the syringe in his hand. Then someone restrained him while the doctor administered the injection.

'Intravenous.' Jinder's voice again. He stood near the foot of the bed, arms across the concave chest, head sunk low, his eyes flitting from the machines to the doctor to him.

Giani, safa around his neck, was keeping his hands busy wiping his face every now and then.

'Blo-cka-ge.' The doctor was slurring now. 'Throm-bo-ly-tic the-ra-p-y...'

A babble. Some feet hurried forward.

The doctor leaned over him, placing both hands beneath his breastbone and began to press downward. His wrist was in someone's hand, the thumb checking for his pulse.

Jinder's brown eyes were looking into him. They were coming closer, closer, until they clouded. A mist enveloped them…

※

Softly, Noor began to cry. A wet tingle, and she looked down to see Pasha licking her hand. She patted the dog's head as a raindrop came splattering down on his brown nose. Pasha sneezed. Noor smiled as he shook himself thoroughly in eager anticipation of the welcome shower that would drench his sweltering coat. Through her wet eyes Noor saw that a drizzle had started.

It was not unusual. In the Punjab plains, a dust storm arrived abruptly, and a cooling shower usually followed.

※

'Baksh puttar!' Maji laughed as she attempted to straighten the wayward head. From a distance came the clanging of a chimta again and Baksh strained his ears to catch the sound. 'Sit still.' Gold bangles clinked as they slid down Maji's arm. A ringing pierced the air, probably from the disc-like chaene attached to the same chimta.

One toss and Baksh escaped his mother's constraining hands and stood up. Turning to face her, he beamed. Maji, white handkerchief in her lap, wide-toothed wooden comb in her right hand, shook her head. Her earrings swung, the encased tiny ruby beads glinting.

The clanging chimta was the summons of a malang. In a flash, Baksh was running out of the kitchen and down the courtyard, bare feet scampering over the cool packed mud floor. Maji's entreating shout followed him: 'Baksh, get your hair tied first. Then go where you want to.'

The head full of curls bobbed above the slight frame. At the iron-studded door of the haveli, the young boy paused, his chest rapidly undulating beneath the blue muslin kurta. As she watched him, he tipped his head to one side, and grinned at his mother. Then he bounded down the steps and into the lane.

There, he cocked his head to determine from where the sound floated: Baghdadi Gate. He started to skip towards the vaulted doorless entrance, its crumbling brick pillars the remnants of a time when plundering Afghans on snorting horses had ridden down that way. A glassy green marble spotted in the dust was pocketed as he paused to sniff in front of the thelewala frying hot jalebis, dodged the fresh cake of cowdung, jogged beside the cotton candy cyclist and waved to Bhaiji sweeping the gurudwara yard.

A malang was singing, and a band of admirers ringed around him. Baksh crept in through a crevice of adult legs and stood inside the ring to watch. The bard—dressed in a saffron lungi, patched in places with other coloured cloth, cream kurta, brown cotton satchel slung from one shoulder—struck the two long flat pieces of his iron chimta together. Rings mounted on the chimta tinkled in rhythm with the Sufi song. As did the iron bangles on his right wrist. His voice rose as he started to spin in a slow circle, leather jutti rustling the strands of straw on the earthen floor.

In accord with the chimta's rhythm, Baksh rocked on his toes, head moving to-and-fro, the curls swaying. Glancing at him, the bard smiled, then looked skyward, his voice cascading around the disparate gathering, lifting it up as one soul.

EPILOGUE: ONE DAY LATER

From behind the meshed windows, Noor watched the first-floor terrace. The sparrows had arrived. Their twitter filled the air as they flapped about, from railing to concrete floor to earthen rim, picking-pecking, picking-pecking. Suddenly, a raucous cawing filled the air. On the powerful flap of angry wings came Long John Silver. The sparrows departed in an upward flutter even as he descended in an angry black swoop.

Like some ghost from the past, Queen had arrived early in the morning, before Mama had finished making her first cup of tea. She had sought Noor out.

She had seen Noor, she said, sitting on the haveli steps that morning, around four—just like Baksh had done, ten days back, before he died. Yesterday night, her son had also come visiting. *Yes*, her son, Prince—the militant, wanted by the police. It was not the first time—he sneaked in, occasionally, from across the border under the cover of night, to enquire after his old mother. A son must do what a son must do. Only, yesterday, he was troubled. He hadn't been able to pass urine properly for ten days, he said. The Jihadi doctor could see no problem and, besides, where else could he go? A true soldier of God, the police on his heels, cannot run to a hospital like a regular guy! Still, the urine refused to flow, burning inside him instead like acid, slowly piling up. It was corroding him from within, and Prince knew a thing or two about acids… He figured out what to do: he had to disclose the truth, and who better than his own mother to do so to? When she heard, Queen sighed, she knew she had to tell Noor—that was why she was here.

Prince was in the same field that night as Baksh. He had crouched at some distance, waiting for the lawyer to go away. But Bhallasaab kept his eyes on him all the while, like he were a scarecrow standing there to guard the crop. And while he stood there, time ticked away. Precious time in which the militant was to plant a bomb under cover of darkness, taking advantage of the moonless night and the lax security cover on the border—the Border Security Force was giving a farewell dinner to a much-celebrated commandant on his retirement! A feast had been laid out, the BSF personnel were sozzled and, after gorging on the Mughlai dishes, satiated as cows in a spring field. The timing could not have been more propitious. A source had indicated that the foreign ministers of India and Pakistan were to hold a joint meeting at Hussainiwala a day later. They were to announce the date of arrival of the gas pipeline to Ferozepur and lay a commemorative stone. One blast would have adequately dispatched the plans for samjhauta, peaceful cooperation, through the skies to the devil's lair where such ideas germinated and deserved to be returned.

But Bhallasaab stood there for an hour or so and, as the pre-dawn light started to lift the darkness, her son had to abandon his mission and crawl back into the undergrowth on the other side of the Sutlej. The lawyer had managed to spoil the party, Prince said, he felt those eyes bore right into his soul. But the lawyer had suffered too. He had lost precious time standing there like a mummy while his heart died. Queen sighed.

She had to tell, she said, handing Noor a newspaper. It was a copy of *The Tribune*, dated a day after Papa's death. The news article that Queen pointed to lauded the success of the gas pipeline and the joint commemorative ceremony conducted at the border by the foreign ministers of India and Pakistan.

Queen had visited Noor for the sake of her son's health, but also, she insisted, because children need to make peace with their parents.

❦

Pasha came bounding down the steps, barking furiously as the tomcat gave him the slip yet again. He did, however, manage to disrupt the victorious gobbling of one fat crow. Long John Silver, abdicating food in favour of life, took off with sudden energy, cawing to let his displeasure be known.

The next instant, the sparrows descended—as if they had been hiding, just out of sight, for their bête noire to depart. They perched on the bowl's rim to peck, their chirruping floating in the air.

Pasha nuzzled his head against Noor. Holding the newspaper to her chest with one hand, Noor patted the dog with the other. 'How well did you know your father?' Jinder Tayaji had asked. That question, coupled with Anant's revelations, had set Noor on a journey: a journey in which a constantly shifting collage revealed a father she thought she knew. Now, with Queen's disclosure, the collage had shifted once again. However, the image added this time would be the collage's leitmotif, Noor knew.

The chance to look into another's soul is the gift of a lifetime—Noor had been fortunate. The question, then, was not how well did you know your father. Rather, it was: did you *know* your father?

To that, Noor had an answer.

ACKNOWLEDGEMENTS

No book is written in isolation, neither was this. It germinated as I listened, overheard, eavesdropped, was told and regaled with the numerous stories circulating in a border town and an idiosyncratic family.

Ferozepur: a dusty little town that holds so much history that no wonder it keeps spilling over its border. For ease of storytelling, I have changed some of its coordinates without, I hope, altering its essence. It is the place to which I ascribe the quixotic element in me. How else do you explain the presence of a crumbling century-old edifice named Baghdadi Gate in the heart of the city, 3,000 kilometres away from Iraq?

I am lucky to have grown up in the midst of an exuberant family, where each person passionately insists on remaking the world in his or her vision. In hindsight, there could not have been richer soil to nurture the latent writer in me.

This book is a tribute to the memory of my father, a true Punjabi, and the spirit of Punjab which remains undiminished despite its travails. I must, however, state that the book is a work of fiction. It is not a documentary on the life of one man or one state. It is an attempt to illuminate the twentieth-century history of Punjab by refracting it through the invented life of one ordinary Punjabi.

For an understanding of Sikh history and the history of Punjab, I read several books and the list is too long to mention here. I would, however, like to note my gratitude to Khushwant Singh for his remarkable work, *A History of the Sikhs*, which I dive into again and again.

I am grateful to my editors: V.K. Karthika, for her belief in this book; and Shantanu Ray Chaudhuri, for meticulously shepherding it. And my agent Jayapriya, for championing it.

My gratitude to the legendary Gulzar saab. Like any Indian of my generation, I have grown up on the myriad offerings of this creative genius. I am privileged, honoured and humbled that he liked this book enough to write a sher for it.

In the seven years it took me to write this book, I faltered frequently and threatened to quit occasionally. The counsel and patience of one person saved me and the book: my husband Prasanna. Thank you for offering your shoulder, and for your insistence—with each draft—that I could write better. You are the wind beneath my wings, and I hope you will like this book.

This is also for my daughter Malvika, who likes nothing better than to be told a story, a frequent request being: tell me a story about me. I finished the first draft of this book cradling you in my left arm as my right hammered away at the keyboard. It is my hope that one day, when you read this book, it will entertain and enlighten you. As a wise hakawati once said, the story of you never begins with you.